Otherkin

Lisa Stowe

Crooked Tail Press

Paperback: 978-1-946380-21-0
Ebook: 978-1-946380-22-7

Published by Crooked Tail Press
Cover Design by Crooked Tail Press

Contents

Dedicated to the Irish legend of Mis,
the original wild woman of the forest, and all those who, like her, descend
into grief and emerge transformed.

As always, this is for Art, and our work of art. Love you both more than you know.

Otherkin

Chapter 1

THE TALL CONCRETE SMOKESTACK, an old historic site in Monroe, Washington now belched fine ash and particulates that filtered down to gently rest on Ramon Saura's shoulders. The fetid air was a harsh reminder of what the smokestack had been repurposed for and the thought that the falling ash, that each breath he drew in, could be his family, almost broke him.

Even though he wasn't sleeping much and exhaustion weighed on him, over the past two weeks he established a routine. Each morning he went to the huge parking lot of the destroyed Coastal store where the few soldiers with the National Guard had set up a base of sorts. A Guardsman in his early thirties, with a name patch sewn on his uniform that said 'McCausland' grew more and more terse and impatient as Ramon repeatedly demanded news of his niece Marie, of where she'd been taken, why they were keeping her, when she was coming back.

His brother and pregnant sister-in-law were still missing and, after this long, he knew in his heart they were dead. Even so, he had hung a tarp behind the ruins of their old home, creating a tiny camp. If his family still lived, that was where they would go first.

His niece Alegria was as safe as she could be somewhere in the woods around Index but Marie was gone and it was his fault and he was here to get her back.

A month ago, the most devastating earthquake in recorded history hit the Pacific Northwest. And not only was it cataclysmic, it released ancient killing myths from the fractured land. Ramon and his nieces tried to escape the destruction. But they only made it as far east as Index before being forced to make a stand alongside the few survivors in the tiny mountain town.

After the initial quake, the first helicopter that came took the critically injured. The second brought emergency supplies. The third brought two men and a woman from a new paramilitary group. The Cascadia Protection Force somehow learned Marie could sense the location of creatures released by the quake and they wanted to use her to hunt.

Ramon refused. He knew the physical and mental toll sensing creatures took on her and she was possibly all he had left. It was on him to protect her. She was just a teenager. His brother's child. Marie, however, begged. She felt she could endure a week. She'd guide them only to the creatures that killed, and away from those that helped. In the end he negotiated with the soldiers and they agreed to take him as well so he could look for her parents while Marie assisted in the hunt. The soldiers even signed the terms he scribbled out.

Ramon was dropped off in Monroe. Marie was picked up for her first hunt.

She never came back.

The ruined city was a lawless nightmare, a landscape unrecognizable reeking of decomposing bodies, a place of despair. People were starving and dying from injuries that wouldn't have killed them before the quake. The National Guard was overwhelmed. There was limited control and no way to enforce laws. Ramon didn't go anywhere without his handgun in his jacket pocket. Grief and despair and anger made his soul a landscape just as unrecognizable as the one he walked through.

He begged for information, grew angry and demanded action. And this morning, like every day, he was left with no answers and no idea what to do.

After the National Guard, Ramon went next to his assigned relief station manned by the Red Cross to get his small allotment of rations for the day. A packet of oatmeal, a couple bottles of water. A military ready-to-eat meal in its foil pack. This time there was a tin of peaches and an honest-to-God tube of toothpaste and toothbrush. It felt like Christmas.

With the rations stowed in his backpack, he joined the long line of traumatized people searching layers and layers of paper posted on a make-shift wall. The scavenged plywood and broken lumber bordered what had been the highway and grew daily, holding heartbreaking scraps, each a tiny story of loss and hope.

He inched along with strangers desperate for news of loved ones, scanning as fast as he dared, terrified of missing something. Descriptions of those missing. Where they were last seen. Who searched for them. Descriptions of bodies taken to the crematorium. Names, if those bodies had been found with identification. His first day in Monroe he added his story to the lists, added his brother and sister-in-law and their descriptions, added a note begging them to come home. At the very bottom he penciled in that he was safe and could be found in Index if not at their old home.

Finally, out of desperation, he added Marie to the lists.

Sixteen years old. Long, wild, curly black hair. Solemn dark eyes that see into your soul.

Taken by the Cascadia Protection Force and it was his fault for letting it happen. His fault.

Ramon knew someone watched him because each day her description was missing from the lists. He scrounged a piece of a paper grocery sack and replaced her name, holding his fingers to the paper momentarily, then swallowed against the loss.

With the uncountable number of those dead and missing, each day the lists grew longer and it took almost three hours to move along the line. By the time he reached where it ended that day it was late afternoon, chilly and beginning to drizzle, and he was emotionally drained and physically exhausted. And he still had to get back to his camp, which meant he needed to be alert because, oddly, the lists were the only safe place in Monroe. Almost as if the scraps of paper and bits of cardboard, the names and stories, were sacred.

Ramon made his way carefully back toward the ruined house on Kelsey Street. More bits and pieces had been scavenged from the abandoned building while he was gone. One day soon there would be nothing left, their home carried away board by nail by stone. Each day he expected to find his camp gone, too, but so far, like the lists, it hadn't been touched.

He built a fire against the coming night and ate a bowl of oatmeal while sitting under the tarp on his damp sleeping bag and watching the small flames. He thought back over the day and realized despair would drive him crazy if he stayed there, searching the lists indefinitely. The reality was, he might never find his family and that possibility cut deep. He didn't know what to do but clearly this futile begging for information, this hopeless moving through the days, wasn't going to accomplish anything. He needed action.

He saw two paths before him. One, to continue as he was, waiting passively in hopes that Marie would be returned. Or two, give himself a deadline and prepare to leave Monroe and walk back to Index. It would be extremely dangerous, but he would be doing *something* and he could search along the way for Marie.

Ramon touched the handgun he kept with him at all times. If he could find the helicopter, if he could find Marie, he was taking her back.

So. A deadline to leave by. He rinsed out his bowl and stowed it in his backpack. He would start eating one meal a day because he didn't know how long rations would be available and he had to be stocked up for the trek home. Had to be stocked up to feed both of them once he found Marie. He would need supplies for her. She'd had her backpack when she left but he had no way of knowing if she'd been allowed to keep it. Maybe, then, a week before he could leave.

He left the fire burning low and crawled under the tarp and into his sleeping bag fully clothed, his gun in his hand, and the bag unzipped in case he had to move fast. He slept fitfully, his nightmares scattered and sleep broken from dancing flames, low voices, footsteps passing, and distant screams.

In the morning it would all start again but now, having a plan, at least there was a faint hope flickering inside. He almost didn't recognize the emotion. He definitely didn't trust it. But it was better than despair.

Chapter 2

Max Douglass hit the nail one last time then dropped the hammer on the makeshift table made out of two sawhorses and a warped sheet of plywood. He pulled up his grimy black shirt to wipe his face and then ran a hand over his dark red hair. His previous, military-precision short hair was getting bristly.

His rifle leaned against a stump of wood. He rested his hand on the butt of his service weapon, a Glock in its holster, and listened. All he heard was the gentle sound of a breeze in the trees and the background rush of the North Fork Skykomish River. The day was cool and overcast, with dampness in the air that promised spring rain. The Index Town Wall was a sheer granite mountain face, now like a high broken curtain. The deep green of what forest remained washed up that wall, and below it, the ruin of collapsed homes and destroyed streets made up the tiny town.

A month ago, he'd been a Snohomish County Sheriff's deputy dispatched to a call in Index with his partner, Casey Richards. A 'dog from hell' had been reported by an old woman and she had been one of the first to die when the quake hit, like so many others, beyond count, killed by the quake. And then killed by creatures that shouldn't have existed outside of myth. Except that now, they did.

The quake took bridges down, isolating them in the tiny mountain town, and attempts to get out became extremely dangerous. In the weeks since, there had been opportunities to leave with the helicopters. But he'd chosen to stay, to help build the rough fort that walled in all their makeshift shelters at night, to help bring some semblance of safety and security to this new world they moved through.

Now here he was, spending a spring afternoon finishing a small shed that was their first barter store. With money meaningless, trade was invaluable. He looked at the shed and grimaced. Construction wasn't one of his skills.

Casey strolled across the street, hands in her jeans pockets, to stand beside him. She, too, wore a black shirt, a left-over piece of their former uniforms. But on her, he thought the shirt looked just fine. With the addition of her holstered gun on one hip, a knife in its sheath on the other, and a rifle slung over her shoulder, she actually looked better than just fine. He'd always had a soft spot for strong women.

"Is that wall leaning?" she asked.

"Not if you tilt your head."

She tilted her head. "Still leaning."

"Forget my construction skills and think about my other skills. Like an afternoon nap?"

"Maybe. But I came to tell you June has cold beer."

"*What*?" Max's eyebrows shot up.

June and her husband Ben were an elderly couple who had come into town after the quake with Ramon Saura and his family. Their even older truck had been stocked with supplies, but he didn't remember beer.

"Cold. Beer. Want some or not?" Casey grinned.

"Lead on," Max said, picking up his rifle and taking her hand. "How did she manage that?"

Casey took the short path to the river that led past the small Fort Curtis, thrown together where the museum had once stood. "June got the six pack from the last bunch of supplies dropped in. Thought you might want one. Since you're working so hard building the barter shed."

"God, yes." Max tugged on Casey's hand. "Pick up the pace, slacker."

The whitewater river was the odd gray-green it got when the high snowfields melted in early spring. It moved fast and deep, over and around boulders. Bobbing gently at the edge was an oar frame raft anchored to a fallen tree and June had used one of the raft's D-rings to tie off and chill the beer in the water. Casey took one can and popped the tab with the most satisfying sound Max had heard in weeks. She handed it to him and he took a swallow, momentarily closing his eyes in bliss.

Then he handed the can to Casey. "We'll share. Six cans won't go far."

Casey took a swallow and sat on one of the boulders along the edge of the river. She handed the can back to Max as he sat next to her.

"Who knew Rainier beer could taste so good?" she asked.

They heard the sounds of boots on rocks and Max turned to see Spike Costa jogging down the path, his unruly black hair wild around his angular face. The kid had once been on Max's deputy radar. Once. Back when school truancy and teen angst had been important.

"June says there's beer," he said breathlessly as he reached them.

"You're not legal age," Max said. "What are you anyway, seventeen?"

"Eighteen, yesterday."

"Not legal age." Max handed a dripping can to the kid. "If I see you staggering around drunk, I'm arresting you."

"Yeah, yeah." Spike grinned and dropped down to sit on the ground next to them. He popped the can open and took a long drink. "Fuck me," he said on a long exhale.

Max shook his head and reached for the can. "If it's that bad, we'll finish it for you."

Spike flipped his middle finger and took another long drink. "I scavenged some more boards for the barter shed. You know it's leaning?"

"Not if you tilt your head," Casey said.

Max raised his can in a toast to her words, then handed it to her. He let their easy conversation wash over him as he kept an alert eye on the river. A week ago, something had grabbed the oar frame boat when their resident white-water rafter, Rob, had been ferrying supplies to people on the other side. The hand disintegrated when air hit it. And right after the quake, people had been killed by a creature that had been chased into the river. There were things out there and Max watched for their return. And since he was watching, he was the first to see the huge raven flying low and coming upriver. He stood.

"What..." Casey started to ask, then fell silent as she followed his gaze.

Spike crumpled his empty can and got slowly to his feet.

The raven circled and came down to rest on a boulder a few yards away. It cocked its head to one side, its eye on them. Spike turned and raced up the path.

"Go." Max pushed against Casey's back. The raven never came alone.

He ran up the trail following Casey, with Spike already out of sight. When they reached Avenue A the mayor, Albert, was at the barter shed with a hammer. Max saw him pause and turn slowly.

A young couple, in front of the tiny town hall with shovels, working the equally tiny garden stopped abruptly. They gripped each other and backed up to the wall.

"What is it?" Albert asked. "What's happening?"

"The raven is back." Max pointed up at the bird, circling above them with long strong strokes of its wings. "Let's get everyone in the fort."

Albert dropped his hammer and ran to the old schoolhouse bell that hung in front of the town hall. He jerked on the rope and the bell clanked loudly.

Max hauled on the heavy gate of the fort and Casey helped him hold it open as people raced inside. There were some missing. Those who were too far way to hear the bell, those that would be slow in responding. But all he could do was give them as much time as possible before he had to shut the entrance to save those he could. At least their oldest survivor, Henry, made it through, clutching an armload of books. Max scanned the gray sky but couldn't see the raven anywhere.

Albert, heading to them, was in the middle of the street when the earth heaved.

Up on the flanks of the Town Wall where, in another life, rock climbers would have been, evergreen trees bent and danced.

People screamed as the thunder of falling boulders from the Wall echoed around them.

Casey fell back on her butt, tried to stand, and fell again. Max staggered to her but lost his balance, coming down hard on one knee. The road heaved under him and he rolled with it, unable to stop himself. Somewhere he heard the crash of something big collapsing.

And then it was over.

Max pushed himself to his feet, his knee a sharp bite of pain that made him wince. Even though there were sounds, tumbling rocks, cracking trees, faint sobbing...they were oddly distant and otherworldly. In these first few seconds of no movement, it felt like silence, like the land held its breath. He reached for Casey's hand and pulled her up. She stood for a long moment just holding on, and he understood the need for something stable.

Casey loosened her grip, took a deep breath, and started to speak.

"Look!" Spike shouted from the open gate, his voice tight with fear as he pointed downriver.

From where they stood, they could see the railroad berm, the remains of collapsed buildings, and beyond it all, the forest.

Mist rose up through the trees, the tendrils twisting like river vapor lifted on a breeze. They caught in tree branches, sifted through, rose and reformed.

A soft, gentle fog in the evergreens on a damp spring day.

"No," Casey whispered. "Sharon took them. We saw it."

There had been aftershocks since the quake and each time more monsters came out. Each time death crept closer. But not these. They were supposed to be buried deep in granite.

The Shadow People moved like fog, looked like mist, and sank through mouths and eyes and ears, feasting. Max's heart stuttered in fear. How did you fight a shadow? How did you shoot fog?

They watched, terrified. If the Shadows turned toward town, they would die. That simple. The mist rose, solidified, took vague human form.

"They're going west?" Spike asked, his shaky voice a whisper.

It did seem that way. Max watched the fog writhe, lift upward, and then move down river.

After a moment, he ran a hand over his face. "Okay, show's over. Let's get the teams out. Look for anyone injured by the aftershock. See what new damage we have to deal with."

"What if they come back?" Spike asked. "The Shadows?"

"Nothing we can do." He briefly squeezed Spike's shoulder. "Nothing we can do."

Chapter 3

T HE FOREST WAS QUIET. Early spring in the Wild Sky Wilderness, one of those damp days where once twilight came down it still felt like winter. Ethan Reynolds pushed his dark hair out of his eyes, shed his backpack and put it on the ground at the base of the yew tree, with his rifle on top. It was a risk but he got so damn sick of carrying a gun all the time.

Anya had buried her stillborn son, Joseph, in the roots of the yew before the quake, before Ethan came into her life. She'd thought of it as a memorial space, but with the quake, Joseph returned. Her son and yet not her son, a young boy from the heartwood of the tree with a massive guardian grizzly. Ethan didn't understand, but it was no stranger than the monsters that now walked the woods.

He zipped up his old canvas jacket and shoved his hands into his jeans pockets. Bad dreams the night before of his friend Curtis had left him unsettled and with raw memories. His friend had died by fire, his ashes impossible to separate from those of the Windigo that had tried to kill Ethan.

He couldn't spread those horribly contaminated ashes under Anya's tree. Instead, he took them to a tunnel bored into granite near Index called the Hole in the Wall where Curtis, a professor with the University of Washington, had worked on gravity experiments. Just because Curtis's ashes weren't at Anya's tree, though, didn't mean that Ethan couldn't come here to remember.

He drew in a deep breath of the scents of life returning after winter. Earth warming, sap rising, all the things that continued season after season as if no catastrophic earthquake had ever happened. Even the robins had come back and sang their early evening bird songs around him as if no myths had become reality when the quake hit.

He couldn't pretend it was a peaceful spring day when he knew the aftershock earlier had probably opened another fault. Somewhere, something new had come into their world. He thought sometimes that they should go back to Index, help out there. But he'd managed to find nights with fewer nightmares and days where grief was a little easier, out in the mountains with just Anya, who also knew grief. It was easier to stay here.

Ethan bent to pull a few weeds from the tiny herbs Anya had planted right before the quake. As he did, the birds fell silent. He straightened and grabbed his rifle then blew out a breath when he saw her and their German Shepherd, Bird.

The dog woofed once, his tail up as he came to Ethan. He still had a slight limp from when he'd been attacked by a huge raven but the dog's wounds were healing into ridged scars across his belly.

Anya, her long mahogany hair in a neat braid, wore a fleece sweater and baggy jeans and looked calm and relaxed if he ignored the rifle she carried. He took her hand in his and as always, the warmth of her eased the hollow ache inside.

"You had nightmares last night," she said. "I figured at some point you'd end up here. The same dream?"

"Curtis burning." Ethan grimaced. "Don't need a psychiatrist to figure that one out."

"No." She reached up and gently stroked the still-healing scars on his face, cut deeply into his skin by the Windigo Curtis had saved him from. "But that doesn't make it easier."

He caught her hand, pulled her in close, and kissed her temple, her skin warm against his mouth. Slowly, the darkness of grief receded and he sighed heavily, stepping back.

"Hungry?" she asked. "Biscuits for dinner just came off the wood stove."

"Huckleberry jam?"

"I think we might still have some left." Anya turned toward the cabin and gestured for Bird to follow.

The dog gave a sudden short warning bark and then growled. By now they both knew what that meant and brought their rifles up, swinging around to look in the direction the dog was staring.

Something low to the ground. Pushing through salal and Oregon grape. Humanoid shape on all fours with long, clearly visible claws. Pale gray with deeply sunken eyes.

It came straight for them with an incredibly fast scuttling crawl.

Ethan and Anya fired at the same time. The thing flipped, hit the ground, and was still, oozing grayish fluid. Anya released Bird with a hand motion and the dog went to the creature, nosed it, and then sat.

Reassured by the dog's behavior that the thing was most likely dead, Ethen moved forward while Anya held back to cover him. He poked the creature with his boot and waited.

Nothing.

The oozing fluid slowed and then stopped. Ethan lowered his rifle. "Dead. I'll haul it back into the woods and bury it. Guess we know what this last aftershock sent us."

Anya also lowered her rifle. "Don't touch that slimy stuff with your bare hands."

"You're not offering to help?"

"Are you kidding? I'm not touching that. I got more important things to do." She pulled a pair of work gloves out of her jacket pocket and tossed them to him.

Ethan caught the gloves one-handed. "Like finding huckleberry jam?"

"Like finding huckleberry jam. Have fun, hero."

He shouldered his rifle and pulled the gloves on as Anya headed back to the cabin. He poked the thing one more time with his boot. Still dead. With Bird at his side, he bent and grabbed the thing's legs.

Just another beautiful spring day in the Pacific Northwest.

Chapter 4

THERE WERE ONLY A few days left before Ramon's self-imposed deadline to head back to Index. The long days of despair and longer nights of disrupted sleep were wearing on him. The aftershock the day before had kept him awake all night, thinking about monsters and the reality of traversing a destroyed landscape.

He trudged to the Red Cross station and took his place in line to receive the rations for the day. It was odd how his life had encapsulated down to two lines. One for food and hope and one for loss and grief. There were similarities in both lines though. Few people, even children, talked or made eye contact with anyone outside their remains of family.

Except for this morning.

In the fresh spring air, a man in line ahead of Ramon was talking to anyone who would listen. His words flowed fast, almost manic, as if the need to relate news overwhelmed him.

"The National Guard guy showed me photos on his phone." The man, hair going gray, clothes tattered, gestured as if he held a cell phone. "Seriously. He had a phone. He said this was a full rip quake. The coast is gone. Seattle, man, the waterfront, Pikes Place Market, it's all sunk into the Sound. Port Authority? Gone. Vashon and Bainbridge islands? Gone. The tsunami flooded Seattle, washed around like water in a tub. And that's just Seattle. They're saying months before any sort of infrastructure is back in those areas, let alone out here. And Bellevue? Guess it was built on an old swamp or something. It sank. Some places dropped more than thirty feet. Ain't no climbing back up out of that."

"Don't, please," a young woman said, holding up her hand.

"The refugee camps in Yakima are overwhelmed." The man continued as if he hadn't heard, or simply couldn't stop. "But at least there you don't got your monsters. Though I hear tell those things are starting to show up outside the quake zone so it won't be long. Even in Japan, like the tsunami carried 'em along. And the Guard guy says-"

The young woman was in tears, hands over her ears.

"That's enough," Ramon said loudly. "Come on, guy, we've got enough to handle here."

"No! You have to hear this – it's good!" The man held his hand, palm up, to Ramon. "Seriously! The Cascadia Protection Force has got a monster hunter! A, you know, myth buster!" He laughed loudly.

A few people laughed as well but it sounded forced.

Ramon's stomach clenched with sudden dread. "What are you talking about?"

"Some girl they've found that can tell where the monsters are. They're using her to hunt them."

Ramon's heart jolted. "Where?"

The man stared. "Huh?"

"Where?" Ramon stepped into the man, grabbing the front of his shirt. "Where are they hunting?"

"How the hell should I know?" the man shoved Ramon back and ran a hand down the front of his shirt, smoothing the dirty fabric.

"The more monsters they kill, the better," a teenage girl said. "Something grabbed my mom in the middle of the night. Right out of the tent. Right here in town. We never saw a thing." She swiped the back of her hand across her eyes.

"I've heard some are okay. Will help you."

"Who is going to stand there long enough to find out? Kill them all."

Ramon let the words wash around him, head down as he tried to control his breathing, his anger. Marie was out there, being used, by now possibly being held against her will. Without him to keep her safe.

His supplies were pretty sound if he was careful. It would be slow going back, especially through Sultan where the Culmback dam had breached and drowned the city. That might be where the hunt was happening, where monsters might be feeding on all the bodies. He moved forward with the line, not really paying attention, thoughts whirling, until he was almost at the station and then the teenager spoke again and her words sank in.

"Probably a dog. There's a lot of starving animals."

"And starving people," a man said with a laugh. "Wonder if they'd barter for the dog. Probably tastes like chicken."

A few people laughed half-heartedly like the man had just made a joke. But only a few. Ramon looked where the others were watching a woman pull a large dog crate off a rusty garden cart. The crate dropped to the ground and the woman shoved it behind the table where the volunteers handed out food packets. He was close enough now to hear what the woman was saying to the aid worker.

"I told you. I'm not feeding him. He's your problem."

"But ma'am, we can't feed everyone here as it is, let alone pets." The aid worker didn't even glance back at the crate.

Ramon scowled. He barely had enough rations for himself, let alone him and his niece when he got her back. He couldn't take on a dog either. But...the poor thing was probably terrified as well as starving. And a dog might be an early warning system when something sneaked up in the dark. He remembered what a good guard dog Bird was for Anya.

"Mind if I take a look?" he asked one of the workers, hoping they would say no. But they just shrugged, too busy to even look his way.

"Guess he wants chicken!" the man said, laughing again. He looked around as if expecting others to laugh with him, but no one did.

Ramon was aware of the hungry eyes of many that followed him as he left the line and went behind the table, hoping it wasn't going to be some ankle biter he had to carry. He squatted down to look through the grill of the crate.

A scrawny little boy in filthy clothes with greasy hair that might have been blonde if clean crouched in the cramped space, looking back at Ramon. His brown eyes were dilated with fear.

Ramon shot to his feet. "Where is she?"

"Who?"

"The woman!" Ramon's voice climbed to a shout. "The one who did this!"

The aid worker shrugged, glanced back, and her mouth dropped open in shock.

Ramon fumbled open the crate and knelt down on one knee as the child flinched back.

"Was that your mom?" he asked, forcing himself to swallow the anger, to keep his voice level.

The boy shook his head, scooting further back. Tremors ran through his skinny body. A little hand came up to clench his shirt over his chest.

"I'm not going to hurt you. I'm not going to let anyone here hurt you. Do you understand? If you come out, I will keep you safe." Ramon's thoughts raced. And he'd been worried about feeding a dog. Now, suddenly, it was a skinny kid.

The boy dropped his chin to his chest for a long moment and then surged forward, throwing himself out. Arms went around Ramon's neck. He reflexively wrapped his own arms around the boy, who buried his face against Ramon's shoulder, shaking with deep tremors. All Ramon could do was drop back to sit on his butt and hold the child. At least until he couldn't help but sneeze.

"My god you need a bath."

The boy tightened his grip.

"Okay," Ramon continued, speaking calmly. "I'm going to stand up. I'm not letting you go, so you don't have to choke me."

The grip loosened. Slightly.

Ramon stood awkwardly with his burden and spoke to the aid worker, who was watching. "Can I get a second set of rations? And who do I let know where this child will be if someone is searching for him?"

"I don't know. The lists maybe? National Guard? They're the closest we have to police." The aid worker gathered the rations, hesitated and looked at the kid, then carefully slid another packet of oatmeal under the first.

Ramon nodded his thanks to the worker and shifted the boy to one hip so he could pull off his backpack and open it one-handed. The aid worker helped him put packets of food and another bottle of water inside.

"Can you open one of these protein bars for me?" Ramon asked as he maneuvered the pack back on.

The aid worker did so, and handed it to the boy who took it cautiously and then took a small bite.

"Go on," Ramon said. "It's yours."

The boy took a huge bite, cheeks bulging.

"Just go slow, okay?" Ramon said. "Don't need you puking on me. There's more."

"You're going to need, like, clothes," someone in the crowd said. "Go to the Coastal store where the National Guard is. The west corner is being used like a thrift store. People piling up shit as they find it."

"Thanks," Ramon said.

As he walked away, an elderly man caught his arm.

"For the boy," he said, holding out a crumpled snack-sized Snickers bar. "I've been saving it for my grandson. But I don't know where he is."

The old man's eyes filled with tears that slowly fell as if he was unaware of them.

Ramon wanted to tell the old man good luck, or that he hoped the grandson would be found, or that things had to get better. But in the end, he simply walked away. Words were inadequate and clichés meaningless. In this new world, words of kindness were simply cruel lies.

He'd already been to the Coastal store earlier, asking for news about Marie. But he worked his way back there now, carrying the little boy. A National Guard truck idled in the far west corner of the lot as two young men tossed more stuff into the piles. They were clearly bringing things they salvaged from their daily routes. People moved through the stacks, picking through remnants of lives now gone.

Ramon approached one of the guardsmen. "Who do I report an abandoned child to? I'm keeping him with me, I just need to know where to document it in case someone's looking for him."

"You been to the lists?" the man asked.

"Every day."

"Best add his name there. There isn't any organized relief yet. Everyone's too overwhelmed. Lots of abandoned kids and old people."

"I can do that," Ramon said, trying not to think of more kids out there starving and alone.

"What is he, five or six?"

Ramon looked down at the boy in his grimy clothes and shrugged. "Damned if I know."

"I seen a bunch of kids clothes in the north section. Maybe start there. And hey," the guardsman said as Ramon moved away. "Thanks. For keeping the kid, you know? Not much kindness for those not your own now."

The guy sounded suddenly weary and Ramon could only nod. He got it. God, how he got it. The overriding need to pull your family tight and protect and provide as best you could, even at the expense of others. It didn't leave a person much to help others suffering, especially when they weren't yours. Ramon knew he had to prioritize finding Marie and getting her home. But this starving child had crossed his path and now was his responsibility.

The boy took the last piece of protein bar and reached inside his shirt. Ramon saw a leather cord around the boy's neck. The kid had to be starving, though he wasn't as bony as Ramon expected. Maybe he hadn't been on his own that long. Either way, it was no surprise he felt the need to save some food for later, just in case. Ramon started to reassure the boy, to tell him that from now on, things would be okay.

The boy lowered his head, holding his hand over the small bag that hung from the cord around his neck. It looked almost like he was praying.

Ramon said nothing as he went to the scavenged stacks. Silence was better than making promises he might not be able to keep.

It took a couple hours but by the time he headed back home, he felt better prepared. He'd found a rusty and squeaky wheelbarrow and the kid now rode in it, sitting on a musty quilt. There was a small assortment of old clothes next to him and a bright pink plastic girl's backpack. Ramon tried not to think about what might have happened to the little girl who had owned it. The most valuable thing they'd found was a sleeping bag with only one small tear in it.

At the lists, Ramon had added a description of the boy, and where they would be. But when Ramon had asked the kid what his name was, he'd simply remained silent. With that task done, he headed back to camp.

Kelsey Street had enough foot traffic that a fairly decent but rough path had developed through the debris of wrecked cars, downed power poles, and ruined buildings. A man came toward them, watching the wheelbarrow. Ramon slowed, tensing. Most people now avoided direct eye contact, either out of fear, or simply too caught up in despair and survival. But this man looked straight at him and kept coming.

Ramon lowered the wheelbarrow and moved out in front of it. He pulled his gun out of his pocket and rested his finger near the trigger.

"That's close enough."

The man held his hands up. "Not looking for trouble. Just wondering if you want to barter."

"For?"

The man pulled a backpack off one shoulder and fumbled inside a broken zipper and gaping pocket. "I got me a can of chicken here. Family size." He shifted to look past Ramon at the wheelbarrow again.

"Sorry," Ramon said. "I need the wheelbarrow."

"I hear you." The man held out the can of chicken. "Not much around with wheels anymore. But I want the kid. Scrawny one like that, he can help me."

"What?"

"That boy you got there. He can get into places I can't. Still lots to scavenge around here. Maybe help me out with other things, too." The man used the can to gesture with. "I'll trade you. One less mouth for you to feed, you know?"

Ramon's stomach clenched. "No."

"Two cans of chicken?" The man reached for the pocket in the backpack.

"I said, no." Ramon lifted the gun. "Back away."

"Look, man-"

"Back away. Not telling you again."

The man dropped the can into his pack, lifted his hands, palms out, and backed up. Ramon kept the gun up and his eyes locked on the guy until he'd rounded a corner and was out of sight.

It was only then he felt the kid gripping the back of his shirt in a grimy fist. He lowered the gun and turned around. The boy's eyes were dilated with fear, his pinched face white.

"I told you. You're safe. To the best of my ability."

Ramon rested his hand on the boy's shoulder and only then realized he was shaking. He hid it by squeezing the kid's shoulder then pocketing the gun. Once the kid seemed a little more settled, he gripped the wheelbarrow handles and pushed it over the rough ground to the back of the house where his camp was, a bearing squeaking loudly and one tire wobbling.

He could have shot the man. Killed him right there and what would have happened?

Nothing.

Not one damn thing.

"We're going home," he said, tilting up the wheelbarrow and sliding the kid out when they stopped at the tarp. "Tomorrow, we get our rations then hit the road."

The kid clutched his shirt, watching Ramon with wide eyes.

"There are monsters out there. And I'm going to be searching for my niece. When I find her, it's not going to be easy to get her back." Ramon thought of the hunger in the man's eyes. "If you want to stay here, I'll find a place that's safe. If you want to come with me you need to know it's going to be dangerous. But if we make it, you'll be part of a family again. And there's this old lady named June who will be your granny and love you until you're sick of hot chocolate."

The kid's chin was down, his hand over his necklace under his shirt.

"Think about it. In the meantime, let's have some dinner and figure out how to get you a sponge bath or something. No offense, kid, but you stink."

The kid's chin came up and something faint, that might have been a sheepish smile if allowed to grow, passed fleetingly over his face.

Ramon poked at the remains of the previous night's fire. "You wouldn't give me a name to put on the lists. Anything you want me to call you?"

The silence held between them a moment, the kid watching him with big eyes.

Ramon thought of Tómas, his missing brother. "Okay then, Tommy it is. You let me know in the morning what you decide."

He rubbed a hand over his face and sighed. What in the hell was he going to do with a stinky, hungry little kid?

Chapter 5

IT WAS LATE. MAYBE getting close to midnight. The gate of the fort was slightly ajar so Max could get back in fast if need be. He sat on the damp grass, back to the wall of the fort, knees up, and arms resting on them.

His watch battery had long since died and he didn't care enough to ask for a shipment of more batteries in their ration deliveries. Besides, the exact time of day or night wasn't important anymore. With no job to go to, no lunch breaks, no appointments, no deadlines to meet, what did it matter? He could roughly guess by the sun and that was good enough.

To have a life without time to govern every action during the day should have been liberating. He guessed it was in a way, but the tradeoff sure as hell wasn't worth it. He wondered if they would ever progress to the point where time mattered again.

Another unexpected result of the quake was the stars. He didn't think he would ever get tired of seeing them. With no ambient light at night, no street lights or neon signs, or even headlights, he could now even see the Milky Way. The stars had always been nice in the Index area because the town was so small, but now it was unreal how many he could see.

The soft breeze was cool on his skin. He wore his only pair of jeans which were starting to show wear and tear, and an unbuttoned wool shirt over a tee-shirt that had once been white but that was now dull, stretched out, and comfortable. Washing clothes by hand was hard on modern materials.

Coming out at night to watch the stars was his escape from the daily grind of having to be responsible. He was still seen as a police officer, and technically he supposed he still was a deputy. He certainly still thought of himself as one and knew Casey felt the same way about herself. It meant that everyone came to them, all day long, with issues from the trivial to the important. They expected him to have answers, to solve their problems, to be in charge and fearless.

Sometimes it left him exhausted and drained and, in those times, the fear swamped him with existential questions. Was this the way it would be forever? Would they never feel fully safe again? Would they all die one by one, killed by mythical beings until humanity ceased to exist?

The other questions that were harder to bear. What if he screwed up? What if he missed something or made a mistake? What if someone in his charge died because he couldn't protect them? Those questions haunted him and when they became too overwhelming, sleep wouldn't come and he'd slip outside the fort to be alone and quiet. To just breathe.

He watched the slow and graceful arc of a satellite passing overhead. It was strange to think that the world existed normally out there. That the east coast was full of people driving cars to work every morning. That other countries read about their horror stories in the news. He'd been told by FEMA that the quake sent a devastating tsunami to Japan and wondered if any monsters had traveled that far, going with the waves. He hoped not.

Max stood and picked up his rifle. He felt like he could sleep now, and looked forward to slipping inside warm blankets beside Casey. He grinned suddenly. Maybe she'd wake up and he'd delay sleep a little longer. But as he turned to go back inside, he heard the creak of wood and the gate moved slightly.

"Who's there?" Max flicked on his flashlight.

He heard a quick gasp and saw Jennifer, one of Ethan's high school students, in the beam of light. She stood with her hand to her throat and her eyes wide with fright.

"What are you doing?" he asked.

"I couldn't sleep." Her voice was breathless, shaky. "I saw the gate open and was going to shut it. I didn't know anyone was out there."

Max stood silently, watching her. Waiting.

"Honestly." Her voice became tight. "I screwed up before but that doesn't mean I'm repeating it. I didn't know you were out there. If I had I wouldn't have been shutting the gate."

"Okay. Fair enough," Max said calmly. "Let's get it shut now though. I was on my way in."

"What were you doing out there anyway?" Jennifer asked, looking past him into the dark night.

Max's cop instinct kicked in and his neck hairs stood straight up. "Couldn't sleep. Just like you." He pushed the gate closed and lowered the heavy bar. "I'll walk you back."

She didn't say anything further as he walked with her to the small tent she used, pitched a short distance away. He raised the flap for her to duck inside.

"Hope you get some sleep now," he said, dropping the flap.

She didn't reply but he heard the sound of the zipper as she closed up the tent.

He kept his flashlight beam pointed at the ground in front of him as he made his way back to the gate so it wouldn't wake anyone. Once there he shown the light around the ground but too many people came and went through that entrance for anything unusual to be there. He ran the light over the gate itself, double-checking that they were secure.

Back in his own tent, he crawled into the double sleeping bag next to Casey. She curled up against him with her head on his chest without even waking. He put his arm around her and lay there, thinking.

Jennifer was just a kid. After the quake, she had been terrified like they all had been. She'd come up with a ruthless way to survive by locking one of the students out of Anya's cabin at night. The boy had died, killed by the Windigo. She'd thought she could pacify the monster by feeding it and she still paid for that action by the way others ostracized her.

Would she repeat the same thing? Shut someone out, bar the gate so they couldn't get back in, leave them out there to die alone? Had she known he was out there, after all?

Maybe.

Except he was pretty sure she had been pulling the gate open.

Chapter 6

IT WAS SO EARLY that the light was the soft pearl gray that could have been dawn or twilight. A low mist hung above the river and the air felt damp. A few birds tentatively chirped but for the most part the world was quiet and still. Max and Casey walked side by side with backpacks, weapons, and fishing poles. They followed what had once been the back road from Index to Gold Bar before the quake, when the world still felt like it would go on forever. Now the road was a rough path cut through the debris of a life gone.

"Do you ever think about leaving?" Casey asked. "Not to the refugee camps, but further east, maybe Montana, where the quake wasn't as bad? Cities are always looking for experienced police. We could get a job anywhere."

Max thought a moment before answering. "Once in a while. It would be easy to just go. Mainly I think about it when I'm missing something. A good scotch. Pizza. Or when I'm watching you and thinking about being naked in a hot tub."

Casey laughed.

"Yeah. It would be easy." He turned off the main track onto a smaller path and held back a tree branch as he passed under it so it wouldn't swing back and hit her. "But then I think that leaving this messed up world also means leaving the people in it."

Casey was silent, following him through the tree line and out onto the rounded river rocks, washed smooth by countless years of high water. The river ran fast but there was a nice deep pool where the current eddied in behind boulders. There, they hoped to find fish.

At the water's edge, they dropped their backpacks and rifles, and Casey unzipped a main pocket to pull out a thermos of hot coffee. Both of them carried their service weapons in holsters at their hips, close enough to pull if needed. She rummaged some more and came out with a box of shiny fishing lures. One of the women in town had made them from pieces of soda cans and feathers. Max watched her open the box and pull a lure out but she just held it in her hand, studying it.

"Casey?" he asked.

She shook her head but didn't respond, just taking the lure and tying it to her line.

Max stepped closer and caught her fishing rod, stopping her. "What is it?"

She wouldn't meet his eyes for a long moment, and when she finally looked up at him, he saw fear there.

"What if I wanted to?" she asked, her voice almost a whisper. "What if I wanted to go? To find some place with no monsters? Some place to build a nice boring life with no fear?"

Max cupped her chin with his hand. "If that's what you want, we'll go."

"Honest?"

"Honest. These people are friends. I have a loyalty to them. Yes, I'd feel like I was abandoning them. But I could live with that. Where you go, I go."

Casey's eyes shimmered as if she were about to cry but then she gave him a shaky smile and tugged her fishing pole out of his hand. "I'm not saying I want to do that for sure. Not yet anyway. It's just some days are harder than others."

"I hear you." Max put his hand to the back of her neck, pulled her close, and kissed the top of her head. "When you're ready to go, tell me. We'll figure it out."

Casey sniffled, then walked to the edge of the river and cast her line out into the green water, the circling currents catching the lure. "Pour me some coffee, big guy?"

Max recognized that to mean the subject was closed and he was willing to let it drop. He meant what he said, but he still hoped it would be a long time before it came up again. He poured coffee into the lid of the thermos and put the thermos down on a rock.

"Changing the subject here," he said. "Had a weird encounter with Jennifer."

He told Casey what had happened the night before. "There isn't anything concrete at this point. I just think maybe we need to keep an eye on her and find out what's going on."

"Fear hits people in so many ways." Casey lifted her pole a little, making the lure wiggle. "Especially fear, like this, that shows no sign of going away. She's a traumatized kid who took an extreme way to keep herself safe."

"Right? I just want to make sure that extreme method isn't something she's going to use again."

"We'll keep an eye on her," Casey said. "And keep this between us, too. I mean, the town is already against her. We don't want fear spreading and people turning on her if she's not doing anything wrong."

"Good point. We don't need vigilante justice."

An odd sound, like a low humming, came from back in the woods.

"What is that?" he asked.

Casey looked over her shoulder at him. "The wind? Can't tell for sure over the river."

Max stood, listening carefully. "Rising wind?"

Casey put her pole down and came back to him, picking up her rifle. "Sounds like howling."

"Maybe. If that's howling though, it's more than one."

They stood shoulder to shoulder a moment longer as the strange sound grew louder. Came closer.

"I don't like this." Max took his rifle and checked that it was loaded.

Casey looked around them as she also checked her rifle. "Not much to put our backs against."

"Tree line. Won't be as visible."

Max pulled on his backpack and jogged back the way they'd come with Casey close behind. Once they were inside the shadowed woods, he found a downed tree and crouched behind the log, resting his rifle across its mossy bark. Casey dropped down beside him, her rifle also across the log. He heard her draw in a slow breath as if steadying her hands. She was good in a fight. Calm and steady. There had been so many times in their past, as partners in the sheriff's department, that he'd been glad to have her at his back.

Just like now.

The sound grew, still hard to distinguish whether it was a low, strong wind or some sort of animal.

"There." Casey gestured by lifting her chin, hands never leaving the rifle.

There was movement through the trees, a massive blackness that rolled, formed wolf-like shapes, darkened into storm, reformed. The sound changed, focused, became more like a tortured screaming.

And then the wind hit like a wall of night, so hard Max was thrown back. The rifle was ripped from his hand and gone. He had no sense of up or down or where Casey was.

The keening voice of the wind, the sound, the power, was beyond breath, became his whole universe, burying thought or reason.

Until a woman bent to him and incandescent pain burned hot and deep in his chest.

And then thought, awareness, pain, was gone.

Chapter 7

RAMON HAD PLANNED ON leaving with the chilly, fog-filled dawn. He'd wanted a full day of walking. But he kept finding reasons to linger. He left the wheelbarrow at camp and picked up last minute rations. Tommy managed the walk okay, although he looked a little pale. At the Red Cross tables, the food had been scarce and he'd come away with only a box of raisins, a little jar of peanut butter, and a single bottle of water. There had been a lot of angry people standing around the empty folding tables. Ramon thought it was a good thing he was leaving, if rations were drying up.

As they walked away, Tommy tugged on Ramon's hand and when he looked down, the kid handed him half a protein bar. Surprised, Ramon took it and stopped walking.

"Where did you get this?"

Tommy, not surprisingly, said nothing.

"One of the Red Cross people give it to you?"

The little boy hesitated, then nodded.

Ramon handed the half a bar back. "Okay then. But I'm not hungry so you keep it. Thanks though."

Tommy took the piece of bar, folded the wrapper around it, then tucked it inside his shirt.

Ramon looked at the dark shadows under the boy's eyes, then bent and scooped him up. "Time for a break in walking, I think. Let's go back to camp."

At the ruins of the house, he decided he had to repack their gear and organize stuff in the wheelbarrow so it would be more comfortable for the kid. Then he did a walk around the site to see if there was anything they could use that he'd missed.

Each chore led to something else that kept him loitering around the remains of their home, debating with himself. What if they brought Marie back and he was gone? Should he head out into unknown dangers on the slim chance he could find her? Should he stay here with known dangers hoping she'd show up?

Tommy slept in the wheelbarrow, on the soft cushion of the old folded quilt on top of their tarp and sleeping bags. His backpack rested next to him and he was surrounded by the last-minute things they'd packed. Even in his sleep he held his hand over his heart, gripping a fold of his grimy tee shirt.

Ramon glanced again at the dirty shirt and dirty kid. Both of them were going to bathe as soon as they reached the river. Though there was dampness in the fog like rain coming. They might end up getting a shower instead of a bath.

He paced a wide circle around the wheelbarrow. Nothing left to pack. He walked to the front edge of what had been the lawn and stood on the buckled sidewalk, looking up and down the street, still clogged with wrecked cars and downed utility poles. People moved through the area, but none were Marie.

It was now late afternoon.

"Come on," he whispered under his breath. "Come home."

He looked back at the kid, stirring awake, and then pressed the palms of his hands hard against his eyes as if that could help him make up his mind.

He drew in a deep breath, hauled up his heavy backpack, and walked back to the wheelbarrow.

"Okay, little man." He gripped the handles of the wheelbarrow. "Okay."

There was no longer any reason to wait.

The bearing on the right tire squeaked as he pushed it forward but when he maneuvered it up and over the hunks of sidewalk the squeak stopped. He started down Kelsey Street slowly. More slowly than the debris and destruction warranted. He argued with himself with each step. What would it matter to wait one more day? And then what? One more day? With supplies disappearing people were going to get even more desperate. He needed to be out of the city before then.

He gritted his teeth and pushed the damn barrow forward until he reached Main Street, then paused one last time. Their house was barely visible from the intersection. No movement. No one running to catch up with him.

If the Cascadia Protection Force hadn't brought her back by now, they weren't going to do so willingly.

The boy twisted around in the barrow to face him and Ramon saw the question in his eyes.

"Yeah. I know. Past time to go."

He pushed forward and the squeak came back, accompanying them all the way down Main Street and to the smokestack. Ramon kept going past the long snaking line of people. There was no reason to stop now and go through the lists.

By the time they reached the junction of Main Street and what had been, before the quake, Highway 2, Ramon was quietly cursing the wheelbarrow under his breath. What had seemed like a good idea now didn't. He wondered which would be easier; hauling the damn thing over such rough terrain or having to walk at the pace of a half-starved kid and carry everything. Either way, they'd be lucky to reach Index before winter.

There were a few buildings still standing. Doors hung off hinges. Inside openings, Ramon caught glimpses of collapsed and empty shelves, cracked sheetrock, hanging light fixtures. It was hard to tell what had been destroyed by nature and what had been further destroyed by desperate people.

The building to his right had been a liquor store. Broken bottles and shattered glass glinted in the small parking lot. Only one corner of the structure remained standing. As they slowly worked their way past it, two men, a woman, and a teenage girl came around the debris. They were all dressed in mismatched and clearly scavenged clothes that didn't fit any of them.

One man had a hand on the shoulder of the teenager but when he made eye contact with Ramon, he pulled the girl behind him to the woman. Both men came closer.

Ramon put the wheelbarrow down and pulled his handgun out of his coat pocket. He'd had the Glock since he'd worked the Port in Seattle, loading on the docks at night, and the weight felt familiar in his hand.

The man who had pushed the girl behind him raised his hands. "We don't want trouble. Not even carrying a gun, here."

The second man moved off to the right.

Ramon put a hand on Tommy's head and pushed him down to burrow low in the wheelbarrow, then calmly raised his gun. "Don't want trouble here, either. So stop flanking me or I'll shoot."

The second man paused, glancing over at his companion.

"No need for that," the man said. "No need for trouble none of us wants. Just hand over your backpack and we're good."

"Not going to happen." Ramon drew in a steadying breath, everything in him going tense and still and waiting.

The man laughed. "You planning on shooting an unarmed man?"

"You think an unarmed man can get this pack?"

Out of the corner of his eye, Ramon saw the flash of movement as the second man reached behind his back and came out with a gun.

Ramon shot him. Center mass. Without thought, without hesitation, without doubt.

The man hit the ground. Ramon turned toward him, watching for movement, barely aware of the woman and teenager screaming. And in that brief second of distraction, the first man charged. Ramon never saw him coming and never saw what hit him. There was just sudden white-hot blinding pain and then nothing.

Chapter 8

THE WIND-SHAPES HIT LIKE a physical force, lifting Casey into the air. Daylight disappeared into deep blackness but she could still feel the pain as she was thrown, hitting something hard. A tree, a rock, she didn't have time to care. She slammed into something again and pain came, deep and profound, and yet distant as if she only observed it. She tried to grab onto something but her fingers touched nothing but cold.

She could feel claws tearing as she was thrown down and rolled by creatures she couldn't fully see. The howling was there inside her head, then screaming around her and through her, and then...gone.

In its place was a woman. Tall, in a long white dress that moved gently around her as if in a breeze. Her skin was as white as her dress, her hair coal black and long, hanging loose past the backs of her knees. Her fingers were abnormally long, and the sharp nails even longer. And somehow worst of all, she was clearly heavily pregnant.

She didn't seem aware of Casey, focused on something on the ground in front of her. She went down on one knee and bent lower, and Casey saw Max there.

Casey's brain shut down, unable to grasp the horror and shock. The woman was taking bites out of Max's chest. Her long fingers reached, grasped, lifted his still-beating heart.

Casey screamed, an ancient, brutal, throat-ripping sound that wiped out all thought. She yanked her gun out of its holster and ran straight for the woman, shooting.

The woman twisted to look at Casey, her night-black eyes widening. She hissed and stood. Casey slammed into her and it was like hitting a wall of ice. As she grappled with the woman her gun was torn from her hand. She fumbled her knife out of its sheath but it, too was torn away by a wind-whipped blackness that bit into her hand. The woman-thing shrieked, and Casey, tasting blood from her own screams, tried to slam her fist into the woman's face.

One thought howled through her. *Not Max. Not his heart.*

But the black wind was back and Casey was ripped from the woman, thrown into the howling wind, and thrown down. And then she was alone.

She was lost in the sudden silence, as if weightless. Somewhere in her mind she wondered fleetingly if she was dead, but the stillness and loss of time was so profound she couldn't latch on to the reality of the thought. Life came back to her in tiny sips. A sense of cold. Numbness. Pain, but that was a faraway thought, not something she could fully grasp or deal with. Something soft touching her cheek.

She became more aware of the pain. Cold moved upward in her consciousness until she gasped with it, like a swimmer surfacing.

The sun was up, the river mist gone. The softness touching her was tiny wavelets of cold river water. She was sprawled as if broken on rocks, close enough to the river that her left arm, hip, and boot were in the shallows. The snow-melt water was frigid, her body numb.

Casey pushed up and the sudden pain was white-hot, bringing her fully back to awareness. She managed to roll out of the water and on to her back on the rocks. She held there a moment, able to do nothing more than gasp. Fine shivering started throughout her body, making the pain throb in time with her heartbeat.

Shock. Cold. Injuries. Gut-clenching nausea. Somewhere in her mind she knew all those reasons for the growing tremors but the knowledge didn't seem to translate to action. She lay there immobile for several long moments until the pain became too much and she struggled to sit up. She turned carefully, looking for Max, her backpack, familiar surroundings.

Nothing. Except for her blood-encrusted knife in the rocks a few feet away.

Moving slowly and cautiously, she made it to her knees, retched, managed to stand, and staggered. The left sleeve of her shirt was shredded. Blood had seeped from multiple slash marks and dried into dark red scabs. More cuts crossed her chest. Her ankle complained when she put weight on it, but held her upright, so probably not broken. There was at least one broken or cracked rib that burned with each breath. There were odd puncture wounds on the back of her right hand. And a feeling of stickiness at her temple that told her she'd been cut and bled at some point. But she didn't feel the warmth of fresh blood so that was one good thing.

She picked up her knife and turned carefully to look around her. The river was the same as always. The woods were as well, to some extent, although there were fresh trails through broken and trampled underbrush. She couldn't see the path she and Max had come down but she knew she could go upriver and eventually, if nothing else, she'd reach Index.

She drew in a breath of pain. "Max!"

No response.

There was no way to know how far he'd been thrown. Or taken. Something stirred in her memory, but thoughts broke down, fled. Slowly, she worked her way upriver, breathing shallow and limping. She shivered harder now, her body struggling to warm her. She kept moving though she'd forgotten where she was going. She had a confused sense that she was looking for something but couldn't remember what. Until she saw the backpack caught on a snag of broken tree.

With her good hand, she pulled it off and fumbled zippers open. She recognized it, and that brought back a rush of awareness of Max. It was his pack and they carried pretty much the same things. She paused, her hand inside the main pocket, resting on the rough canvas material, and looked around. She was so tired.

It was peaceful here. The sound of the river, a breeze in the tree branches. Her eyes closed and she swayed a little. She was just so very tired. She could lie down here and rest for a bit.

She slid down and the sudden sharp pain in her side shocked her again back into awareness. She was half-lying on Max's pack. Gritting her teeth, she pulled out his fleece jacket, then a space blanket, a bottle of water, and a chocolate bar.

Sometime later, Casey came back into a clearer sense of self, as if she'd dozed off and was just waking. She'd managed to get the fleece sweater on and the space blanket around her shoulders, but couldn't remember doing it. She tore open the chocolate bar and took a bite, choking it down. Her shivering eased slightly though, as she warmed slowly, and as the sugar kicked in. Carefully, she pushed the space blanket back into the pack and zipped the pocket. Even more carefully, she stood again.

She tried calling for Max, her voice hoarse, but heard no response. Her throat felt raw, as if torn all the way into her chest. Shrugging the pack onto her good shoulder, she pushed her left hand through the front strap to support her arm.

There was no sense of time passing as she limped her way upstream. But the sun, partially hidden in gathering clouds, wasn't directly overhead yet so maybe late morning. She had to move so slowly that she also had no way to judge how far she'd gone. But at some point, she saw a break in the tree line that was the trailhead they'd walked that morning. Oddly, her fishing pole was still there, wedged into rocks. The sight was so incongruous that she had to stare for a moment before shaking her aching head and calling out again for Max.

She heard fear and deepening desperation in her voice but heard no response. She'd have to get all the way back to town for a search party. The thought was daunting and she ached with the need to just give in, sit down, and wait for help. But then she thought of Max, that he might be out there injured worse than she was, and started limping forward again. Her breath was shallow and caught on pain with each step as she entered the tree line.

And then she saw the blood.

And then she saw what was left of Max.

And then time stopped again.

Chapter 9

R AMON ROLLED TO HIS side and tried to push up onto his knees but the wave of vertigo and pain held him down, vomiting. When he finally heaved up nothing but bile, he used his shirt to wipe his face. It came away bloody, which explained why he couldn't open one eye. He rolled over onto his back, groaning.

A cool, wet cloth came down on his face and he jumped, causing sharp pain to fire his whole head and another wave of vertigo to roll his stomach. A little grimy hand clumsily swabbed the cloth over his face and every movement sent more pain arcing. Ramon reached up and caught the hand.

"It's okay, Tommy," he mumbled. "I got it."

The hand shook and Ramon felt like the top of his head was going to shoot off into thousands of burning stars.

"No, really, I got it."

He managed to roll onto his side and prop up on one elbow. He took the cloth and wiped at his eye as the boy shoved a water bottle into his other hand. He pushed himself up to sit, head hanging and the world spinning.

"Damn," he said, fingering his face. "What'd he hit me with?"

There was a gash over one cheekbone and another at his temple. Both had bled profusely down the side of his face and neck. But at least the bleeding was now just a trickle. Tommy didn't answer but he pointed with a still shaking hand and Ramon looked at a rock and half a bottle, both with his blood on them.

"Okay." He slowly maneuvered up on one knee but then had to stay there until the world stopped spinning. "Okay."

His thoughts were sluggish, like words weren't connecting right and that there was something else he should be asking. Slowly, thoughts coalesced.

"They're gone? Are you hurt?"

Tommy shook his head, pupils dilated with fear.

"No, what? No, they're not gone or no you're not hurt?"

The kid pointed again.

The man Ramon had shot was clearly dead. But the boy wasn't pointing at that body. He was pointing at the other one. The first man was crumpled only a few feet away, also dead. But there was something wrong with his body.

Ramon heaved himself up and had to grab the edge of the wheelbarrow to steady himself for a moment before he could go closer. The kid climbed into the wheelbarrow and burrowed down out of sight under the bedding.

The man was full of holes. Like he'd been stabbed thousands of times. But as Ramon moved closer, he saw the ragged edges. They looked more like…bites. And the man's eyes and ears and pieces of scalp were gone.

"What the hell?" Ramon whispered.

He staggered back to the wheelbarrow and uncovered the boy, who was curled in a fetal position.

"Hey." Ramon put a hand on the boy's head. "It's okay. They can't hurt us now. Did you see what happened?"

Tommy shook his head but wouldn't open his eyes.

Ramon kept his voice low and soothing. "Did you see that man die?"

Another shake of the head.

Ramon gripped the edge of the wheelbarrow and leaned on it for a long moment. His stomach settled but his head pounded and the wounds burned. As he drew in a deep breath, he focused on the damp, blood-stained cloth still in his hand. Where the hell had the kid found that?

Finally, he rested his hand on the boy's shoulder and spoke, still with his voice calm. "It's okay, little man. You hear me? We're okay. We're going to be fine. We're going to get out of this hell hole."

He turned, scanning the ground around them and it was only then he realized his backpack with all their carefully saved food was gone. And his gun.

Chapter 10

Casey was alone, hollowed from sobbing so deep she was empty.

She would have gone with the first helicopter, back when they'd started airlifting people after the quake. Max would have gone with her if she'd asked. Just like they'd talked about earlier. This morning, or a lifetime ago, she wasn't sure anymore. They could have been in the refugee camps in Yakima right now. There, together, sitting in the hot sun, safe, holding each other's hands.

Instead of this.

There was enough left of Max to know it was him. But he was a mangled body that was so very, very wrong. Broken from being thrown by whatever that darkness had been, but also torn apart as if shredded, his lungs gone, his heart half-pulled away. His blood had stopped flowing but when she carefully lay down next to him, it was still warm under her hand, under her cheek where she rested against what would have been his shoulder. She curled against him, put her hand on his heart, on the remains of his beautiful, beautiful heart, and closed her eyes.

Chapter 11

RAMON SAT ON THE ground under the tarp he had tied up for shelter. They were back at the ruined house and he wondered briefly if he'd ever get free of the place. It didn't feel like home so much now as it did defeat. All they had was what had been in the wheelbarrow; the musty blanket, the two sleeping bags, the tarp and its ropes, and Tommy's pack. There was no way they could start the trek back to Index without some sort of weapon, with no food or water, with nothing to start a fire.

The need to get out of Monroe was like a huge fist at his back, pushing and pushing at him, the desperate need to *do* something to find Marie. But the reality of what had happened was sinking in, now that his pain was easing some and he had time to process it.

Rain pattered lightly on the tarp but it didn't drown out the sounds of the remnants of the city around him. He could hear distant shouts and occasional shots being fired. It sounded like desperation, like growing fear, worse than it had been.

Or maybe it was just him. After all, he'd just shot and killed a man and absolutely nothing had happened. He'd been beat up and robbed and nothing had happened.

No one cared. There'd been no reaction at all. And the bodies of those two men might very well still be lying in the parking lot. Somebody might have hauled them off to the smokestack, but still. In this strange new world, he could kill someone, walk away (or stumble, in his case) and be completely free.

He tried to focus on those abstract thoughts but the reality kept pushing into his aching head, twisting his stomach with nausea, making his hands tremble.

He'd killed a man. Shot him without even hesitating, simply reacting to the threat. He'd been in fights before but never, ever, something this violent, something he, himself, had done. There should be consequences. He shouldn't be allowed to take another's life, to end someone so brutally. But that's exactly what happened. No sirens, no arrest, no jail, no one to even ask why.

What did that make him? What was he becoming?

It was a clear sign, if any more were needed, that this wasn't the place to be. Especially if you had a kid to look after. Yet he was left with the same dilemma. Leaving and taking the chance Marie may be brought back to this dangerous city and be left alone here, or staying and taking the chance that she was out there somewhere, needing him.

Ramon glanced to his right. Tommy was a small lump in his sleeping bag, not moving. He shivered and considered getting in his own as well, trying to get some sleep. He'd taken the old blanket from the wheelbarrow and spread it on the ground under the tarp, then put the sleeping bags on top so they'd have some sort of insulation from the dampness. But he knew sleep would only bring nightmares, a never-ending reel of the gun in his hand firing, the man falling.

What was the plan now?

Someway to protect them was the highest priority. He had to get some weapon and he had no idea how. He had nothing to barter with and wasn't about to steal from someone else in need no matter how desperate he was.

Food and water would be the next priority. They might be able to forage or fish on the way home but this early in the spring there wasn't much coming up and he didn't trust his foraging abilities. He'd probably poison them before they starved.

If the monsters didn't get them first.

Ramon dropped his head to his hands, sinking his fingers into his hair and pressing against his aching scalp. They couldn't stay and they couldn't leave.

And he couldn't see a solution.

He shifted slightly to lift the side of his sleeping bag and carefully maneuvered inside. He thought about the need to keep watch during the night but then realized it no longer mattered. If someone came into their camp now, mythical monster or human monster, there was nothing he could do about it except try to hold them off long enough for the kid to get away.

Ramon's eyes were gritty with exhaustion and he was bone-deep discouraged. He fell asleep while thinking there was no way he would sleep, while the city around him slowly continued its collapse.

Chapter 12

IT WAS LATE EVENING, cool and misting rain, but Casey had no idea of the exact time. Not that time mattered anymore.

Two days since Max died. She wasn't sure she'd slept much. Not that sleep mattered anymore, either.

She hadn't spoken to anyone since they'd found her curled up against his body. She could still feel his heart in her hand as warmth faded and his blood soaked into the ground, into her skin. She was sure that's what had happened. His blood, joining with hers, because she felt him still there, somewhere inside.

She saw the worry in Ben's eyes and the understanding in June's. But seeing the elderly couple's concern didn't ease the ache. Someone had once said grief was a hollowed-out place but that was a lie. It was a huge, massive weight that suffocated her, bore her down into darkness.

And she went down into that darkness willingly.

She couldn't settle. She finally left the fort, limping around the perimeter in the dark silence. She thought about going to the little cemetery, where the others had buried Max. But the spot didn't mean anything, since he wasn't there. Couldn't be there. She hadn't even gone with them. What they put in the ground, what they cried over, wasn't Max and seeing the others grieving angered her.

Max's words about Jennifer's behavior stuck in her brain, gave her something to focus on, and she watched for the girl. She knew monsters came out in the dark but she didn't fear them anymore. What could they do but kill her? And what would death do but reunite her more fully with Max?

But, oh god, how she missed resting her head on his broad shoulder at night. She missed his breath. His chest rising under her hand. The way he would reach for her in his sleep, restless until his fingers touched her. How he would settle deeper into sleep once he found her.

How could he find rest now, without her?

So she slipped through the evening hours, following the darkness, continuing their job to keep people safe and giving her purpose for the moment. But deep inside anger was restless and waiting.

The mist fell, collecting on leaves and dripping softly to earth. A light spring rain that couldn't penetrate the fleece sweater she wore. She had Max's backpack, a new rifle from Ben, and her headlamp, although it wasn't on. She also had her knife and Max's handgun. Hers had been lost by the river, but his, oddly, had still been in its holster. She was fully armed and knew that, even injured, she was ready for whatever the night brought her.

She started another perimeter check but the creak of the fort's heavy gate being pulled open made her pause. She stepped into the deeper shadows under a tree, rage a fire banked for now under the grief, but waiting for a spark. If it was Jennifer setting someone else up to die again, Casey would stop it.

Max would want that.

When the gate opened enough, a person slipped through but in the darkness, it was hard to tell who it was. They paused by the gate, head turning as if to make sure no one followed. After a moment, they stepped away from the fort and flicked on a small flashlight that they kept pointed at the ground. Casey gave them time to get a short distance ahead and then straightened and walked quietly across the street.

Whoever it was turned down the short trail to the river. Casey stayed several feet behind them, beginning to get a sense of who it might be. That was confirmed when the person reached the river and put the flashlight on top of a stone so they were outlined in the low beam.

Rowan O'Reilly, one of Ethan's high school students, tall and with a thick auburn braid, was now easily identifiable. As Casey watched from behind a cedar tree with its crown sheared off, Rowan unbraided her hair and fingered it loose. As the girl started slipping out of her clothes, Casey realized she was probably going to bathe and shifted to turn and leave. But movement in the water caught her eye and she reached awkwardly for her gun with her bandaged hand. The tiny spark that could ignite her rage flickered.

The river was no longer a safe place to be. The rushing water hid things that needed to be destroyed.

Casey, jaw clenched, moved silently forward as she pulled out her gun. She willed whatever it was to come fully forward, to try and take Rowan, so she could kill it and kill it and kill it.

The movement was there again, faint at the farthest edge of flashlight beam, something underwater. The river current rippled around it but Casey couldn't see what it was. Rowan was watching it though and wasn't reacting with fear. Instead, the girl stepped carefully out of her clothes, her pale skin glowing and haloed in the faint light. Casey hesitated, not sure what was happening.

Rowan went into the cold river until it was to her waist. The current rushed around her and she was clearly bracing herself against it. Whatever was in the river rolled like a large fish and circled her once, then again, closer.

She sank underwater.

Casey limped forward, stopping at the water's edge. From Rowan's flashlight beam, she could see the girl out there, swimming underwater, her long hair fanning out into the current.

Someone else was there, swimming with her. Casey could only see outlines but it was clearly a young man, blue with cold. She could catch the flash of skin as he came close to Rowan, touching her, floating away with the current, coming back to circle her again.

Rowan came up for air and Casey saw she was laughing. Taking a deep breath, she sank again, this time letting the current carry her downriver a short distance. The young man went with her, caught her, rolled with her, their bodies sinuous underwater, disappearing into the darker shadows beyond the reach of the flashlight.

Casey's racing heart slowed as she holstered her gun. This had nothing to do with monsters. She didn't know who the young man was, but there were a couple guys in the small town, and clearly a rendezvous had been planned. She started back up the trail and once on Avenue A, walked down the street in the darkness, heading back to Fort Curtis.

Tears tracked down her cheeks but she didn't feel them and didn't wipe them away. They were nothing. Just a tiny, tiny piece of her greater grief. If Rowan had found someone to be with, Casey sure as hell wasn't going to be the one to take that away from her. Maybe Rowan wouldn't end up with her heart broken and shattered and empty.

Let the girl have a brief moment of happiness.

Max's voice was there, with her, a sudden blossoming warmth inside. She stopped, breath hitching on a sob. She'd known. Even when they buried those pieces of a body, she'd known he hadn't truly left her.

"You're here." Tears coursed unnoticed down her cheeks.

I told you, love. Where you go, I go.

Chapter 13

S PIKE SAT CROSS-LEGGED ON top of a boulder at the edge of the river. He watched the rushing water intently, shivering slightly in the damp breeze of an overcast morning. At the edge, the remaining cans of beer bobbed against their tether. He couldn't look at them and the thought of drinking one twisted his stomach with something heavier than nausea, something like fear.

When Ethan had left after the quake, going with Anya to her cabin, he'd left Spike in charge of their high school group. The ones, like him, who'd been on the fieldtrip from hell. He sucked at the whole being-a-leader shit. He'd been secretly relieved when Payton and Michael had decided to leave for the refugee camps. Payton with her perfect hair and perfect boobs and feigned helplessness had driven him nuts. And Michael, overweight and belligerent had just made him want to punch the guy.

The group of students shrank when Lucy also decided to go. Though he'd understood her need to find her parents, he missed her presence in the little family he'd created with her and Nathaniel. And now he was left with the Index survivors. Like an extended family that had been created by proximity and danger. He even liked a few of them, like the old farts, Ben and June, the grandparents he'd always wished he'd had.

But now, Max was dead. He couldn't wrap his head around it. When they had first met, when their group had stumbled into town, terrified, he'd seen Max and Casey as just cops. Like the ones that used to come for him, for all the trouble he sought to escape his life. Cops that would take him from home and then send him back. Over and over and over.

But Max and Casey had been different. Like Ethan, they'd treated him like they did everyone else. They didn't look at him with disgust in their eyes. Or worse, pity. And the quake had changed everything.

Max had become someone he respected.

But he was dead. No coming back from that.

Nathaniel, Connor, Tessa, even a few others, now treated Spike like he was the new leader of their little group. Even Albert, the mayor, was starting to rely on him for shit like he was an equal instead of a fucked up newly eighteen-year-old. He felt the pressure of needing to have answers, of needing to be one of the strong ones.

The reality was, he was scared shitless.

Ben and June had asked him that morning to help them secure the barter shed. Someone was stealing supplies. Then June asked him to carry up some buckets of water for her. And Tessa wanted help reinforcing their one chicken coop to keep rats out. It never stopped.

He needed to be alone where he could be scared and no one could see. So, he went to the river for a few minutes. Just to grieve for Max.

Except there was something in the water. Not quite to the middle of the channel. He only caught flashes of movement, of blue in the green water. If it got too close to the surface, it almost dissolved into a rainbow sheen, like oil on water. He briefly considered getting Rowan, to show her in case it was a weird kind of fish. She somehow managed to catch more than anyone. But then he realized it was too big for a fish. Fear briefly clenched him, but if this was a monster, it wasn't coming to shore.

He heard the soft clatter of dislodged river cobble and looked over his shoulder to see Nathaniel coming down the trail with a lined canvas jacket over one arm and a steaming mug in his hand. He took a deep breath, forcing himself to relax, to not scare Nathaniel.

"Grannie send you?" he asked, glad to hear no echo of fear in his voice.

Nathaniel nodded, handing over the coat first. Spike pulled it on and zipped it up over his shirt.

"Coffee." Nathaniel lifted the mug. "Instant, with powdered milk. But hot."

"Thanks."

Spike took the mug and glanced back at the river. What would Max do? Tell people so they would be warned? Keep it to himself and deal with it on his own? Spike didn't know what that would look like, and sure as shit, didn't feel up to saving the world. And Nathaniel lived in this new world, too. He'd seen monsters and what they could do.

Spike gestured toward the water with his mug. "Something's out there in the river. Too big to be a fish. Not big enough to be a fucking monster."

Nathaniel walked to the water's edge and Spike tensed, wanting to pull him back.

"I don't see…oh, there. Wait. No. It's gone. It was like, almost swimming against the current. It's kind of pretty. And it's not coming closer."

"Yet." Spike took a swallow of hot, bitter coffee and felt the warmth track down to his stomach like false courage. He slid off the boulder. "Throw a rock at it."

"What?" Nathaniel's eyebrows shot up. "Wouldn't Max, like, want us to warn people? Want us to stay away from the river?"

"I'm not Max." He knew he sounded defensive, but Nathaniel didn't react. "Throw a big fucking rock and see what happens."

"You mean, like some monster breaching up to eat us?"

"Yeah, like that." Spike bent, picked up a palm-sized rock, and threw it into the current.

Before either of them could move, the rock came flying back out of the water and hit Spike in the chest, making him stumble backward.

"Shit." He managed to not drop the mug and Nathaniel caught his arm to steady him. "That hurt."

"Bright idea." Nathaniel bent, picked the rock up, and threw it. It fell short of Spike's throw but still made it out to the current.

There was a brief flash in the water and the rock came flying back. Prepared this time, Spike caught it one-handed.

"Okay," Nathaniel said. "This is weird."

"But not man-eating weird."

"Not yet anyway." Nathaniel took a nervous step back.

Spike squatted down at the river's edge, studying the rushing emerald-green and white water. He took another swallow of coffee but didn't taste it as his thoughts rolled around in his head. Still no breaching monster coming to eat them. Was it friend or foe?

"What should we do?" Nathaniel asked.

Before Spike could answer, they heard someone else coming down the trail, fast. He straightened to see Rowan slide to a stop before them, her eyes wide in surprise. Her auburn hair was in its usual long braid and she had an old towel over one arm.

"Oh!" She glanced quickly at the water and then back to them.

"What's going on?" Spike asked, suspicion flaring.

"What do you mean?" Rowan asked. "I was just going to bathe."

"In snow-melt, ice cold water?" Spike put the mug down then threw the rock into the river as hard as he could. It went into the deep center of the river with a heavy, low, splash.

And came right back up. This time Spike let it fall at their feet.

Rowan stared at it, then surprisingly grinned. "You've met. He likes playing games. He gets lonely."

"He?" Spike asked. "Just who the hell are you talking about?"

Rowan came the rest of the way down the path and put her towel on the boulder Spike had been sitting on. "I don't know his name. I've been swimming with him but, you know, it's kind of hard to talk under water. He helps me catch fish."

Nathaniel put a hand on her arm and spoke, voice gentle. "Rowan, you do know it's not human, right? No one has come up for air."

She laughed. "I'm not crazy. This isn't me escaping into my dreams and drawings. I came down here one night to swim and we met. We've been swimming a lot together since. I think maybe Casey saw us, but she never said anything.

You wouldn't believe how magical that moonlight is underwater. It was like everything terrifying on land, was just gone."

"Okay, happy for you," Spike said. "But what exactly is your new boyfriend?"

"A guy," she said, confused. "Just like us."

"Except he can't come out of the water. You do realize that's not normal, right?"

"What's normal?" Rowan asked, her voice suddenly bitter. "You think because he can't breathe air, he's a monster. But he doesn't hurt me. We swim, we ride the rapids, we touch. He's real. He's lonely. And he likes my company."

"Great," Spike said. "But you can't keep doing this. It's not a person. It's not safe."

Rowan pulled her tee shirt over her head and then unzipped her jeans, stepping out of them with no embarrassment, standing in her bra and panties. The cool air raised gooseflesh on her pale skin. "I'm fine."

Spike caught her arm. "You're not going into the water. Seriously. What if that thing decides to keep you?"

Rowan tugged against his grip, then pulled harder. "Let go, Spike. He won't like it if he thinks you're keeping me from him."

"All the more reason this ain't happenin'." Spike bent and slid his arm behind her knees, lifting her up. "Nathaniel, grab her clothes. We're getting the hell away from here."

Rowan was tall for a young woman, taller even than Spike. She struggled against his grasp and he stumbled, his grip slipping.

"Let me go!" Wild panic came into her voice and she lashed out, hitting and kicking at him. "Let me go! Let me go!"

A stone came flying out of the river and hit Spike between the shoulder blades. Another one hit Nathaniel on his shoulder. And as Spike went down on one knee, losing his grip on Rowan, more rocks came flying out of the river, drops of water arcing out from them as they flew true to their targets. Spike let go of Rowan and bent over Nathaniel, shielding him from the raining stones.

Rocks pelted him and he grunted with pain, one arm coming up to protect his head.

Rowan lunged to her feet and sprinted for the river, wading in until it was deep enough that she could slide under water.

The rocks stopped.

Spike stood slowly, his bruised body aching. He reached out to Nathaniel and managed to pull him to his feet. Together they went cautiously to the edge of the river.

"Rowan!" Nathaniel called. "Come back!"

They could see her, swimming toward the center of the river. She surfaced, shaking water out of her eyes, and raised her hand to them.

"See? It's fine. I'll meet you back by the fire."

She slid back under water.

"What do we do?" Nathaniel asked. "I mean, she seems okay. Like she knows what she's doing."

"She's swimming with something that isn't fucking human," Spike said.

"But it's not hurting her."

Rowan surfaced again, laughing. Her braid had come undone and her hair washed out away from her, waving in the currents like auburn seaweed.

"I'm fine!" she shouted.

And then she was jerked under and didn't surface again.

Nathaniel grabbed Spike's arm and they froze, staring at the rushing river, willing her to come up, to shake out her hair, to laugh. Spike held his breath and clenched his jaw, waiting, waiting, waiting. When his fingers tingled and his lungs burned, he gasped and sucked in a lungful of cold air. And still the water ran fast and churning and no Rowan.

Nathaniel, his slight frame shaking, jerked down the zipper of his coat and yanked his shirt up. Spike caught him.

"No."

"We have to do something!" Tears streaked Nathaniel's pale cheeks.

Spike swallowed against the thick lump in his throat, the bottomless fear in his gut. "You're not going after her. I am."

He yanked off his coat. Kicked off his boots.

Nathaniel reached out to him, but Spike was already running for the river. He pushed out until the current took him and he had to swim. He went under, eyes open, seeing nothing but green and foam and boulders. He came up, shook hair out of his face, sucked in air, and went down again. And again.

Each time he surfaced, he was farther down river, until he could no longer see Nathaniel. The river was so cold his body burned and it got harder to control his movement. And it got harder to get enough air into his lungs as his body slid into shock. The current shoved him into boulders, bruising him, but he barely felt the impact.

Finally, he gave up and let the river take him. He couldn't fight it anymore. He couldn't force his body to move. He could see sparks at the edges of his vision as his oxygen-deprived brain fired. And then Rowan was there, beautiful hair fanning out around her in a thick halo of rich autumn in the forest-green of mountain water. Her arms came around him, her eyes looked into his, and he saw peace there and it was enough.

Spike heard Nathaniel's voice but couldn't answer. He coughed and gagged and coughed again, unable to open his eyes. His chest burned, his ribs ached, and his whole body shook uncontrollably. His teeth chattered so hard he thought his jaw was going to break.

"You stupid, stupid motherfucker!"

Nathaniel seemed to be shaking him, but Spike was shaking so hard on his own he couldn't tell for sure. He got his eyes open and saw Nathaniel's hands on him, but he couldn't feel them.

"Wrap him up." Connor grabbed Spike's shoulders, heaving him up and folding a wool blanket around him. "Get that other blanket tight around him."

"Samuel says warm him up slow so he doesn't have a heart attack." Tessa's voice came from somewhere above him.

"You...you...you stupid motherfucker!" Nathaniel shouted again. He rocked back on his heels and collapsed in a heap, crying and shaking almost as hard as Spike.

Spike tried to speak, coughed, and could do no more than lay there, boneless.

"Don't try to talk," Samuel, their sole paramedic said, and he sounded oddly exhausted. "We need to get you to the fire."

Spike's throat burned. "Nathaniel...doesn't...cuss."

"I said don't talk." Samuel pulled a wool hat down over Spike's ears and cinched another blanket around him with someone's belt. "We're getting you on a stretcher so we can carry you. Don't move. You'll just waste body heat."

The stretcher was an old cot with the cot's siderails still in place. Spike could smell the musty canvas and felt the roughness of it against his cheek but it was distant as if not real. His brain felt fogged, his body non-existent. But he saw Nathaniel stand and grab the edge of the cot as the others lifted him. His weight made the material sag until he was cocooned and couldn't see anything but sky and treetops. He coughed and had to turn his head to the side to bring up river water and bile. Nathaniel grabbed a corner of the blanket and wiped his mouth.

"Had...to do it," Spike said hoarsely. "Or you would have. Couldn't...lose you, too."

Chapter 14

WHEN RAMON WOKE LATE in the morning the only good thing was that the rain had stopped. It was chilly and even his jeans and coat felt damp. His muscles had stiffened up during the night and he groaned as he rolled over.

Right in front of his face, lying on the ground, was his gun.

Or at least, it was a Glock. But he was sure it was his because it was sticky with dried blood.

Ramon sat up too fast and pressed his arm to his side as his breath caught on the pain. After a moment he shifted more slowly, reaching for the gun. Tommy was still under the sleeping bag. Surely, Ramon would have known if the kid had left during the night. So where had the gun come from? Who else could have known that his had been taken and how much they needed a weapon? Who had seen the fight? The woman and the teenage girl. But how would they have known where to find Ramon if they'd wanted to return the gun?

Ramon grabbed up the gun, ignoring the dried blood, and checked the chamber. Empty. The clip, which should have still had bullets, was missing. He sighed heavily. He'd wished for his gun and it was here. He should have wished for bullets, too.

Could Tommy have slipped away during the night without him realizing it?

But that was crazy. The boy would have had to search the whole city to find the woman and teenager who had been with the two men.

Well, it was a crazy world. He put his hand to the ground and got to one knee, then slowly pushed to stand. He'd talk to Tommy when the kid woke. For now, it wouldn't hurt to let him sleep as long as possible. There was forgetfulness in sleep.

Ramon slipped the empty gun back into his coat pocket. Maybe people would assume it was loaded. When the kid woke, they'd pack the wheelbarrow then head over to Coastal where he might be able to scavenge some clothes or a backpack for himself. And maybe the Red Cross had come up with more food and water. Whatever they could find would determine their next steps.

Someone behind him cleared their throat tentatively. "Uh...hello? Ramon?"

He turned too abruptly and grimaced as his body complained sharply. Standing at what would have been the back corner of the house were two of Ethan's high school students. It took Ramon a moment to switch gears, to think about the days in Index, to remember their names. Michael and Payton.

It looked like Michael had lost a few pounds in the month since Ramon had seen him last. He also looked like he'd lost some of his angst and belligerence. Or at least, at this moment anyway. Payton stood behind Michael, half hidden, head down, dirty hair hanging over her face.

He gestured them forward. "Come on in. Home sweet home and all that happy crappy."

Tommy stirred under the sleeping bag and sat up, and both Michael and Payton jumped nervously, grabbing on to each other.

"Relax," Ramon said, gesturing them forward. "It's just an abandoned little kid."

Michael led the way tentatively to the tarp with Payton staying close behind him.

"What are you two doing here? How did you find me?" Ramon asked.

"We saw your note on the lists," Michael said. "The one you left for your brother."

"Oh, right. I thought you two were headed for the refugee camps in Yakima."

"We were," Michael said. "But the helicopter dropped us here and the guy said this was as far as they were taking us. That the camps were full. Asshole laughed at us. We've been here since. I couldn't find my family. Payton...uh, she found her parents. Her kid brother. I mean, found their names on the lists. You know?"

"Yeah. I know."

"And there isn't any food left. When we saw your name, we thought maybe you could, you know, help us. We didn't know what else to do. Didn't know where to go. And this place…it's getting scary, man. You know? I mean, not that I'm scared but…"

The words poured forth, fast and desperate and tears shimmered in Michael's eyes. And then the words faded. Dried up.

"I don't have anything," Ramon said bluntly. "Lost it all yesterday. But you can stay with us until we figure out the next step. As soon as I can get provisions we're heading home to Index."

"You're going back?" Payton's voice was a sudden whisper. She stepped out fully from behind Michael and her chin came up. "Will you take us? Get us out of here?"

Shock robbed Ramon of breath. She had been traditionally pretty, one of those popular high school girls with the perfect makeup and the confidence that comes from knowing life was held in her hand, and knowing how to manipulate her world to get whatever she wanted. Now, her face and throat were covered in fading bruises and scabs from healing cuts. Where she used to wear low-cut, tight-fitting shirts that showed contours and cleavage, now a grimy, cut up hand gripped a too-big shirt tight at her throat.

"I'm getting us the hell out of here one way or another, and yes, the two of you are definitely going with me."

Tommy's eyebrows shot up to his hairline.

Ramon gestured at the wheelbarrow. "Michael can help push."

Michael snorted. "A wheelbarrow? I'm not pushing that to Index."

"I'm not taking any of your attitude," Ramon said. "You lose it, or you don't go. And if you act like you used to when we're out there, you're left behind. Get it?"

Michael raised his hands, palms out. "Sure, sure. I'm sorry. I'm trying, really. It's just sometimes things come out of my mouth. But…I'm trying to be better, man. Seriously."

Ramon saw fear in Michael's eyes and maybe something else. Maybe shame. Maybe loneliness.

"Then I guess we understand each other. We're going to hit the Coastal parking lot and see if we can find anything to help us survive. Then we're leaving. Today. Even if we can't find stuff we need. You both okay with that?"

When the sleeping bag and tarp were packed into the wheelbarrow and the kid was sitting there hanging on to the sides, Ramon picked up the handles and headed for the street. As they left the remains of the house, Payton walked next to the wheelbarrow with one hand gripping the edge.

Ramon pushed the barrow out into the street, hoping that maybe this time it would actually be the last time they saw the remains of his home. He couldn't help but pause though, to scan the few people walking by, hoping for a familiar face. Hoping one final time for family.

After a moment he cleared his throat as if that would ease the ache lodged there, and moved forward.

The bearing on the wheelbarrow started squeaking.

Chapter 15

THE SUN WAS PAST its zenith and casting shadows in the small valley between the river and the Index Wall even though it was only late afternoon. With the shadows came coolness in the air that reminded Casey winter hadn't been gone all that long. It was almost time to head back to town.

Tessa and Connor were foraging for early spring greens and roots and mushrooms to supplement the resources of their tiny community. Tessa was also carefully digging up some to replant in a garden. She'd told Casey that if she could get native plants to thrive there, it would be safer than going out into the woods to forage.

When they had started out with their baskets that afternoon, Casey had silently joined them, handgun and knife in their holsters, backpack on, rifle slung over her shoulder, and obviously ready to guard them. She hadn't asked if they needed her and they didn't say anything either. They all understood the need to be watchful.

And Casey, deeply unsettled, needed a job. She was lost and something inside wanted to flame up and rage. Max was still there inside, with her, of that she had no doubt. After all, she'd held his heart. His blood had soaked into hers. But yet, who was she now, when her mind and body seemed fractured, filled with pain and oddly empty at the same time?

She trailed the other two silently, limping on her sore ankle, as they worked through the day, finding early salmonberries and picking handfuls of miner's lettuce, young nettles, and cattail shoots. And now, as the day ended, snipping the tips of new growth from a spruce tree.

"Anya said it makes a tea high in vitamin C," Tessa said. "And you can make a cleaning solution, too."

Casey stepped away, letting the young couple work, checking her service revolver, the rifle across her chest. She didn't take her eyes off the trail ahead of them, feeling no need to reply. Words were worthless.

Tessa and Connor lifted their full foraging baskets and Tessa nodded to Casey. They started back down the trail toward Index and she fell in step behind them, scanning the woods. Sudden movement in the trees made Casey pull up her rifle and jack a shell into the chamber.

The sharp noise of the rifle made both young people run back to her and she used her hand to gesture them behind her. She rested her finger alongside the rifle's trigger and sighted along the barrel, focused on the movement in the trees.

"What is it?" Tessa whispered, voice shaky.

Casey shook her head, for a brief second not sure. But then she recognized Jennifer and lowered the rifle slightly.

"What are you doing out here?" Her words were sharp, her voice hoarse from disuse.

Jennifer came out of the trees and stopped, standing several feet away from them. She scowled and held up a small basket. "Same as you. Just finished."

"Alone?" Connor asked in disbelief. "Unarmed?"

"Why not?" Jennifer asked. "Being armed or with others didn't help Max, did it?"

Casey shut down instantly, a deep flash of agony followed by blankness. She pushed past Jennifer, starting down the trail to town alone. She didn't look back as she walked away, numb to what might happen to any of them. But she still heard Tessa's voice.

"That was intentionally cruel."

"Why?" Jennifer asked. "It's true, isn't it?"

Casey was several feet away now, picking up speed, almost jogging to get away.

"Casey deserves better than your cruelty." Connor's voice was fainter, dropping away behind her.

Watch that one. Max was there and Casey slowed, tilted her head, listened. *Don't trust her.*

"I don't," Casey whispered as Tessa and Connor caught up to her.

"What a bitch," Connor said.

"I think she does it on purpose," Tessa replied. "I think she's scared and acts tough like that so no one knows how lonely she is."

Connor met Casey's eyes over the top of Tessa's head, his eyebrows raised in disbelief. He put his arm around Tessa's shoulder. "You keep believing there's good in everyone," he told her. "Someone around here needs to."

Casey said nothing but she glanced back at Jennifer, coming down the path a few yards behind them with her basket.

She's up to something.

Casey almost smiled. Max would do that, state the obvious to be corny and make her smile.

He agreed with her, though. And if they both picked up on the same thing, Jennifer needed watching.

Chapter 16

B Y LATE AFTERNOON THEY'D managed to find a few supplies and Ramon called for a break. They gathered around the wheelbarrow to spread out their treasurers. Michael and Payton had both found beat up backpacks. Michael's had a hole in one pocket but was still functional. They had all managed to find at least one change of clothes and best of all, Ramon had found an all-purpose tool, one of those foldup jobs with a little screw driver, pliers, two knives, and a can opener. It had been in the pocket of a torn-up coat. Maybe he'd end up with a can to open.

The Red Cross had added another relief station in the same lot and Ramon left his charges in line with instructions to get all the food and water they could. He told them to stay together and when they were done at the relief station, to wait beside it for him to come get them. He then crossed the rough parking lot to the National Guard tents as a few tentative raindrops fell.

He waited in a long line of people who looked as bad off as he did. Scavenged clothes, healing wounds, signs of hunger and illness and grief and desperation. Soldiers had set up battered traffic cones to try and create some sort of order. People shifted forward slowly, each one with something to ask, to beg for, to demand, and Ramon inched forward with them, shivering, queasy from hunger and a headache. He could see McCausland, the Guardsman he'd been dealing with, sitting with three others at a folding table.

The teenager in front of Ramon leaned heavily on a broken broom handle. His left knee was bandaged but the bandages were dirty and fresh blood seeped out under them. There was a sweet, sickening smell of infection like a fetid bubble around him as he hobbled slowly under the canopy.

McCausland didn't look up from the forms he wrote on. "What can we do for you?"

"Antibiotics," the teenager said. "Or, please, a ride to the refugee camps in Yakima."

McCausland gestured to another soldier as he spoke to the teenager. "No ride to the refugee camps for a couple days yet."

The second soldier stepped up to the folding table. "Sir?"

"Take this kid to the medical tents and find someone to help him."

The soldier put his arm around the teenager's waist and helped him limp away. "Next."

Ramon stepped under the canopy. McCausland looked up and scowled as recognition came into his exhausted eyes.

"Anything?" he asked, not wanting to waste time with repeating what he'd been saying for days.

"What happened to you?"

Ramon shook his head and then winced. "Got beat up. All my supplies stolen. Have you heard anything?"

McCausland leaned back and tossed his pen down. "Looking for your niece, right? The one assisting the Cascadia Protection Force?"

"Assisting?" Ramon struggled to keep his voice from rising.

"Assisting," McCausland said firmly.

Ramon put his hands flat on the table and leaned forward. "She was supposed to *assist* them for one week. I have a contract. I've told you this." His voice rose, anger and frustration leaching into the words.

McCausland raised a hand to interrupt Ramon. "Cascadia knows you're looking for her. But they aren't bringing her back. You really think a contract means anything with those guys?"

"We had a deal," Ramon said. It felt like his heart was clenched into a fist beating against his chest.

"They changed it." McCausland leaned closer and lowered his voice. "And you're not doing your niece any favors. You're making too much noise, coming here every day. What you don't get is *you're* expendable. They need her, not you."

"I do get that!" Desperation tightened Ramon's voice.

"You won't get her back until they have no more use for her," McCausland said bluntly. "Why do you think those guys make us take her name off the lists every day? They're keeping her."

Ramon lunged across the table, grabbed a fistful of the man's shirt and half-lifted him out of his chair. He barely registered others moving forward or McCausland quickly gesturing them to stop. "No, they're not."

He looked down at Ramon's fist. "Can I have my shirt?"

Ramon released him, pushing back slightly. As soon as he did, McCausland came around the table, grabbed Ramon's arm, and propelled him out into the rain and away from the soldiers who stood, alert, watching them. They stopped in an open space where no one was close enough to hear.

"Listen, you stupid shit. You're being a pain in the ass asking about her. These guys. This Protection Force. They act like the military but they're not. They act like the law but they're not. Some of us who have pushed back against them have even disappeared. No consequences anymore. You understand?"

Ramon thought of the man he'd shot and his stomach twisted. "I understand."

Water dripped off the brim of McCausland's uniform hat. "Look, brother, this is reality. You got others to think about, right?"

Ramon glanced over his shoulder. Tommy in the wheelbarrow. Payton standing next to him, a hand on his shoulder. Michael behind them, shoulders hunched, miserable.

McCausland sighed heavily. "I'll watch for her. But you? You need to get out of here. Like I said, they don't need you and you're making too much noise."

"Maybe if I had my niece. Or a working gun. Or supplies to keep these kids alive. Until then I can't leave."

McCausland threw up his hands. "It's on you then, whatever happens. Watch your back."

Ramon stood there in the rain as the man left him, the cold wetness soaking the thin jacket he'd scavenged, barely feeling the rain dripping through his hair and down his face. After a moment he walked back to the others. Without a word, Michael took hold of the wheelbarrow handles and started pushing it back towards Kelsey Street and the remains of home.

"We'll get a fire going, get the tarp up, dry out," Ramon said after a few blocks. "Then we're going to need a plan. It may be that you have to go without me."

There was fear and worry in their eyes, but no one asked any questions. And that was a good thing because he had no answers.

Chapter 17

J ENNIFER ANGRILY SWIPED TEARS away as she walked back to town. Casey and her tough woman act. Connor and Tessa with their hippy, back to earth, hug everyone shit. Except when faced with reality. Then they weren't full of sunlight and peace.

They were so blind to what needed to be done. So blind they couldn't see all she did to save them. It hurt.

She'd been friends with everyone in her environmental science class. She'd even been kind to Michael, patient with his stupid awkwardness. With the quake, with the monsters, she'd been the one to not only know how to keep her friends safe, but also know which ones were strong enough to have a chance at surviving. She'd been the only one brave enough to do what had to be done.

And they hated her for it.

It was so, so hard. After all, it wasn't like she'd killed Zack. She'd just set the scene to keep the others safe. So, of course, his death saddened her. She'd even cried when he died.

She was scared all the time. She knew the consequences of her actions, what the cost was. Even now, heading along the trail. Casey with her rifle. Thinking *she* was the one keeping them safe. Casey had no idea what walked out there in the trees.

But Jennifer did.

She glanced down at her foraging basket and paused to pull some fiddlehead ferns over the blood stains. Luckily Tessa hadn't looked too closely.

Well, mostly, Jennifer knew what was out there in the woods. But now there was something new. Whatever had killed Max. She didn't understand what it wanted yet, but she would. She'd figure out this newest threat. Figure out how to placate it.

But right now, she was lonely. She swiped tears away again. She missed her friends. Not knowing if her parents were alive, was a deep frustration. She wished she had someone to talk to, someone who understood, someone who recognized her value.

She reached the edge of town and saw people moving around, going about useless tasks like they could bring some sort of order to the new chaos of their lives. Completely oblivious to the real dangers. And over at the remains of the general store, she saw old Betty behind her locked door, watching the world through her window. Betty had stockpiled the store's few remaining supplies and refused to share. She rarely came outside and when she did it was to publicly pray for God to take back the demons and keep them all safe.

Jennifer realized suddenly that they might have something in common. Other than Betty being crazy, of course. Maybe the old woman got lonely, too. Plus, she was unappreciated in her mission to save everyone with her religion, like Jennifer was unappreciated in her efforts to keep monsters away.

Maybe it was time to make an overture of friendship. Be kind to her. Encourage Betty to trust her. Not only for the shared loneliness and that Betty might be the only one to fully understand what Jennifer was trying to do, but because one never knew what might come in handy.

Chapter 18

THE RAIN WAS LOUD on the tarp. It was only early evening but the others were asleep already, huddled together for warmth. Ramon sat cross-legged in front of a small fire, keeping it burning with scraps of wood from the remains of the house. Crowded under the tarp were their meager possessions, hopefully drying. It was hard for him to get comfortable. The pain from his injuries, his whirling thoughts, his fears for their future, weighed on him.

Hanging up the tarp again had felt like failure. Spreading out the musty blanket and sleeping bags felt like letting his family down. He hadn't wanted to use their rations but they were shivering, cold, damp, and miserable. Not to mention discouraged. So he'd splurged, opening two bottles of water to boil for their dehydrated packets of something optimistically labeled as chicken and dumpling stew.

Now, in the growing dark their situation felt more like despair.

Ramon added another piece of lumber to the fire, feeding in bits of his old life and watching it burn. He held his hands out to the warmth and worked through their options, their supplies, and how long they could wait. He was back at the beginning, stuck in the loop of no answers to the questions running through his brain.

Out there, beyond the tiny circle of light made from the fire, the night was a bottomless dark with stars of other tiny fires. The normal night noises of distant gunfire, punctuated by faint screams and shouting only brought home how defenseless they were. And over it all was the ever-present smell of decay and death. The weight of this new reality pressed down on him so heavily that he wondered if he would ever be free of the smell, ever be able to move without underlying fear.

There was the sound of a sleeping bag zipper behind him and Michael came to the fire, dropping awkwardly down next to Ramon. He was too heavy to sit cross-legged like Ramon, so he sat, knees up, blearily watching the flames.

"Did you mean it?" Michael asked finally. "Us having to go without you?"

Ramon didn't answer for a minute. Then he sighed heavily. "You might have to. I don't know what to do, honestly."

"We won't go without you." Michael gestured to the darkness. "Out there? We'll die. You're like, the only safety we have."

There was movement at the edge of darkness and Ramon jumped up, breath catching on pain. He stepped in front of Michael and heard the kid struggling to get to his feet.

McCausland stepped into the faint firelight. He wore a backpack, carried two more, and dropped all three on the ground.

"The helicopter landed about half an hour ago. I think she's with them. No guarantees but we got to go now." He pointed at Michael. "Hey kid. We're either going to be caught or Ramon will be coming back fast. Get everything ready to leave."

He tossed a head lamp to Ramon, gestured for him to follow, and turned toward the darkness and shadows. Ramon, heart racing, started after him then looked at Michael. The kid's eyes were wide with fear.

"If I don't come back, you make the choice to go or stay. They'll be after me, not you. If you go, I'll find you if I can."

"But-" Michael stopped, sucked in a big breath, and straightened. "Okay. We'll run, man."

"I need you to keep the others safe."

Michael puffed up. "You got it, man."

Ramon jogged after McCausland, everything in him humming, suddenly alive and flushed with adrenaline. By the time he pulled on the headlamp, all thoughts of Michael and the others at camp were gone. He turned the headlamp on, the beam of light mirroring McCausland's.

He handed a gun to Ramon. "If you have to use it, brother, we're screwed because their weapons will make these nothing more than peashooters. But it's yours, for after, if you succeed."

"What's the plan?"

"I'll get you to the helicopter and then you're on your own. I have to live with these guys. Can't risk them knowing I was involved."

"No problem. I can handle it." Ramon's stomach clenched. He'd been counting on McCausland's experienced help.

They moved through the dark city, past the glow of other small fires, past shadowy movements of people, carefully making their way over and around the remains of destruction. Anyone out this late at night had no more desire for contact than they did. There was no meeting of eyes, no nods of heads, no words. Just slipping by each other and hoping not to get noticed.

In the distance, at the Coastal parking lot, generators ran and lights worked and the military gathered resources. They headed towards it, and the helicopter.

Chapter 19

T HE BOULDER CASEY SAT on was cool, the granite rough under the palm of her hand. Her backpack rested against the stone at her feet and she propped one worn work boot against the splintered trunk of a fir tree that seemed to think it was still alive. It had come down during the quake but new growth was still showing green at the tips of broken branches. She wondered how long it took a tree to realize it was dead.

How long had it taken Max to realize it was the end? Her mind skittered away from the thought.

The light was leaving the day and she watched shadows lengthen around her. The Hole in the Wall was a deeper shadow under the boulders that had been placed to close it off after Sharon died. A cool breeze fingered through the prayer flags that hung on lines tied to tree branches. Some tattered, some new scraps torn from bits and pieces. Were they messages of hope? Petitions for help? Names that shouldn't be forgotten? She didn't go close enough to see but imagined they were all those things and probably more.

No one had seen Casey leave Index. By now they were used to her going off on her own. She bent to retrieve her pack and slid her arms through the straps. Raising one finger to her forehead, she gave a small salute to the Hole in the Wall, to Curtis and Sharon who had died to save them. She clambered awkwardly and painfully over the trunk of the fir tree.

The rage inside simmered slowly and steadily. The only thing that could make it turn into incandescent flames of joy would be to kill the thing that had taken Max from her. In the last few days since he died, she had tried fitting back into her life. She'd tried being around the others in Index, tried to continue doing her job keeping them safe. But the heat inside just grew and grew, flames feeding on her soul.

She needed revenge.

She needed the one who did this to die. The one who came in her nightmares, a vague shape of a woman, a faint memory of white cloth and black hair and blood.

She needed to hunt.

But the Snoqualmie National Forest was well over a million acres. She was a miniscule speck in that wilderness. She thought being out here in the quiet would show her the path, but it hadn't.

She headed back to town, jogging painfully until her heart pounded and sweat ran into her eyes and her lungs burned and the rage slid into a sleeping smolder. Almost, but not quite, banked to embers.

Finally, gasping, she had to slow down. She walked the rough ground, one hand over the butt of her gun, ready to come up in a second and fire if anything came out of the woods. But instead of cool metal in her hand, her mind slid away and she felt a heart no longer beating, warmth cooling, blood congealing. Her own heart seemed to tighten, to grow cold, to falter, and she fisted a hand to her chest, unreasonably afraid she would feel nothing.

Hey. Focus.

Max was there. She could almost see him in her peripheral vision. Her breathing slowed. She'd held his heart. His blood had seeped into her skin. With him beside her, she'd always felt able to face anything. Now, with him inside her, he would see that their heart kept beating as long as needed. She drew in a deep, ragged breath. He was still with her. His warmth spread through her.

That's my girl.

They could do this. They would find the bitch. Together they would kill her.

She picked up her pace again. Max's strength flowed through her and she thanked him as she climbed up and over a downed tree and broke into a steady, limping jog. She'd figure out what she had to do. She'd be ready for the fight to come.

Her heart beat steadily now, in the same rhythm she used to feel under her cheek when she slept with her head on his chest. Max would never leave her. Just like she would never leave him. There were tears on her cheeks but she wasn't aware of them. She smiled for Max alone and moved through the forest, promising death to the woman they hunted.

Chapter 20

S PIKE WOKE TO HIS stomach growling. His chest felt like a weight was on it and each breath ached. He knew he was warm and the cold was just a memory, but he could still feel it deep in his bones. His head ached like the worst hangover he'd ever had.

And his stomach growled.

Nathaniel's head was on Spike's shoulder, his arm over Spike's chest. The sleeping bag was zipped and snug around them and Spike drifted, sliding back toward sleep.

And his stomach growled.

Nathaniel shook with quiet laughter. He rolled over, unzipped the bag, and climbed out, kneeling to zip the bag back up around Spike. "Don't move. I'll be back."

Spike couldn't have moved if he wanted to. As he came more fully awake, more hurt and ached and felt bruised. He closed his eyes and drifted again until the sound of the tent zipper going up brought him back and Nathaniel came in carrying a steaming mug, followed by Samuel with his stethoscope. Both sat beside the sleeping bag and Samuel tugged the zipper down again.

"Breathe for me," Samuel said, placing the icy stethoscope against his chest.

They went through the motions of a painful exam and then Samuel sat back. "Your chest hurts when you breathe because of CPR. I'm sorry but I probably bruised your ribs. You're bundled up because, besides being dead, you were hypothermic. You've been out of it for a while."

Spike tried to speak but his throat hurt too much and when Samuel leaned forward it was a good excuse to stay quiet.

"Don't ever do anything that stupid again. You hear me? All of us here, what's left, we can't lose anymore. Understand?"

Spike managed a nod. He did understand. Samuel, their lone medical technician, had seen too much death. Including his own brother Artair, friend to Ramon's niece, who had died from a burst appendix. Something that Samuel hadn't been able to fix, and something his brother wouldn't have died from before the quake.

"Good. For now, you get broth. That's it."

"Fuck." Spike's voice was a raspy, hoarse whisper that scratched his throat.

Samuel lightly punched Nathaniel on the shoulder as he stood wearily. "Cussing. He's back."

When the zipper came down, closing the tent, Spike met Nathaniel's eyes and the tears he saw there hurt as much as his bruised ribs. Nathaniel put the mug down carefully and then covered his eyes with his hands, his shoulders shaking. Carefully, Spike reached out and tugged Nathaniel down to hold him against his chest. It hurt but not as much as it did seeing Nathaniel cry.

"I'm sorry," he rasped out.

Nathaniel sat up and wiped his eyes. "Did you know I had a crush on you in school?"

Spike shook his head.

"You were the ultimate bad boy. All the girls had crushes on you. Wild hair, in trouble all the time. You were a walking cliché. A tough guy. I didn't even exist in your realm."

Spike struggled to remember those days that now felt like the life of a stranger. The neglect at home, the constant anger, every step he took the wrong one, leading in the wrong direction with no way to change his path.

"And then there was this day when the buses were late." Nathaniel stared at his hands, folded in his lap. "A bunch of us were waiting in the bus yard and a couple of the guys got bored so of course they started picking on me. The smallest one there, the one everyone just knew was gay. The girls were laughing."

Spike thought back to that other world. "I showed up," he whispered.

Nathaniel managed a soft laugh and wiped his eyes again. "Rode in to my rescue on a black steed."

"That old beater Bronco." He could barely remember it, as if the earthquake and all that had happened since had wiped those days out.

"You got out, told them to knock it the fuck off, grabbed the collar of my jacket, shoved me in the passenger seat, told me to buckle up and shut the fuck up, and drove me home."

Spike nodded as the memory surfaced. Nathaniel, the slight, quiet kid, being pushed around.

"I was so happy."

"For getting a ride home?"

"No." Nathaniel shook his head. "Because you knew where I lived. You never asked me for directions. You knew. And then when the quake hit and we were out there in the woods, you took care of me and Lucy. I knew it was just because we were the smallest. The most vulnerable. But you were my hero."

Spike reached carefully for Nathaniel's hand.

"And then you go and do something so stupid!" Nathaniel's eyes filled with tears again and his voice rose, bright with anger. "You risked everything! You died!"

"Had to," Spike whispered. "You were going to."

Nathaniel sniffled and they sat there silently a moment, holding hands.

Spike drew in a painful breath. "Broth?"

Nathaniel reached for the mug. "No more heroics from you."

"No more cussing from you."

Nathaniel gave a wobbly smile. "Damn it."

Spike managed about half the mug of broth, sipping carefully as Nathaniel helped him. The warmth eased the burn of his aching throat but he drifted, asleep and awake. Nathaniel put the mug on the ground and eased him back down, tugging the sleeping bag up to his chin.

"I'd do it again," he whispered, eyes closed, sinking, sliding away.

"What?" Nathaniel leaned forward.

There was a long moment before Spike roused himself enough to answer. "Take you home. But home is gone."

And so was he, giving in to the bone-deep exhaustion.

Chapter 21

O THE EAST, THE black night lightened minimally to a dark charcoal but it couldn't be called dawn. Ramon and McCausland turned off their headlamps, made their way cautiously into the Coastal parking lot, and to a row of canvas tents. McCausland went to the third one, bent and unzipped it, then gestured for Ramon to follow. He ducked inside and stood impatiently while McCausland pulled a large frame backpack out from under a cot and opened it. He rummaged past a few books and brought out a heavy, ribbed pullover sweater and pants similar to the Carhartt ones Ramon used to have but in the gray-green of McCausland's National Guard uniform.

"Get these on."

Ramon quickly shed the thin coat and tee shirt, still damp from the rain. The pullover was thick and warm. As he undid his worn jeans, and pulled off his boots, McCausland tossed him heavy socks.

"If you're in uniform you won't be as noticeable. Might buy you some time. You understand I can't help you, right? Wish I could but this is my career."

"Hey," Ramon said. "You've helped more than anyone else has. I appreciate it."

The pants were a little big but a belt helped. Ramon felt warm for the first time in weeks. He balled up his damp clothes and hesitated. In this new world, nothing was wasted. These were his clothes, hard-found scavenging through piles. Plus, the blood-encrusted gun was still in his coat pocket. But it was empty and now that he had a loaded one, there was no need to carry the other one around.

"Get moving," McCausland said.

He was right. Marie was the priority. Ramon shoved the clothes and gun under the cot but pushed the valuable headlamp into a deep pocket. "Get rid of these when you can. You don't want to get caught with them."

"No shit."

Ramon went to the tent entrance and turned back. "Thanks. For everything. Sorry I've been such an asshole."

"It's the times, brother."

Ramon went outside and stood a moment to get his bearings. There were floodlights behind the store and he saw a few men headed that way. They were wearing black, not the olive-green of National Guard. He started forward but stopped when he heard the tent flap tossed back.

"Guess I can't let you go alone," McCausland said angrily. "You're a pain in my ass."

"It's the times, brother," Ramon said, relief so overwhelming it felt like nausea.

McCausland snorted.

They went toward the back lot of the store and Ramon quickly saw the wisdom of swapping out clothes. There were others moving around the camp but no one paid any attention to him.

They stopped at the corner of the building, standing in the shadows and scanning the area. The helicopter sat in the middle of the lot, lit up with floodlights. Generators at the bases of the floodlights ran, making enough noise that it would be hard to hear over them. McCausland gestured at two men and a woman in the black uniforms of the Cascadia Protection Force who stood near the helicopter. Ramon nodded, recognizing them as the three who had originally taken Marie. He scanned the area but couldn't see his niece anywhere. His heart raced. What if she wasn't here?

One of the two men shouldered a large assault rifle and headed toward the building. Ramon and McCausland stepped back against the wall. Ramon hoped the bright floodlights ruined the guy's night vision. The woman pulled open the access door on the helicopter and climbed inside. Lights came on and the rotors began a slow turn as the chopper warmed up.

"Getting ready to leave," McCausland whispered.

"Then he's going for Marie," Ramon replied. "Let's move."

They stayed close to the wall and shadows. The man went inside and Ramon thought to himself that this would be easy. Slip in after the man, grab Marie, knock the guy out or something, and take off.

Except that the door had locked behind the guy when it closed. Sudden panic made his breath come fast and shallow but McCausland grabbed his arm.

"When the door opens, I push him back inside." McCausland spoke low, even though no one could have heard them over generators and the helicopter starting up. "You get your niece and get the hell out of here. Back to camp, out of the city."

Ramon nodded, barely aware of the nausea of fear, of his hands shaking. McCausland gripped his upper arm.

"Breathe, brother. Focus. Your niece needs you in control."

Ramon sucked in another breath.

The door opened. McCausland pushed right into the opening. Ramon heard scuffling but kept his eyes on those around the helicopter. There was a muffled gunshot inside the building and he jumped, everything in him going weightless and breathless with adrenaline. His racing panicked thoughts shrunk to a pinpoint focus.

Marie.

There was movement in the doorway and she was there, small and frail, eyes wide in terror. Ramon grabbed her arm and tugged her out to him. Keeping tight hold of her, he propelled her ahead of him along the building wall and around the corner into the deeper shadows. He didn't look behind him for McCausland, didn't hesitate.

Marie stumbled and he pulled her upright. At the front of the building he stopped, scanning the parking lot.

Others had heard the gunshot inside the building. People were running in the side doors, drawing weapons.

Now, he thought. *Now, before they organize outside*. He pulled Marie close to him and used his free hand to gesture, palm down, in a calming motion. She nodded but he could feel her shaking. Slowly, he led her along the side of the building.

Dawn lightened the sky a few more degrees. Behind them the sound of the helicopter spinning up drowned out the shouting of those headed inside and those wise enough to start forming a perimeter.

They couldn't cross the parking lot. It would be too visible. They couldn't hide in one of the tents. That would just allow others time to organize and find them. They had to stay to the shadows and keep moving. Ramon knew enough to realize that stopping meant getting caught.

He pulled out his gun and leaned down to his niece. She was breathing fast and shallow, eyes so dilated with fear they were black. "Stay to the darkness. If we get separated go to our old home. There are friends there who will help you until I catch up."

Marie gripped the sleeve of his sweater and wouldn't let go even when he started moving again.

He kept his finger alongside the trigger of the gun and rounded the corner to the front of the building. Here, the floodlights at the back didn't reach so the shadows were deeper. By now they had to know Marie was gone. Their window was rapidly shutting. He touched Marie's shoulder and pointed. To the west, before the quake, there had been some shops in a small strip mall in the same parking lot. Then a street behind them, then a gas station, diner, and big grocery store. Now of course, all that was destruction and debris and lots of hiding places.

They just had to get across the street and they could get lost in the ruins.

The sound of the helicopter changed as it lifted up behind the building. Ramon could hear commands being shouted behind them. They had to go now, before the chopper was fully airborne. He caught Marie's arm and ran, towing her with him.

Dawn was getting more determined to bring the day and pale light started erasing shadows. Marie stumbled again but Ramon kept her from falling, dragging her up and over and around torn up pavement and wrecked cars.

On the far side of the street the small row of shops had once had an overhang roof, where cars could park in something like a carport and go into the fish store or lawyer's office. Now the roof had partially collapsed. Ramon pushed aside broken timbers and ducked under the still-dark alcove formed by the fallen roof. His boots crunched on broken glass.

Behind them, he could hear the sound of the helicopter, growing louder. It had clearly lifted off and was flying in their direction. Ramon squatted and pulled Marie down beside him so that they were pressed up against what would have been the wall of the fish store. There was no way they were visible unless someone had seen them running. He heard no shouting, no voices drawing closer, and the chopper was clearly circling a wider area, not hovering over them. The semi-darkness of the alcove gave him a semblance of safety but he knew better than to think that was true.

"We can't stay here long." Ramon spoke low and put his arm around Marie's shoulders. "It's too close. You holding up okay?"

She nodded, but she still had his sweater sleeve in a death grip.

He waited a few moments listening to the sounds of activity and the sounds of the helicopter, trying to interpret movement from them. When the chopper sounded like it was out toward the highway and the smokestack, he gently disengaged Marie's hand and stood, motioning for her to wait.

He moved carefully over debris to the far end of the alcove, opposite where they'd come in. There was the familiar scent of something dead that grew stronger as he got closer to the far opening. He pulled the sweater up over his nose and carefully looked out through broken roof timbers.

There was enough pearl-gray light in the coming dawn now that he could easily see back across the destroyed street to the Coastal building and all the activity. Tents were being searched and his stomach knotted as he remembered his old clothes shoved under McCausland's cot. Too late now, especially if they'd caught the man, or worse, shot him. He spared a moment to hope the guy was okay and then worked his way back to his niece.

"We'll go out that way," he said quietly, helping her to her feet. "Once out of this space, we go left and uphill where the grocery store was. If we get separated, stay close to quake damage. If you hear the chopper coming back this way, get under something. Go slow and mark your next spot where you can hide before you move. If something happens, can you make your way home if I'm not with you?"

Marie nodded.

He started back to the other end and she followed. They'd only gone a few feet though, when she grabbed his sweater and pulled him to a stop.

"Something's there."

Ramon froze, trying to see or hear what his niece was sensing. "Something's where?" he whispered. "Something real? Something monster?"

"Something," Marie whispered back. "To the left of the opening."

Ramon frowned as if that would help see into the shadows better. He raised the gun and moved forward, Marie still gripping his sweater. He hadn't seen anything when he checked this opening out moments earlier but he trusted his niece. And yet he still couldn't see anything that shouldn't be there. Using his boot, he pushed back some chunks of wood. Took a few more steps forward. Listened so hard he could hear the pulse of his own blood beating.

"It's gone," Marie whispered. "Did you see it?"

Ramon jumped at the sound of her voice. He lowered the gun and ran his other hand over his face then took a deep breath. "No. What was it?"

"Something small. A butterfly?"

"Are you shittin' me? I almost shot a butterfly?"

Marie quivered with a hand over her mouth and he realized she was stifling a small giggle. "Not a butterfly. But something small. Watching us. I saw it and then could just, kind of, faintly sense it."

"Okay," Ramon said and drew in another deep breath. "Great. A butterfly. Spying on us."

He was rewarded with another small giggle but she stifled it and her face sobered when he gestured for her to follow him again. He checked the surroundings and saw the activity all still centered around the Coastal store and parking lot. The chopper was out of sight. It was now or never. Taking his niece's hand, he tugged her out of the shelter and they ran uphill.

A little red Subaru Justy was on its side near the entrance to what had been the Safeway grocery store. Ramon headed for it and tugged Marie down on the far side of the banged-up car. It looked like a truck or something had gone right over the top of it but there was enough left to squat down behind it and watch back the way they had come. Ramon saw no signs they were being followed.

"Now we move fast. These guys know where we lived and they'll head there next." He grimaced. "If the chopper isn't already there. We need to get the others and run."

Chapter 22

E THAN RUBBED A HAND over his morning stubble and pushed hair back out of his eyes. He didn't want to leave the warm cocoon created by the heavy pile of quilts and furs. But he knew by now that Anya always woke early and would have the fire stirred up and the kettle warming. He reached for chilly jeans, a tee shirt, and a green crewneck sweater that had been part of military surplus clothing dropped by FEMA right after the quake. It was warm and that was all he cared about. Bending, he reached for his heavy socks and boots and then paused.

It was too quiet. Too chilly.

There was a lantern hissing and giving out a faint light, but no flickering glow from a morning fire.

He heard the low whimper of Bird, over by the door and a cold weight settled on him. He dropped his boots and went to the lantern, raising the flame and illuminating the cabin.

Anya was gone.

He ran for the door and yanked it open on a gray morning and saw nothing but forest. No movement, no Anya. Back in the cabin, he quickly stirred up the fire and opened the shutters letting what light there was in.

He scanned the room. Her rifle was gone but her pack was still by the door. Panic rose deep in his bones but then he stopped, breathed in, and shook his head. Focus. Evaluate. Act. His old mantra from growing up in war zones eased the panic.

Her clothes were still at the foot of the bed. Her boots sat where they always did. Her old ugly orange slip-on crocs that she wore to collect eggs or use the outhouse were gone, though.

Feeling stupid at his overreaction, he pulled his boots on and went outside, gesturing for Bird to come as well. But once out there, Bird didn't run around as usual, doing his morning happy dance. Instead, he whimpered again and came close to Ethan's side. Fear stirred.

He stared at the dog, hesitated, and then ran for the chicken coop.

No Anya.

He ran for the outhouse.

No Anya.

But her rifle was there, lying in the winter-dead leaves. And resting on the barrel was a raven feather.

Ethan took the rifle and worked circles around the cabin, the outhouse, the perimeter of the clearing, but found no other signs. No tracks, no signs of a fight. Thankfully, no signs of blood. Bird went with him, snuffling the ground, then raising his head and scenting the air, but also clearly finding nothing. Finally, as the late morning grayness coalesced into a fine drizzle, Ethan slammed his hand against a tree trunk in frustration and went back to the cabin.

Inside, the quiet was unsettling, wrong. Their home was chilly and still empty. Anya's book lay face down on the arm of her chair where she'd left it the night before. Her heavy winter coat hung on a nail by the door. The blankets on her side of the bed were still in disarray because she never straightened them.

Bird paced in front of the door, nails clicking on the wood floorboards, eyes never leaving Ethan.

He got his pack, checked supplies in it, added wood to the small fire in the woodstove, and went out onto the porch. He could hear Bird still searching inside the cabin. He sat on the top step and the old boards creaked under him.

The need to go, to do something, flooded him but he didn't know where to start searching for Anya. Maybe he was overreacting. Maybe she'd just gone for an early hike, didn't realize she'd dropped her rifle, and forgotten to leave a note.

Too much time was passing too quickly. He instincts told him this was all wrong. Anya's son or Ramon's niece with their spirit animals might help but he didn't know how to find them, either. Each time they had been needed, they'd appeared. He didn't know what else to do but wait for Anya to show up or for them to come to him. Even Bird didn't know where to go and didn't seem able to pick up a scent.

He had to wait.

Everything in him yearned to be up and moving, searching, bringing Anya home. The alternative, that something had grabbed her and she was never coming home, terrified him and he worked to keep pushing that back out of his mind. He'd learned during his childhood how to box up terror, close it away, shut down and simply function until it was safe again. It had been easier when it had just been him.

Movement caught his eye and he looked up to see a raven circling high above him on currents of wind he couldn't feel.

"Please," he whispered, hoping it was the Stone Woman's raven. "Bring her back. Or bring me help."

He waited until afternoon, pacing, circling the clearing, as the light slowly faded, as shadows lengthened under the trees that still stood. He waited until the solitude became a threat he couldn't fight. He waited until he was queasy from exhaustion, worry, and no food.

Eventually he felt his way into the shadowy cabin where the fire had long since gone out. He fumbled for matches with chilled and shaking fingers and lit a kerosene lantern. Mechanically, he moved to the wood stove and started another fire. He spread honey on a thick slice of homemade bread and ate it, standing in the middle of the floor, barely tasting it.

Bird was curled on Anya's side of the bed and as Ethan paced, the dog whimpered. Suddenly overwhelmingly exhausted, Ethan lay down next to him, fully dressed and boots still on. Bird moved close, shivering. He draped his arm over the dog and dug his fingers into the thick fur like Anya always did.

Dog breath next to him instead of soft snoring. Dog warmth beside him that wasn't the warmth he needed. The fire crackled in the wood stove, giving out a sense of coziness that was a lie.

"What do we do, big guy? Where do we even start searching?"

Bird pushed closer and he stroked the dog's fur. Giving Bird comfort eased his own fear a tiny bit. Or maybe it was just the growing warmth of the fire.

He might have slept but he wasn't sure. When Bird stirred, he got up, eyes gritty, body aching.

He crossed the main room and pulled open the door to see nothing but the woods. No mythical help.

In a sudden rage, he slammed the cabin door so hard a cup fell off an old shelf. He damped down the wood stove. He gestured sharply for Bird to follow but the dog was already at the door. He had to move, to go, to do *something*. No more waiting. He got his pack, stuffed in some protein bars on top of his gear, picked up his rifle, then jerked open the cabin door.

The grizzly was there, massive head lowered to show the distinctive hump on its back. It gave the odd coughing sound they made to warn you away, and clawed at the ground, talons raking long cuts in the dirt.

Ethan took a step back before he could stop himself. But then the young boy came out of the trees and stood next to the apex predator like it was a teddy bear, putting his hand on the bear's side. Bird, tail wagging, went to Joseph and stood at attention, ears up and forward, waiting.

Overwhelming relief swamped Ethan. He collapsed down to sit on the top step, dropped his gear next to him, and put his face in his hands. For a long moment he couldn't speak, couldn't do anything but breathe. Finally, he looked up.

"I need help."

The boy tilted his head to one side. "The raven told us."

"Is Alegria here, too?"

The boy looked over his shoulder towards the trees and Ethan saw movement. It wasn't that Alegria simply walked out of the woods, stepping between trees. She moved through a massive cedar, still standing but damaged, merging until he couldn't separate the girl from the deeply fissured bark of the old tree. For a moment she was gone.

As she became visible again, for the briefest second, she was made of bark and moss and glowed with the deep red-gold of the cedar's heartwood. As she neared there was movement again back in the trees and Ethan saw her moonlight wolf following.

"Anya's gone. I don't know where to look," he said when Alegria stood next to the boy. "I don't know what's happened or even if she's still…" He couldn't say the word. "Can you help?"

Alegria and Joseph took hold of each other's hands and were silent so long that Ethan reached for his pack and rifle, not able to wait, to just sit there, any longer.

"I can sense my mother," the boy said. "But alive like me, or alive like you? I am not sure."

The overwhelming relief was instantly submerged in equally overwhelming dread. Ethan clenched his hands into tight fists. "Where?"

"We need Alegria's sister." The boy gave a very human shrug. "My mother is a whisper under the sound of the otherkin coming. With Marie we will be stronger."

"Otherkin?" Ethan asked sharply. "Is that what took Anya?"

"Otherkin are…all." Joseph seemed to struggle with finding words. "The creatures you call myth. The life in all things. Trees, stones, river. All we are connected to. What we can feel. But now there's…a roar, an avalanche of beings."

"There is something massive trying to cross over," Alegria said. "I can feel its need and longing and joy. Each time there is an aftershock it gets closer to breaking through. It wants something desperately and we aren't strong enough to understand. Marie can help us."

"Last I heard she was in Monroe." Ethan paced, gripping his rifle. "But Anya is here. I need you to find her."

Tears on Alegria's cheeks glowed like drops of amber. She wiped them away with the back of a hand. "And I need my sister."

"Fine," Ethan said. "You help me find Anya and I'll help you find Marie."

The wolf raised its head, suddenly alert. It took a few steps away and looked back at Alegria. Bird, watching it, followed.

The wolf headed west into the trees with Bird loping at its side. The grizzly didn't move until they followed the wolf. And only then did it come. The unreality of jogging into the woods with a grizzly behind him caused a brief moment of vertigo.

He focused on Anya. Wherever she was, he hoped she knew they were coming for her.

Chapter 23

J ENNIFER STOOD JUST INSIDE the gate of the fort in the overcast morning, watching Samuel come out of a tent with his med kit. Probably checking on Spike again.

Rowan was gone.

How many left?

There had only been around 150 people in Index when the quake hit. Over half died then, some later. A few had left for refugee camps. So well under fifty left, probably.

And now Rowan was gone, having served Jennifer's purpose. She didn't know what the thing was in the water, but she'd told Rowan about it one day when the girl had been going fishing. She didn't know if it could leave the river, but it was best not to take any chances and keep it happy where it was.

It was too bad Samuel had known CPR. Otherwise, Spike would be in the river, too. He'd never paid any attention to her when they were in high school but right after the quake, when she'd been trapped in the bus, he'd been kind. He'd helped free her, helped calm her down. But now he shunned her, just like the others.

Still, though, she might keep them safe if she could afford to. She knew after Max's death that something awful was close. She may not have had Marie's abilities to sense monsters, but she was smart and it was obvious whatever had killed Max stalked the woods around Index.

She didn't know what it was and hadn't seen it yet. But she'd been experimenting with feeding it because she needed to know what it liked to eat. She needed to be able to plan, for her own safety. No one in town, so busy with day-to-day survival, had noticed that animals were almost gone. Or when they did notice, they attributed it to the woods and wild animals and monsters. It was to be expected that they would lose a few chickens. A few cats. A small dog or two.

Jennifer studied the results of feeding and had learned something that could be important. Whatever was out there seemed to only feed on males. That was her theory anyway because they were sliced open and the hearts and internal organs taken. She'd also noticed a change recently. It was like the monster was getting tired of what she was bringing it. The last rooster had been killed but its organs tossed aside.

Clearly Jennifer was going to have to change its diet. Find something bigger. She wished briefly that Michael hadn't left for the refugee camps. He'd been easy to manipulate because he was lonely, grateful for any kindness. Plus, he was fat. He'd have fed monsters for a week at least. But he was gone, so wishing didn't accomplish anything.

Maybe Betty. She was like Michael in a way, so very grateful when Jennifer gave up some of her precious time to pray with her. There wasn't much meat on her bones, but it would prove or disprove Jennifer's theory that this monster wanted only males. And since she kept herself locked in her old store most of the time, it would be a while before anyone missed her.

The more information she gathered, the more she had to work with, the higher her chances of surviving became. But what if she couldn't appease it? She felt a faint twist of fear, of shakiness, and clenched her jaw, clenched her fists.

She couldn't afford to be afraid. If she failed, she could so easily die. And if others found out what she was doing, what would they do? Would they kick her out into the woods, alone?

No. She couldn't fail. She shook out her hands and breathed deep, settling the fear. There were no other options. She *wouldn't* fail.

Chapter 24

Ramon and Marie never made it home. They were still a couple blocks away from their camp when he heard someone call his name. Pulling Marie behind him, he turned. Michael leaned out from behind a large rhododendron bush and gestured frantically.

An old brick home had once stood there but all that was left was one corner that the rhododendron grew against, and a pile of bricks, timbers, and broken glass. The bush was a poor hiding place but Payton waited there, squatting down against the corner next to Tommy.

"Hey man," Michael said breathlessly. "We saw those guys. Those Cascadia guys." His hand shook as he gestured down the road. "I thought we should get out of town like you said, but Payton thought we should head toward Coastal in case we could find you. And it's, like, kind of on the way. I think those guys were headed to your place. Our camp. You know, where-"

Payton reached out to put a hand on his arm and Michael paused, gulping a big breath.

"Okay. Right. I'm rambling. I'm scared shitless. I mean, you know, not scared. Just stressed, man. You know? Oh, hey Marie. Morning. Good to see you."

Marie, eyebrows up as if confused, nodded to him.

Ramon gestured for him to be quiet and then leaned out to look the way they had come. There were people milling around but no one in uniform. He pulled back.

"Smart, leaving when you did." Ramon kept his voice low.

The wheelbarrow was nowhere in sight and they'd taken the gear and had it rolled and tied to the backpacks McCausland had left them. Michael wore one,

Payton had one, and the third rested on the ground next to her. Tommy, with his pink backpack, sat on the ground next to her.

"They're searching for us so we need to get out of town now and move fast," Ramon said. "You up for that?"

"Yeah, man. We're up for that. We can move fast." Michael swallowed. "Or fast enough."

"Good. I need a jacket or something to put over this uniform." While Ramon had been glad to have the disguise earlier and was still glad to have something warm and dry, now the military clothes had to be covered.

"Haven't had time to go through these packs yet," Michael said, slipping one of McCausland's backpacks off his shoulders. "But they're heavier than shit. Should be something in there."

He unzipped the main pocket and rummaged around. Ramon shifted his weight, impatience eating at him.

"Shit. Nothing but emergency supplies. No clothes."

Ramon, itching to be on the move, just shrugged. Nothing he could do about that now.

Payton stood, hefting up her pack.

"Can you manage that okay?" Ramon asked her, nodding to the backpack.

She simply nodded.

"We left the wheelbarrow," Michael said. "Figured it was too noticeable and might slow us down. Plus, it squeaked like shit. I asked Tommy if he could make it."

Ramon took the third pack and handed it to Marie, who slipped her arms through the straps.

"That was a smart idea, leaving the wheelbarrow. I'll piggyback Tommy for now," he said gesturing to the little boy. "We can move faster. Later we can trade off or he can walk."

Ramon bent and helped Tommy on to his back then straightened. "Okay. Same goals. We get out of town and head east to Index. If we get separated it's up to each of you to decide if you want to keep going on your own or come back here. And same decision – these guys are looking for Marie and me, not you. You don't have to do this."

"Quit wasting time, man," Michael said. "We're going home."

Chapter 25

JENNIFER'S HANDS SHOOK AND she gripped the handle of her basket tighter to hide her fear. Shadows were deepening in the forest as the late afternoon sun slanted downward. She and Betty moved carefully over and around broken trees.

"We should go back now," the older woman said. "We really shouldn't be this far from town. It will be twilight before long."

"We have time," Jennifer replied. There was a tremor under her words. "This is a shortcut to the Hole in the Wall."

"I'm not comfortable leaving my store unattended. I prefer to be inside and have the doors locked before it gets dark."

Sudden irritation swamped the trepidation and Jennifer turned back to face the old lady. "But aren't you always telling me the Lord will protect us? You do have your bible with you, right?"

"Of course, but-"

"Then we're fine. We both have our faith to keep us strong." Jennifer turned away before Betty could see the grimace she couldn't quite suppress. Yes, she had faith. Just not the same as Betty's.

"You're sure this is the right way? It seems dangerous to go all the way to the Hole just to pray."

Jennifer didn't bother looking back. "It will be worth it. I told you. People have created a sanctuary there. It feels like a holy place. You've been missing having a church to go to. And like we talked about, it's good for you to get out of the store. For people to see you out."

Betty carefully stepped over a tree root. "Yes, but someone's been stealing from the barter shed, you know. My place will be next."

Jennifer did know, since it was something Betty rehashed tirelessly. She stopped again and turned suddenly enough that Betty stumbled back, clutching her bible to her chest. Jennifer stepped closer.

"I understand. You can go back if you want. I don't mind going on to pray alone. It's just...I keep thinking of those verses in Jeremiah and Galatians about God rescuing his believers from the evil around them. We're definitely surrounded by evil right now. And we sure could use rescuing. Wouldn't it count more if we prayed for rescue for everyone? I need your faith to save us because I don't think mine is strong enough. Definitely not like yours."

Betty gripped her bible and looked around at the lengthening shadows. "Well...maybe a little further. But then we really must turn back."

Jennifer agreed and turned away. The nervousness was making her queasy. The fear made her knees shaky. The doubt made her walk more slowly than she otherwise would. Was she doing the right thing? A year ago, she wouldn't have recognized the person she was now.

A year ago, she wasn't alone. Wasn't forced to do the unthinkable in order to survive.

The wind was rising. She could hear it in the trees, see the leaves shivering as it came toward them. The ending daylight faded quicker than it should have. Jennifer's shaking deepened. She was so afraid. So terribly afraid. If she had Betty's faith she would be praying by now. She stopped and closed her eyes, not to pray, but to gather her own strength.

She could do this. She needed to do this. She was pretty sure the thing only fed on males, but she had to be positive. And if the monster only wanted males, she had a backup. The carcass of a cat was in her basket covered with a cloth. She would leave it to feed the thing and she and Betty would be able to get away. This was an experiment to learn what she had to do next.

"There's something out there." Betty grabbed Jennifer's arm.

"Yes," Jennifer said, prying Betty's fingers loose. "But we'll be fine. I've brought an offering. I'll leave it and we can go. We're almost there now."

"I don't like this. I don't like this at all. I want to go home."

Jennifer put the basket down and pulled the cloth off, then pulled Betty back with her. When they were a few feet away she put her hand on Betty's shoulder, pushing down. "Pray for us, Betty. I have an offering. We'll be fine. Just pray."

Betty dropped to her knees and opened the bible with shaking hands. The wind, blowing harder, whipped the fragile pages as if turning them for her, seeking help that wasn't there.

Jennifer backed up. There were no words in there to save them. There was no rescue coming. There was no help. No parents to keep someone safe. No home to provide shelter. The only way to survive was to bury who she used to be and stand strong. Do what needed to be done. Mourn later. Let guilt visit in nightmares.

The wind roared around them bringing darkness into the woods. Jennifer backed away a few more feet. Betty started to turn and get up, to come after Jennifer, but the howling of wolves came on the wind and she curled downward, bent over her bible.

A woman came out of the shadows. Tall and slender except for the swollen belly of advanced pregnancy. Her flowing white gown and long black hair lifted around her in the wind. She glided to the basket and pulled out the carcass, turning it in her long-fingered hands. She tossed it to the ground and looked at them. At Betty.

Jennifer stumbled back. Her heart pounded in terror and she couldn't do it. Couldn't stay next to Betty and watch what happened to the old woman.

The wind grew in roaring strength and Betty fell to her side. Jennifer backed against a tree, breathing fast and shallow. When the monster moved toward Betty, she stared at the ground, tears running hot down her cheeks. She was sorry. So very sorry. She hated this.

Betty screamed. Jennifer squeezed her eyes shut, her breath coming short and panicked. The icy wind grew stronger and knocked her away. Unable to hang on to the tree, she rolled, banging into debris, hitting rocks, her hands struggling to catch anything that would stop her. But there was nothing. The storm threw her at the monster's feet.

Jennifer dug her fingers into the ground, shaking so hard her teeth chattered. She pressed her face into damp and decaying leaves, unable to move or look up.

The wind slowed. The howling storm eased.

The screaming stopped.

Something touched the back of her neck and she squeezed her eyes shut, digging her fingers deeper as if trying to hold on. But her hair was caught and pulled so painfully that she rose to her knees and cried out. The pregnant woman shook Jennifer and she flopped, boneless. The long fingernails dug into her scalp, forcing her head to turn.

Jennifer opened her eyes. Betty had been torn apart and fed on by the wind-wolves. The woman kicked disdainfully with a bone-white bare foot at a bloody piece of Betty's heart.

Jennifer understood. It wasn't enough. "I'll do better. I promise."

The woman shook her again and Jennifer sobbed.

"There are men here." Her thoughts raced to find a path to survival. "You won't even have to hunt them. I can bring them to you."

The woman spoke, her voice like storm wind, heavy, cold, felt more than heard. "Bring me the one who carries a man's heart."

Jennifer was released, tossed to the ground. The wind stilled. The air warmed. The low fading light of the setting sun came back through the trees as the storm passed. Going back to wherever it came from. The woman moved through the filtered light and shadow under the trees and was gone.

It took Jennifer a long time to be able to stand. She had lost track of time, there on the ground, sobbing. But she was alive. She'd done it. Once again, she'd found a way to survive. Yes, she was terrified. Yes, she mourned the loss of Betty. But now she knew for sure the monster would only feast on males. She pushed herself to her feet and wiped her eyes with dirty hands. Females fed the woman's wind-wolves. And she'd come so close to being dog food like Betty.

She straightened and took a deep breath.

Obviously, she now had value to this monster.

She picked up the basket, hesitated, and picked up Betty's bible. It seemed wrong to leave it in the dirt and blood. It had meant a lot to Betty, had given the old woman hope and comfort. She could honor Betty's sacrifice by taking care of the book that had taught the old woman the value of sacrifice. She tucked it into the basket and turned toward Index, drawing in another deep, deep breath. Her hands steadied.

The one who carries a man's heart? She just had to understand what the woman-thing meant. Didn't all men carry a man's heart? Luckily, she was smart enough to figure it out. Someone else would have to die, but it wouldn't be her.

Chapter 26

There was no clear border, no delineation that Ramon could step over and know the destroyed city was finally behind them. What had been the highway was now cracked and heaved up pavement riddled with wrecked cars. Debris was everywhere, from downed trees and buckled roads to hillsides that had slid. Makeshift graves scattered the land, marked with whatever could be used. He saw signs of the floodwaters from the breach of the Culmback dam in Sultan that had reached this far west. The waters had flowed through, moving and piling debris, flattening grass in fields, leaving behind mud and pools of stagnant water.

The cool late afternoon spring breeze smelled of decay.

The biggest surprise though, was the number of people living in makeshift camps. He had assumed leaving the city meant he and the kids would be on their own. That made him worried about how they would travel, fearing they'd be visible if moving by day, and equally visible moving at night by the light of headlamps. But there were so many people outside the city limits, they could easily move through the camps without being visible. He realized, slightly embarrassed, that he'd expected some sort of border, that people would have gone into the city proper for safety.

Instead, his group went past camps made from tarps, shelters made against wrecked cars, a few scattered actual tents, and rough shelters made from scraps of lumber or old roofing material or whatever could be scavenged. Many had clearly chosen to stay away from the crowded city. Ramon wondered if these camps were any safer than within the city limits.

Some watched them cautiously as they passed but most were too busy with their own tasks to pay any attention to a small group of survivors like them, moving through, making do, seeking someplace safe.

"This is kind of freaky," Michael said quietly.

Ramon agreed but didn't say so. "Maybe they're out here because it doesn't stink as bad as back there."

"Maybe," Michael said. "But kind of seems like they're sitting ducks when it gets dark."

"No shit." Ramon adjusted his grip, his arms beginning to ache. "Feel like walking some, little man?"

He felt Tommy's nod against his shoulder blades and paused to let the boy slide down to the ground. He then took the backpack from Marie, who stifled a sigh of relief. When he started walking again, Tommy stayed right at his side. Marie was on his other side and Michael and Payton close behind them.

"Marie needs a hat or something," Michael said. "Won't they recognize that hair? No offense."

Michael was right and Ramon should have thought of that. He'd been so focused on getting them out of the city that disguising Marie hadn't crossed his mind. She'd braided her long curls but he wondered now if that would be enough. It would have to wait though, just like disguising his clothes, until they had a safe place to stop and had time to look through their supplies.

They'd only gone a couple miles when Ramon heard the distinctive sound of a helicopter coming from Monroe.

"What do we do?" Michael whispered, as if he could be heard by the ones in the chopper.

"Spread out," Ramon said quickly. "Get close to a camp or a vehicle and sit. They'll be anticipating us to be together or running."

Michael immediately went left, headed toward an old VW van on its side. Payton followed without hesitation. Ramon went toward a small camp where two young people stood next to a campfire with a tiny pup tent behind them.

"My kids are cold," he said. "Mind if we sit by your fire for a minute?"

The young man looked at them and cautiously nodded. Ramon herded Marie and Tommy forward to the fire and pushed down gently on their shoulders until they sat on the ground. He could see Michael and Payton, also sitting on the ground, against the side of the van.

"Thanks," Ramon said.

The two looked similar enough to be brother and sister, both with thick blonde braids and wearing second hand, well-used camouflage pants and coats. She was maybe eighteen. He was maybe a year or so younger.

"You doing okay out here?" he asked.

"Better than in the city," the girl said. "Nothing but death there. You?"

"Like you said. Nothing but death back there. I'm getting my kids away from it."

"We've got a safe place," Marie said unexpectedly. "If we can get to it."

Ramon didn't like the idea of anyone knowing where they might be going. Or even that they had some place to go. It wasn't like Marie to speak up and he didn't want her to say anything more. The sound of the chopper grew closer and Ramon looked over his shoulder, checking its progress, then used it to change the subject. "Think they might be coming out here to drop some supplies?"

The young man scowled. "No way. Not those assholes."

The chopper was flying low. Two people with rifles were visible on each side, leaning out and searching the ground, their dark sunglasses reflecting light. Marie and Tommy scooted up tight against his sides and he put his arms around them. The chopper continued by then circled back. After another pass, it headed east away from Monroe and kept going. He took a deep breath and eased his grip on the kids.

Ramon stood, his knees shaky. "Well, thanks for the fire. Good luck to you."

"And to you," the younger woman said, and then lifted her chin toward the departing helicopter. "Looks like you're going to need it."

He hesitated, but there was no use denying anything. He gestured to Marie and Tommy, and together they joined Michael and Payton.

"Keep going?" Michael asked quietly.

Ramon looked around at the scattered rough camps. It was late afternoon by now, and the overcast day was finally starting to drizzle.

"Yeah," he said. "We keep going."

Michael's stomach growled and he flushed.

Ramon acted like he hadn't heard and took Tommy's hand. "Let's go a couple more miles then see if we can find a place to hole up, get out of the rain, get something to eat. Do a more thorough look at these packs and figure out what we've got."

"Cool," Michael said. "And Marie can tell us if any monsters show up."

"No," Marie said softly. "Not anymore."

"What?" Ramon felt the sudden airless, weightlessness of dread. "What do you mean?"

After the quake, after her head injury, he hadn't believed her when she saw and sensed things no one else could. But when circumstances proved her newfound talent, it had been a godsend to help keep them safe. Of course, it had also made her a target for the military. But now, with the hike ahead of them, that talent was vital and he'd been depending on it.

"It's being drowned," Marie said quietly. "I'm sorry, Tió Ramon. There's something massive out there and it's like loud, constant white noise. It's getting harder to feel much beyond that."

"You felt the butterfly." Ramon touched her shoulder. "So you can still pick up on things. Right?"

"Yes. But because it was close enough, I think. Those soldiers didn't like my failures. But they kept taking me out anyway. We'd stop to refuel and eat, then go again and they said they'd keep doing it until I stopped faking."

"Okay," Ramon said, giving her a quick hug, ignoring the heavy weight of trepidation. "We'll make do."

"Maybe that means they won't be so anxious to get her back," Michael said, but his voice was hesitant as if he didn't believe it either.

Ramon didn't bother responding. He simply started walking, heading east, and the others fell in step with him. Now, with Marie's ability gone, it felt like they were even more exposed. And what did she mean by something big out there?

How the hell was he supposed to protect them against something massive if Marie could no longer tell when it got close?

"What now?" he asked, under his breath. But Payton heard him anyway.

"One step at a time," she whispered next to him.

He looked at her in surprise. Her head was still bowed down. Her shoulders were still hunched forward, her hands tightly gripping her backpack straps. But she'd spoken, and that was rare.

"You're right," he said, wishing the words helped. "One step at a time."

Michael sighed heavily and loudly. "A shit-ton of steps if you ask me. And probably all uphill. And probably nothing in these packs except cardboard protein bars."

Marie's hand came up to cover her mouth and Ramon knew she was smiling behind her fingers. He saw her meet eyes with Payton, who also smiled slightly.

"At least there's no squeaking wheelbarrow," Michael said.

At that, they all laughed except for Ramon. He walked in silence, letting them have their moment of lightness.

Something massive, she'd said. Something coming.

Chapter 27

IT WAS TWILIGHT WHEN Spike finally fully woke. His second day of being alive and not dead in the river. He was alone and could hear dripping on the tent like it was drizzling outside. Carefully, he sat up, one arm pressed against his side supporting his aching ribs. There was a big bruise in the middle of his chest and he put the palm of his hand over it almost reverently. A mark of life. A sign that others had worked hard to save him. The old, pre-quake Spike would have thought he didn't deserve their help. The post-quake Spike still thought that but was grateful.

He worked his still-damp jeans on slowly and carefully then managed to sit up enough to tug on a flannel shirt. He moved up onto his knees, wincing, but couldn't manage to stand. Stuck on his knees, he shook his head at the stupidity of it and wondered if he could crawl to the tent opening. But before he could attempt it, the zipper was yanked upward and Nathaniel came through, followed by Connor. They helped him up carefully and then supported him out of the tent.

"What's going on?"

"Bad news, dude," Connor said softly.

For the briefest second, Spike wanted to pull back, to get back in the sleeping bag, to not hear what was coming.

They half-carried him out of the fort and across the short distance to the barter shed. A fire burned there and people were gathering. It was clear they were scared, watching their surroundings, clutching at each other, gathering in a close circle.

The pain in his ribs made it hard to breathe, let alone say anything. He couldn't even stand easily by himself, but both Connor and Nathaniel kept hold of his elbows, supporting him.

Albert, the mayor, and Samuel came into the circle and it grew quiet.

"As some of you have heard, about an hour ago Connor and Tessa were out foraging and found Betty." Albert paused and ran a hand over the white stubble on his face. "She was dead."

Spike thought of the stories about the old woman, her attempts to get them all to pray with her to fight off the demons. How she'd locked the doors to her store and refused to share the few remaining supplies she had right after the quake. The story about how she'd kept those doors locked when an old couple needed help. They'd died because of that.

"What happened? Maybe just a heart attack?" Nathaniel's voice was almost pleading.

"I don't know what killed her but she..." Samuel swallowed, tried to speak, and closed his eyes a moment before continuing. "She was torn apart. Maybe the same thing or things that killed Max because there were similarities. But her...her heart was still there."

"What was she even doing out there?" Tessa asked, her voice high with horror. "She rarely left the store."

"I don't understand," June said, tears on her cheeks. "Why would she have gone out alone?"

"Mayhap she didn't go alone," old Ben said, putting an arm around his wife's shoulders.

Spike felt a pit of cold dread in his stomach, as if he was still in the river. "Where's Jennifer?" His voice was still too hoarse to carry far but others repeated the question, looking around.

"I'm here," the girl said from the back of the group. "And thanks for assuming this is my fault."

"You hung out with her," Connor said.

"Sure. Keeping an old lady company. More than any of you did. Doesn't mean I had anything to do with this!" Jennifer's voice rose as did tears in her eyes.

Spike pressed a palm against his aching ribs and drew in a painful breath. She was right. He knew what it was like. One mistake, one screwup, and after that everything that went wrong was automatically your fault. And yet...what she had done right after the quake hadn't been a mistake. She'd planned and manipulated, thinking to keep herself safe. And he remembered Max's words. Max hadn't trusted her. And Max had a cop's instincts.

"You're right," Albert said. "Innocent until proven guilty. I'm going to need volunteers to bring her remains back and bury her."

"I'll help," Nathaniel said.

Spike grimaced. "Wish you'd stay here. It's getting dark and I can't go with you. But do what you need to."

Connor started toward him with a hand out, but Spike waved him away. "Go with Nathaniel. I can make it back."

The circle of people shifted and the conversation slowly turned to the business of death. Actions that had almost become commonplace. Spike wanted to also help with the burial but he was in enough pain just standing there. He watched Nathaniel and Connor follow Samuel and thought about trying to get back to the tent and his sleeping bag, if he could even make it that far on his own. Instead, he carefully made his way down to the short path to the little Pickett Beach.

The river pulled at him now, as if with the mountain water he'd sucked in, he'd also swallowed some of its soul. Become part of it, like Rowan now was. That sure as hell wasn't a thought he was going to share with anyone. And he sure as hell wasn't going to go swimming ever again, just in case. Yet he made his way carefully to the water. Where he'd almost died.

Once there, he leaned against a boulder, sure that if he sat down, he'd never get back up. He watched the green and white water rushing away as if there'd been no drama the day before. Nature was so...oblivious. That was the word he wanted. Not uncaring, just in its own world.

Or, fuck. Maybe it didn't care. What did he know? Something moved out there in mid-channel. A flash of auburn, undulating like seaweed, there and gone.

He bent, groaning, and straightened with a rock in hand. He threw it out into the water and shook his head at the lame attempt. His ribs hurt too much to allow tossing the stone very far.

He waited.

Nothing.

Just the loud rush of the water. But the flash of red came again, a little closer. Was Rowan happy out there in the emerald water with her friend? Would he have joined them if he'd drowned?

A little self-consciously, he talked, telling her what had happened, letting his fears and worries flow out of him and into the river. He had no idea whether she still existed as the Rowan he knew, or if she could hear him there under water. But he talked anyway.

After a few minutes he straightened painfully and made his way back to the path, one arm across his chest to brace his ribs. A deep tremor moved through him, making him wince in pain. Underwater, being taken by the current, there had been that beautiful, unworldly emerald light. But not so beautiful that he wasn't profoundly grateful the river had given him back.

As he made it to Avenue A, Spike's thoughts turned to Betty and he crossed the rough, torn up pavement to the general store. The front door was locked and he knew the back of the store was blocked from the collapsed wall. He cupped his hands around his eyes and tried to see in the window but it was too shadowed inside. Turning, he saw Ben near the barter shed.

"Hey! Got a crowbar?" Raising his voice made him bend with the sharpness of pain, but Ben waved a hand in his direction and went to the back of his big old truck, rummaging inside the camper.

Spike waited until the old man came to him carrying a crowbar and bolt cutters.

"What're you looking for, son?" Ben asked.

Spike shrugged. "No idea."

The old man worked the crowbar under the hasp holding the padlock. Spike watched the old fart do all the work while he stood there useless and ashamed.

"Sorry," he said. "That I'm not, you know, helping."

The hasp came out of the wood with a splintering sound and Ben, not expecting it, slipped, hitting his knuckles on the wood of the door jamb.

"Fuck. Now I feel even worse."

Ben chuckled and shook out his hand. "You've been helping. Right now, it's your turn to step back and heal."

"Maybe, but it sucks. Need to get your hand looked at? I could find Samuel."

"No, no. Not that bad. And it will give Mother something to fuss over."

Ben leaned the crowbar up against the jamb and then tugged the door open. The inside of what had once been a stocked community general store was dim and shadowy. Ben went through the door and Spike followed.

Betty had cleaned up a path to the back of the store and they moved past collapsed shelves and broken glass. Anything that had survived the quake and wasn't perishable, she had moved to the back and used to set up a small living space against the collapsed wall. Canned goods had been stacked neatly, creating a corner for one of the cots FEMA had dropped off. There was a sleeping bag on the cot, a pillow, and next to it, an overturned crate that acted as a table. On it was a kerosene lantern and her bible with a box of matches sitting on top of it. She had made an attempt to create a sense of home by tacking up a couple old religious prints.

"Did you know her?" Ben asked.

"Nope. Just what Max said, that she isolated herself in here after the quake and wouldn't share food with anyone."

"Trauma takes some people that way."

"Yeah, but...I mean, she was religious. Aren't you supposed to take care of your fellow man or some shit like that?"

Ben walked over to the cot. "Mayhap people see what they want to see. Interpret things in their own way."

Spike just shrugged.

"What do you believe in, son?" Ben asked.

Spike walked over to board that had been set up on top of cans to make a rough shelf. Betty had used it for her clothes, all folded neatly. "Don't know anymore. But I sure as hell wouldn't let someone starve just to make sure I had a stack of pork and beans."

Ben gestured. "This here comes from fear. She chose to isolate herself but mayhap we should all have tried harder. Jennifer, with all her mistakes, at least befriended Betty. Spent time with her."

"Yeah, about that." Spike turned toward Ben and caught his breath on the sharp pain in his ribs. "Max was watching her. Didn't trust her."

"That was his job."

Spike looked at the neatly made cot again, at the neatly stacked canned goods. At the life Betty had created in the dark remains of her store. Maybe Jennifer had nothing to do with this. And yet, he'd trusted Max.

"Huh."

He turned carefully back to Ben who was holding Betty's bible. "What?"

"She took this with her everywhere."

"Maybe not for a walk in the woods," Spike said.

"Mayhap…but this here looks like blood."

Spike made his way back to the old man. The book's cover was black and the thin onion-skin pages were gilt edged. On the lower end of the well-bent spine was a small stain, darker than the cover. Easy to miss. He watched Ben rub it with his gnarled fingers and then raise them to show Spike the crusty bits that came away.

"Maybe she cut herself or something."

Ben nodded, putting the book back on the table. He rested his hand on it for a moment. "Mayhap. All this broken glass around here. That'd be just common sense."

Spike waited, watching the old man as he kept his hand on the book a moment longer. Ben was frowning.

"What?" Spike finally asked.

Ben shook his head and gestured toward the door. "Nothing, son. Just an old man worrying."

Spike made his way slowly through the ruins of the store and to the door then turned to Ben, holding his hand out to stop the old man. "I'm worrying, too."

Chapter 28

PAYTON WAS LIMPING. RAMON saw her put one hand on Michael's arm as if for support. It was early evening, raining lightly, and they'd been walking steadily, trudging along with hoods up, damp and chilled. And now they were close enough to Sultan to smell it.

The highway was barely negotiable between the upturned pavement, broken earth, and skeletons of abandoned vehicles. Occasionally they came across a decomposing body, although the military, or someone, had made an attempt to retrieve most of those who had died. It should have bothered him more than it did, but the grief for those who hadn't survived was swamped by his low simmering weight of failure and fear. He had nothing to protect these four with him except the gun and few clips McCausland had given him.

And now Payton was limping.

Ramon finally called a break. They followed him to a truck on its side down in a deep swale that ran along the side of the highway. There were other wrecked vehicles but this one had partially rolled into a thick stand of bamboo which would make it less visible from the air. Plus, it had a canopy.

Gun in hand, he checked the back to make sure no one was there. It had clearly been used as a camp but not recently. The back was full of spilled toolboxes and lumber as if the owner had worked construction. But at least there was no body and no monsters.

He gestured the others to come forward and watched Payton limp her way down the slight incline of the swale. "Are you getting blisters?"

Payton shook her head, her long, greasy hair falling over her face as she looked down.

"You're limping. Those boots look too big. We should have found you something back at the lot."

"We did," Michael said. "But she wouldn't take them. She just found more socks."

Ramon was startled by the sudden warmth of anger that rose inside. "You get blisters, they get infected, what do you think is going to happen? You think you can find some antibiotics? You think you might be able to stop blood poisoning by just ignoring it? Even little things, things that didn't matter before, will kill you now. Don't you get it?"

Payton just stared at the ground, her hand with its torn nails and fading bruises coming up to grip her shirt at her throat.

"She won't give up the boots, man." Michael stepped in front of her. "They belonged to her friend Amy. She died when our bus rolled when the quake hit. These boots, man, are all that's left of her. We had to leave Amy in that bus. Out there alone. So yeah, we get it!"

He'd never seen the kid speak up like that before and his burst of anger suddenly shamed him. He sighed then ran a hand over his face.

"Okay. I'm sorry. But the reality is, you need better boots."

Payton simply sat just inside the camper, pulled her knees up, wrapped her arms around them, and lowered her head. The action wiped out the last of Ramon's anger.

"We're doing the best we can," Michael said quietly.

"Things like this, that would have been no big deal before, are huge."

"And like I said, we're doing the best we can." Michael went to Payton, dropped his pack on the ground and sat awkwardly next to her with a grunt.

Ramon biceps and shoulders ached from carrying Tommy and then the pack. He had a headache that just wouldn't go away but throbbed with each step he took. He was still stiff from the fight when he lost their supplies. He saw Marie sit down on the other side of Payton and put her arm around the girl's shoulders. Tommy watched him carefully and hopefully. Ramon gave up, dropped his pack, and joined them in the shelter of the canopy.

"Okay. Let's go through this stuff McCausland gave us. See what rations we got and how long they're going to last."

Michael opened all the zippers of his backpack and dumped it. Payton raised her head, used the backs of her hands to wipe at her eyes then did the same. They organized the piles and Ramon realized they were better stocked than he'd feared. McCausland had either put time into gathering what they might need, or else simply stolen already stocked packs. Plus, Michael had tied their meager supplies from the wheelbarrow to the packs, including the sleeping bags, tarp, and musty blanket.

"We're going to be sick of protein bars by the time we get to Index but at least we won't starve if we're careful." Ramon tossed one of the bars to each of them. "Best eat something now before we repack and head out."

Michael groaned. "Not looking forward to Sultan, man."

Ramon wasn't either. He remembered the mad escape from the city before the water from the breached Culmback dam hit. Would the place still be flooded? How would they get through?

"Do you think..." Michael paused, glancing at the others before continuing. "Do you think maybe we could just stay here for the night? I mean, it's already late. This is a good place to hide out. And, you know, the others are pretty wiped out. Not me, man. I could go for miles yet. But girls...well, you know."

Ramon looked at each of his kids. Even Marie looked pale, with smudges of weariness under her dark eyes. They hadn't covered a lot of ground, but they'd covered a lot of emotional ground. No wonder they looked exhausted. And Michael had been the one to realize it. Ramon let Michael's boast fall unanswered, not pointing out that the kid was obviously as wiped out as the girls.

"Yeah, okay," Ramon said. "And Michael? It's now your job to speak up if I'm pushing you guys too hard."

Michael's shoulders squared and he blushed. "You got it, man."

"Let's see what hasn't been already scavenged in these tool boxes and make some room for our bedding. Payton, Marie, Tommy, you three get everything back into our packs. Divide stuff up so not all the food is in one, in case we get separated."

Michael heaved himself to his knees, puffing, and crawled toward the back of the camper. It didn't take long to make room for them all inside and to go through stuff. The thing had been pretty thoroughly scavenged. It was Payton who found the most valuable item when she went into the bamboo to pee and came back with a can of applesauce. Dented, but unopened.

"There's dinner sorted." Michael laughed. "Payton the provider!"

Ramon gently patted her shoulder and he thought there might have been a tentative smile. "And I just happen to have a can opener."

They'd finished making their rough camp by the time darkness thickened. A few travelers had gone by on the ruins of the highway, most headed west toward Monroe as if they hoped to find sanctuary there. If they noticed Ramon's group down in the swale, he saw no sign of it.

Tommy burrowed under the musty blanket spread on an opened sleeping bag. In moments he was asleep. Ramon didn't start a fire against the dark. He didn't want light for those wandering in the night. As it grew later and colder, one by one the others gave up the battle against exhaustion.

Ramon sat just inside the opening, listening to the rustling behind him as his kids settled down. He made sure his gun was next to him and zipped up his coat. The rain grew heavier and the metallic sound of it hitting the canopy drowned out night sounds. There were signs of life around him though, in small, distant campfires and the occasional flash of a headlamp or flashlight. But no one came near their site.

Those signs of people out there reassured him that the helicopter, even with night vision, wouldn't be able to single his group out. He listened for the sound of approaching monsters, even as he knew if something came for them, he'd probably not even know. All he heard was the rain in the dark, as nights might have been hundreds of years ago, before traffic on a highway. Heck, before the highway.

His thoughts drifted, thinking about how far they had to go, what Sultan would hold, how friends in Index might be doing. Max would keep them all safe. June would make hot chocolate. He daydreamed that sense of home and drifted into sleep.

When Ramon woke, stiff and sore, in the early gray of morning, a small pair of women's hiking boots sat neatly at the opening of the camper next to him.

Chapter 29

Max's heartbeat surrounded Casey. She could feel the pulsing in the earth under her feet. She could hear it in the trees and the wind, as if she held a shell to her ear. It never left her, that constant pulsing that pushed her forward into the hunt.

A sickle moon was still faintly visible in the pale dawn light. Casey had made it to the fishing hole where Max died and found a place to hole up and rest briefly. The river was the quiet murmuring of deep water in early morning. Early birds were chirping, unconcerned with anything other than greeting the new day. The night rain was gone but water dripped from trees.

Casey yawned and stood to stretch out aching and tight muscles. She shivered in the chill air and her stomach growled. She rubbed it and then caught brief movement under one of the trees. Clearly not the woman she hunted because there was no howling wind-wolves, but something. Maybe just a wild animal. But maybe not.

She should have been scared. Dawn and a ruined forest and monsters. But she was just icy. Ready. A little queasy from adrenaline and an empty stomach.

The dark shadow shifted and took form as it neared. She raised the rifle. Finger on the trigger. She drew in a deep breath and let it out, controlled.

Max was there with her. She could feel his steady presence, just like in the old days.

Movement shifted again and she saw a glint of red then recognized the shape. A dog, but bigger than anything she'd seen before. The red came from its eyes as if firelight reflected there, in the depths. Except there was no fire. The dog moved forward, huge paws silent on the deep, mossy humus of fallen needles and decayed leaves.

Casey waited, rifle steady. It wasn't one of the wind-wolves that had taken Max, but it sure as hell wasn't someone's lost pet.

The dog came, its bared teeth glinting in the low light. She remembered Curtis talking about the legend of a black dog. What had he said? Something about it being a guardian of crossroads. That didn't help her at all. There were no crossroads here. Not anymore.

Shadows shifted and she realized the dog was closer. Watching her. Waiting.

It's hunting, too.

"How do you know?" she asked Max in a whisper.

It's a mythical dog from hell. What else would it be doing?

She almost smiled as she lowered her rifle slightly. "You better be hunting the same thing we are."

In her mind, Max raised an eyebrow. *It came to us for a reason.*

"Maybe. Maybe it's just hungry and I look like breakfast." Casey unzipped her pack and pulled out a protein bar. She was hungry, too, and needed food to function. "Stay or go, dog."

As she unwrapped a hated protein bar, the Black Dog moved closer then sat, watching her intently with its red eyes.

No wind whipped through the trees bringing wolves. Not even a small breeze to ripple leaves. Just the dog, staring at her.

She crumpled up the wrapper, put it in her pack, and shivered. With a little to eat, the queasiness from exhaustion eased.

What's that dog want?

"I don't know," Casey answered. "But I wish it would quit staring at me."

She heard Max's chuckle in the wind and smiled. But then the smile chilled, tensed, became a focused scowl as the dog growled low. It took a few steps away, then looked back at her.

Might as well go see what it wants. The walk will warm you up if nothing else.

"Why don't you go follow it then?"

I plan to. With you.

She could hear his chuckle as she shook her head and picked up her gear. When she went toward the dog, it moved away, looking back as if making sure she followed. She did, deeper into the trees.

There's something...coming, I think. Can you sense it? Watch your back though, love.

Casey moved carefully through the woods, listening to the whisper of wind in the trees. Max was right. There was something, like her body had fallen asleep and was tingling awake. She could sense something nearing.

Let it come.

Yes. Let it come. She was ready.

Chapter 30

J ENNIFER HAD LOVED HER parents, especially because they'd understood her fears and coached her in the ways to manage them. What was the worst that could happen? What would you do to survive? They'd had so many hypothetical scenarios at the dinner table. What if this happened? What would you do? What would you be able to do? What would you be *willing* to do? And always, the understanding that God only helped those who helped themselves.

When the quake hit, she realized her parents had been right. To survive, she had to be stronger than the others. More willing to sacrifice.

She left the fort, zipping up the yellow sweater June had given her against the chilly morning air. It was warm, and she appreciated that, appreciated June's thoughtfulness as she walked to the general store. It was weird to not see Betty on the other side of the locked door, clutching her cross necklace, sticking to her barricaded space. It made Jennifer sad and she briefly regretted what she'd had to do. She actually missed the old woman. Betty isolated herself out of fear, but she'd also understood that in order to survive you had to depend on no one but yourself.

There was no way anyone would figure out Jennifer had anything to do with Betty's death. She'd been careful to cover her tracks. But then last night in her tent, she'd woke up in the darkness breathing fast from the remnants of a nightmare. In the adrenaline-sharpened thoughts, she had a sudden sick feeling she'd missed something. She started second-guessing her decision about the bible and hadn't been able to get back to sleep.

In the morning she waited until people were busy with tasks and then made her way to the store. Betty had always been afraid of losing her key so she hid a spare at the back of the building. Jennifer knew where. She figured she would go in, just for a minute, just to reassure herself that all was as it should be. But it wasn't. The padlock plate was broken. Someone had been inside.

Jennifer stared at the splintered door jamb and reached out to touch the door, watching it as it swung open.

"Lookin' for something?" Spike asked behind her.

Jennifer jumped and let out a startled squeak, hands coming up to her chest. She backed up to the door frame. "Don't do that!"

"Sorry."

He didn't look sorry.

"I'm not looking for anything," Jennifer said, getting her breath back under control. "I just...I miss Betty. She'd talk to me."

"Go on in then," Spike said, pushing the door open wider.

Jennifer hesitated but Spike lifted his chin in the direction of the shadowed space on the other side of the door. She entered the store slowly, glancing back at him. Was he the one who had broken the lock? Why?

"I don't need company."

"I don't mind," Spike said.

He was too close behind her, crowding her, and her knees were suddenly shaky. "You don't need to be here. I'm okay alone. Like I said, I'm just missing her."

"She left her bible," Spike said. "You know, when she decided to go for a walk alone in the woods. It's back there in her sleeping space. She'd probably want you to have it."

"Maybe." Jennifer wished he would leave.

"Especially since it's got blood on it."

Sudden dread liquified her insides.

Spike took a small step forward. "But, you know, maybe she just cut herself on all this broken glass or something."

Jennifer drew in a deep breath. "Maybe."

"What do you think got her? Out there alone in the woods?"

"A monster, what else?" Jennifer stepped around Spike and started back outside. "Probably the same thing that got Max."

"Yeah, maybe." Spike followed her.

"I need to go to the barter shed," Jennifer said, hoping he didn't hear the waver in her voice. "See you around."

Spike caught her arm. "Don't you want that bible? The one with the blood on it?"

"No!" Jennifer tugged her arm free. "I told you. I was just missing her, that's all."

Spike raised his hands as if in surrender. "Sure. Right. Didn't mean to upset you."

Jennifer tried not to walk too fast, but she wanted to get away from him. He knew. Somehow, he knew. She stumbled, almost falling, but caught herself and stood still, heart racing and shivering in the sudden cold of dread.

Was he watching her?

She clenched her hands into fists to stop their trembling. She drew in a controlled breath, and then another, willing her heart to slow.

Maybe he wasn't watching her.

Maybe he wasn't following her.

Feeling more in control, she looked over her shoulder at Spike, who still stood at the door. He raised two fingers to his temple as if saluting her.

Jennifer smiled at a sudden thought that instantly calmed her.

Maybe he *would* follow her.

Chapter 31

"**B**UT WHY QUESTION IT, man? I mean, it's stuff we need, right?"

Michael stood outside the camper, staring at the pair of hiking boots while Ramon paced back and forth, agitated.

Ramon pointed at the boots. "But who's leaving this shit, and how the hell do they know what we need?" What he didn't add was the even more disturbing idea that someone had been able to walk right up to him and drop off boots without waking him.

"No clue. But kind of nice having something good happen for a change." Michael scooped up the boots and bent to hand them inside the camper. "Hey, Payton. Wake up. Try these on."

Tommy crawled out of the camper opening, his eyes wide in fear. Ramon grimaced. The kid always looked terrified when any of them raised their voice or got mad. He ruffled the kid's hair.

"It's okay, Tommy. I'm just a little freaked out."

Marie came outside zipping up her coat and dragging a backpack behind her. "It's a good thing, isn't it? Something watching out for us instead of wanting to eat us?"

"Yeah, about that." Ramon, calmer, squeezed her shoulder gently. "Aren't you supposed to tell us when something is close enough to practically sit in my lap?"

Marie cupped her elbows with her hands in a self-contained hug and shivered in the cool air. "I can't sense things like I did. I told you."

Disgusted with himself, Ramon headed for the bamboo trees. "You did. And I'm sorry. It's not your fault and not your job to take care of us. I need to piss. Start packing up, guys."

When he came back, he went to Marie and put an arm around her shoulders. "I'm angry at myself that something got so close and I slept through it. That's on me, not you."

Marie leaned into him. "I wish I could help more."

"You're not feeling anything? Not even a little?" He wondered briefly if that meant she'd finally healed from her head injury. If, all along, her ability had been tied to that after all.

"I can still sense things but I have to work harder. It's like when you're at a loud concert and your best friend is trying to tell you something. The noise is so loud you can't hear what's next to you."

"What's the loud noise?" Ramon asked. "You said something was trying to come through."

"It's more like strong emotion," Marie said, frowning. "An overwhelming, aching, longing. Hunger. But not like being hungry."

"Can you tell how close it is at least?"

"No. I can't even tell for sure where it's coming from. It's just...everywhere I guess."

"Okay." Ramon sighed. "Anything changes you tell me immediately."

Marie raised an eyebrow that clearly said he'd just stated the obvious.

"I know," Ramon said. "You're not stupid. Just humor me, okay?"

She gave him a light shove and went back to the camper, bending to go inside.

"Pack up guys," Ramon said. "We'll eat on the road."

He watched their surroundings as they packed up their bedding, strapping things to their packs. He was still deeply unsettled. What could be big enough to carry a pair of boots and get so close and yet not wake him? What clearly followed them, knowing what they needed, and yet invisible to them? What could he do about it? Did he even need to do anything about it? Nothing so far felt like a threat.

He sighed heavily, zipped up his pack, and checked the kids' progress. The day was lightening to an early spring brightness that felt like something they hadn't seen in too many dark days. A light breeze from the north even smelled cool and fresh and that, too, was something that hadn't happened since he'd first arrived in Monroe. It made him feel hopeful. Maybe.

Payton had put the new boots on but her old ones hung from her pack by their laces.

"How do they fit?" he asked. "Okay on your blisters?"

"Perfect," she said softly, lifting a foot.

"That's good." Why *wouldn't* their mysterious benefactor know her exact size? He turned to Tommy. "You up for walking a bit or you want to ride?"

Tommy slid his little pack on and squared his shoulders, pointing east.

"Right. Let me know when you get tired."

Michael backed out of the camper opening and stood with a grunt. "Everything's packed up."

"All right," Ramon said. "Same thing as yesterday. Watch your surroundings. Stay together. Listen for that damn helicopter. Right now, there's people around to use as camouflage but I'm thinking the closer we get to Sultan there may not be. So, pay attention."

The sky to the east was a bright pink behind the mountains with the rising sun, breaking up the last few scattered gray clouds. It felt symbolic that they were headed in that direction.

That fleeting hopefulness lasted until they reached the outskirts of Sultan.

Chapter 32

MORNING WAS A HINT of pale sunrise above the trees. But within the forest, or what remained of it, night shadows still held tight to the earth. Max's pack was a solid weight on Casey's shoulders, straps cinched tight. It gave her comfort.

The rifle was a weight in her arms, chamber loaded. It gave her purpose.

The only thing missing was where to begin her hunt. Which was why she followed the Black Dog. She was like an aching, empty abyss, something that had been cratered out when she held Max's cooling heart in her hands. The only thing she felt was the grief-scorched need to avenge. There was no place for comfort there in that raw space.

The wolf pack had been like spirits on the high wind, similar to the Shadow People they had faced before. Substance without substance. No way to kill them. But she faintly remembered a woman standing in the midst of the swirling wolves. Not the Stone Woman they had encountered before. This one was tall and pale and Casey had a crazy sense that the woman had been pregnant. Either way, she had seemed to have substance where her wolves had not.

If there was substance then there was something a bullet could cut through. And if she was wrong, if she was going toward her death rather than her revenge, then that was okay, too, because in death she'd no longer grieve.

The air was clear and cool but she was barely aware of her shiver. Birds began to sing around her and her boots crunched on broken branches. Wet leaves and soggy ferns damp from the night's rain brushed against her jeans and chilled her hand when she pushed them away as she walked. The air smelled of saturated earth and new growth and spring. It should have been a wonderful spring morning to be out in the woods.

She followed the Black Dog grudgingly, scanning the woods around her, hoping to hear the howling wind. But now the animal had stopped and she realized she was back at the Hole in the Wall. Where Sharon had died. Where Curtis had worked. Why had she been led back here?

Get a little closer, I think. It's here for a reason.

Casey nodded in agreement. There had better be a reason for that creature to have led her here. If she'd just wasted time following it, she might have to shoot it.

Movement above her made her stop and look up. In the treetops, touched by the rising sun, a huge raven circled. It was so black its feathers glowed in the light like the sheen of oil on water. She knew that raven. It belonged to the Stone Woman. It had once attacked Max and Bird.

The raven circled once more, slow on drifts of a high breeze and called, a rough broken sound that was like the voice of the Stone Woman. And then it plunged downward, landing in front of the Hole and folding its wings.

"Okay," Casey whispered, her voice as hoarse as the raven. "Okay."

They wanted her at the Hole, which meant she had to figure out why. She could only hope their reason mirrored hers.

Chapter 33

THE CLOSER RAMON AND the others got to Sultan the stronger the smell of decay grew. It wasn't just the scent of death, as in Monroe. This was the odor of wet, rotting earth, of mold and mildew and rank mud. The ground grew boggy, and their path became one of circling around low-lying pools of stagnant water.

The massive wall of water from Spada Lake, that had been held back by the Culmback dam, had sent a tidal wave higher than houses through Sultan, over the berm of railroad tracks, wiping out everything in its path. The quake brought the city to its knees and the dam failure finished wiping it out.

When the dam breached it had been chaos and terror as people tried to evacuate. Ramon and his nieces would never have made it out alive if it hadn't been for Ben and June and their old truck. It made Ramon shaky, almost as if finally, after all that had happened, he was reacting to what might have been.

For a second his knees wanted to give out. He wanted to sink to the ground, borne down by devastation and horror and helplessness. How could any of them go on? How did one make it back from the darkness that life was now? He bent, hands to knees, and the others slowed, faltered, came to a stop around him. Ramon's heart pounded, assailed by a sudden cascade of grief.

Payton moaned, almost a deep sob, and sank to the ground, curling around her knees. Tommy went to her and bent to rest his forehead on her shoulder.

Marie wrapped her arms around Ramon's arm and put her head on his bicep.

Michael turned his back, shoulders hunched. He glanced over at Ramon. "It's just the smell. You know. Makes me want to barf." But he brushed the back of his hands over his eyes. "All those people, man."

Ramon straightened. He had to pull it together for them. He had to hide his emotions, be strong, hold them up. He tried to speak, coughed on the lump in his throat, and tried again. "Grieve for them. Be thankful we made it. And focus on our next step."

"We need to remember them," Marie said. "Someday. A memorial or something here."

"Someday." Ramon drew in a deep breath. "Come on, guys. It's not going to be pleasant but let's get through Sultan and get out of here."

They regrouped, Michael retched, and then shrugged. "This sucks, man."

The closer they got to what had been the city limits, the slower they walked.

There were scattered rough camps around the outskirts of the city and a few people went about tasks. Even a woman with three scruffy dogs and a canvas bag over one shoulder that sagged with weight. It was quiet and Ramon heard the sounds of water lapping against things and the gurgle of it in newly formed creeks and rivulets.

The woman with the dogs had seen them. She lifted a hand in greeting slowly, as if not sure she should, and then came toward them. The dogs, half-starved, hung back behind her legs, wary.

"Nice dogs," Michael said.

"They aren't for barter." The woman put her hand on the head of the tallest dog, a brown and white mutt with long floppy ears.

"What would we do with a dog?" Michael's eyebrows rose. "It's hard enough finding stuff for us."

"People eat dogs now," the woman said. "Don't you know that?"

Up close she looked to be around fifty or sixty, with skin beginning to sag from the loss of muscle and weight. Her jeans, red shirt, and thin raincoat hung loosely on her.

"No way, man," Michael said, disbelief in his voice. "Seriously?"

Ramon flashed back on the moment he'd pulled Tommy from the dog crate, and how someone had mentioned the same thing. "We're just passing through," he said, hoping to reassure her they weren't starving.

"Good luck with that," she said. "Climb up on the railroad berm and walk that first. You may change your mind about passing through. You might want to go back where you came from."

"That's the thing," Michael said. "We *are* trying to get back where we came from. Have you seen Monroe? You don't want to go there."

Marie stayed behind Ramon, head down. Payton, though, went forward and sat on the ground a few feet from the woman. She held her hand out and a smaller dog came to her, body low as if it thought it was in trouble, but rear end tentatively wagging. Payton scratched under its chin and the dog climbed into her lap.

"I call that one Scrappy. Only because I can't believe it survived everything." The woman hesitated, then shrugged her shoulders. "I'm Gloria."

"Are you here alone?" Ramon asked, and then realized the question could have been seen as a threat. He held his hand up. "Just wondering if you need anything."

Gloria shook her head. "I'm getting by. Got a camp that's kind of secure. Foraging every day to see what I can find. Collecting abandoned pets and books, I guess. Got a couple cats back at the camp."

"Books?" Ramon asked, surprised.

"I used to work at the library. Everything was lost in the flood. But I'm finding books, scattered and water logged. I spread them out to dry, hoping to salvage them. I'm looking for books on myths."

"About...monsters?" Payton asked quietly.

"Human or myth?" The woman laughed and Ramon heard the bitterness in the sound. "Myth. Trying to see how to get rid of monsters."

"Lots of both around here?" he asked. "Human and myth?"

"Lots of both," she replied. "Like I said, walk the railroad berm first."

Gloria called to the dog in Payton's lap, lifted her hand to them again, and walked away, eyes already on the ground, searching for anything that might help her survive.

"Wait up!" Michael called. He dropped his backpack, rummaged in it, and went to her with a couple protein bars in one hand. "Here. You know, for taking care of the dogs."

"You sure?" Gloria asked, shock in her lined face.

Michael patted his stomach. "Sure. I need to lose a few pounds anyway."

"Thank you." Gloria took the two bars and added them to her bag. "Thank you."

Michael came back, looking sheepish, and wouldn't meet Ramon's eyes. Ramon shook his head as Gloria left them. It was stupid to dip into their limited rations when they needed everything they had for their own survival. He reached out and squeezed Michael's shoulder.

"That was stupid," he said quietly. "But I'm proud of you."

Michael's cheeks reddened. "Just...you know. Dogs."

Ramon gave his shoulder a pat and stepped away.

The railroad berm that ran east and west through Sultan and had bordered the highway when there was still a highway, had taken a beating. In some places it was still intact. In others it had washed away completely, or been left with huge scoops of earth missing. The tracks themselves twisted and uplifted, some still spanning the gaps. Ramon looked around him and pointed to a big root ball of a downed cedar tree. The roots, still full of dirt and rocks, stood like a five-foot-high pancake on its side.

"Head over there," he said. "I'll go check things out. It gives you something to put your backs to."

"You're leaving us?" Marie caught his sleeve.

"Just long enough to see what Gloria was talking about. No sense all of us being up on that berm, exposed to any helicopter. Visible to anyone or anything."

He saw fear in their eyes, in the way they glanced at each other and clustered close. "Go on," he said. "I'm not going far."

They moved reluctantly, but they moved. Marie held one of Tommy's hands and Payton the other. Michael led them to the root ball and started untying the tarp roll from his backpack to give them something to sit on besides mud.

Ramon climbed up the berm where it was only a few feet high and looked solid. Even so his boots sank into wet dirt and sent clumps sliding downhill. He caught the edge of the train tracks for balance and then stood. The tracks were twisted and torn free but looked navigable for maybe a quarter of a mile before the first break where the trestle over the small Wallace River had been. Carefully, he made his way over creosote boards and bent iron. It wouldn't do to slip and break an ankle or leg.

He was so intent on watching his footing that he didn't realize he'd reached the remains of the trestle until the sound of water grew louder. He stopped and looked up.

The sound of lapping water should have been peaceful, like small waves on a beach, or the calm edge of a lake on a summer day. And in a way, the sound was. As long as you listened with your eyes closed.

When they'd tried to get out of the city before the water hit, the highway had been a blocked mass of cars and trucks and panicked people. It was why old Ben had taken his truck through back yards and back roads. When all those cars had been swamped by the flood, some washed up and over the railroad berm. More piled against it and against each other. Smaller vehicles were completely submerged and water lapped against tires and through openings of broken windows. A small bird perched on the axle of an upside-down pickup truck and flew away when Ramon moved to wipe the sudden tears from his cheeks.

Debris from houses taken down by the flood added to the mess, with pieces of walls and roofs smashed into vehicles and torn up pavement. The water was muddy and full of debris. A child's tennis shoe floated, tapping gently against a window that somehow, miraculously, wasn't shattered.

But all the signs of lives broken and destroyed were nothing compared to what moved above the water.

Cold dread gripped Ramon's stomach. He sank to a crouch, helplessness coming down like a heavy weight on his shoulders.

The Shadow People were here.

Chapter 34

E THAN WENT AS FAST as he could through the ruined woods, full backpack cinched tight, rifle in hand, moving between light and shade as the weak morning sun broke through the splintered openings in the forest canopy. Bird loped at his side. He followed Alegria and the boy who were somewhere ahead of him. He caught glimpses of the moonlight glow of the wolf but he couldn't move through the ruined landscape and thick underbrush as easily as they did.

They seemed to be following some sort of sense, or scent, of Anya. Or at least, he hoped so. He figured he'd give it one shot and if it didn't work, he would go to Index for help. Get a search team or something. He scanned the woods as he ran, watching for monsters and trying to watch the rough ground at the same time.

He stumbled, regained his balance, and lost sight of Alegria and Joseph. He started to yell after them but Bird backed up against his legs and growled.

He brought up the rifle, finger on the trigger.

Bird was on point against him, ears up, hackles up, braced.

The faintest movement to the north of Ethan in the shadowed trees could have been the wind in branches. He waited, getting his breathing under control, watching and evaluating.

The cedar branches shivered again, as the soft breeze grew stronger. He saw something pale and for a brief second thought it was Alegria's wolf. But even as he thought that, he realized this was too tall.

There was movement on both sides of him, as if something flanked him. He turned in a circle, trying to figure out the biggest threat. Bird, snarling, moved tensely with him.

Ethan caught a quick glimpse of black, half-formed shapes. Maybe dogs. But then the pale figure in the trees came closer and took form. A woman. Tall and willowy. Long skirts. Pregnant.

Bird snarled again. The black shapes were closer, taking form. Definitely wolves moving in.

The woman came fully out of the trees. Long black hair that fell to the back of her knees and blew around her in the rising wind. Skin so pale she seemed bloodless. She moved with one hand resting on her swollen belly, watching Ethan with dark eyes that reflected no light.

Bird growled again but stood rock solid and didn't move from his side.

The howling started as if from a distance and as it grew in volume the wind rose with it until the woman's hair and clothes became a maelstrom around her. The wolves formed in the wind and their circle around him tightened.

Ethan raised his rifle. "Stop or I shoot."

The woman raised her hands, skeletal, long nails reminiscent of the Windigo they had battled before. The idea of firing on a pregnant woman horrified Ethan and he almost lowered the rifle.

For a brief moment it was like the wolves, the blackness, shivered inside her, part of her. Then, riding the wind, they gathered form again and blew through the woman, closing in on Ethan.

Ethan, no longer hesitating, shot at the wolves but there was nothing solid to hit. The wind grew so strong he couldn't stand against it. He fell, struggled to stand, lost his grip on the rife, fell again.

The earth lifted in a sudden, strong aftershock. There was no holding on against this roar, this upheaval, and Ethan rolled, slamming again and again into the ground. Something hard in his pack jammed into his lower back and his breath caught on the sharp pain but there was nothing he could do. He caught a glimpse of Bird tumbling away from him, of Alegria and the boy racing back through the trees, toward the woman.

Wind rose, cracking and splintering fir and cedar. Ethan rolled into a fetal position, trying to protect his head as branches and debris hit the ground around him. It lasted seconds, minutes, hours. There was no sense of time, just finally the growing quiet as the roar of wind diminished and the earth slowed.

At some point he was able to roll onto his side. Blood seeped from a small gash on his chin but seep he could handle. He heard the crack and thunder of trees still falling. The ground under him felt shivery as if the aftershock still trembled. He rubbed his hand over his eyes and gingerly touched a small, tender knot at back of his head.

Bird, a few feet away, shook his head and limped carefully to Ethan. He nuzzled Ethan's face then collapsed on top of him, trembling. Ethan grunted in pain but didn't push him off.

The forest floor continued to shiver under him, almost matching the trembling in his body. He was nauseated, his heart raced with lingering fear, and it was hard to catch his breath under the weight of Bird.

They were alone.

No pregnant woman. No weird wind-wolves. No ethereal other beings and their spirit animals.

Ethan ran his hand over Bird, checking for blood, then gently pushed the dog off and managed to sit up. He held still, head hanging, waiting for the pain to ease then slowly worked his way to his feet. Around him, broken branches fell through the still-standing trees with the loud cracks of splintering wood. The earth still quivered. The motion was almost subliminal, but enough to add to his nausea. He retched and wiped his mouth with the back of his hand.

When he thought he could move without falling over, he slowly and carefully searched the area until he found his rifle sticking out from under a cedar branch. He bent, wincing, and pulled it out, then straightened and looked around.

Still alone.

"Okay," he said quietly. "Focus first. This doesn't change anything. We have to find Anya."

Bird limped over to him.

"Evaluate next. We're pretty beat up. We're on our own. No idea where everyone went. We could use help searching. We can't just wait here hoping

Alegria and Joseph come back. Or sit here until whatever that woman was comes back."

Bird shook himself, sending dirt flying, and stared at Ethan, ears up, alert.

"And then act. We need help. We can't do this alone." He stroked Bird's head with a shaking hand. "Whatever the hell that was, hope it's gone. I think the aftershock just saved us."

Chapter 35

Carefully, Ramon dropped from his crouch to his hands and knees and worked his way backward across the broken railroad tracks. He moved as slow as he could but still dislodged rocks and dirt. Did the Shadow People have ears? Could they hear him? He knew they sensed people somehow. Curtis had told them about the Gray Men, or Shadow People, how some people thought they were ghosts and some thought they crossed over from parallel universes, which was why they never fully formed a human shape. Whatever they were, they were bad news.

If he looked at them directly, they looked like low-lying fog moving over the water. It was only when he saw them out of the corner of his eye that they took on vaguely familiar, unsettling, bodily shape. No clear facial features such as a nose or a mouth. Just tall, thin, shadow-fog. Except the late morning sun did nothing to dissipate this fog.

They had also been in Index. He remembered how they entered into people, then slid back out, fuller somehow, leaving the person dead. Sharon, the woman dying of cancer, had gone into the Hole in the Wall and taken them with her. And the Stone Woman with her raven had also destroyed them.

But Sharon was dead and there was no ancient old crone with a raven close by.

Ramon paused, raising his head enough to look again, unable to resist. Maybe he was just paranoid. Maybe it was just fog.

But no. They moved with a sinuous purpose, sifting in an almost gentle way, like mist on a breeze, but slipping into debris and under water then emerging and flowing to another spot. As if searching.

He realized, with horror twisting in his stomach, that was exactly what they were doing. Looking for anyone still alive.

Ramon slid down the berm and bent, hands on his knees, shaking with cold fear and icy shock. There was no way they could make it past that. He straightened, and still shaky, made his way back to the tree roots where the kids waited.

Silently, he picked up Tommy and gestured for the others to follow him. Without asking questions, they did so. He saw the sudden fear in their eyes, the quick, quiet ways they gathered their things, the way they kept looking back over their shoulders.

He led them back to where they had met Gloria and saw her there, waiting. She nodded to him as they neared.

"See what I mean? They haven't left the water yet, but it's just a matter of time."

Ramon also nodded then took a deep breath and gestured back where he'd come from. "Shadow People."

The kids didn't need him to say any more. They'd been there when the Shadows had come into Index. Except for Tommy, but he apparently knew what Ramon was talking about, too, because he buried his face in Ramon's shirt.

"Okay." Ramon took another deep breath. "Okay. Let's find a place to regroup. We got out of Sultan before by going back roads and high ground with Ben and June. If we did it before, we can do it again. It just might take longer. We just...I just...I just need a minute to figure this out."

The kids clustered around Ramon and he saw their fear in the way they reached out, catching on to his backpack strap, his arm, his shirt. As if by touching him they would be safe. It scared him as much as seeing the Shadow People, that awareness that they assumed he'd save them. He met Gloria's eyes and saw the sympathy there.

He didn't know what the hell to do.

Gloria gestured. "You can come back to my camp. I'll show you a book that might help."

A book? Ramon seriously doubted any book would help them get around a city full of mist monsters. But with no other ideas, he followed her as she left, shepherding his kids ahead of him.

They didn't have to go far. Gloria had made a rough shelter against the back of what had been a small grocery store. She'd scavenged boards and created a shaky lean-to in a corner of collapsed walls that was surprisingly hard to see. As they neared, a calico cat came out to greet the dogs.

They didn't go into Gloria's tiny home space. Michael shook mud off the tarp he'd carried from the tree and draped it over chunks of concrete from the store's foundation. Payton and Marie sat down together in the shadow of a partial wall and when Ramon put Tommy down, the boy joined them.

Ramon paced, thoughts jumping through memories. Ben and June had the old truck with the heavy winch to move quake obstacles. They'd had well-thumbed Green Trails maps showing back roads and logging roads. They'd had a big homemade camper full of supplies. They'd had shotguns for monsters. They'd had Marie, full strength. Later, they'd had Alegria and her wolf. Now, they had nothing.

Michael sat on a round of firewood next to a stack of three tires with a board on top for a table. "We can do this, right? We just have to go uphill and then go east."

"Sure," Ramon said. He didn't think he convinced Michael. He didn't convince himself.

Gloria came out carrying a book, the cover swollen and warped from water. She turned pages carefully releasing a faint scent of mildew. Some pages were stuck together, some torn, but she seemed to be looking for something in particular. Finally, she sighed and nodded.

"This might help. You might be able to just go straight through them."

Ramon seriously doubted that but he didn't want to hurt the woman's feelings. She'd probably never seen what the Shadow People could do.

Michael snorted. "Like a book is going to keep monsters away."

Gloria put the water-logged book on the tire table and pointed a finger at him. "Books are knowledge. Stories are past, present, and future. Your monsters have been around since the beginning of time. People in the past knew how to protect themselves or get rid of strange creatures. We've just forgotten those old ways. But books haven't."

Michael shook his head. "Like what, sprinkling holy water or waving a cross in the air?"

Gloria gestured abruptly with her hand for Michael to vacate his seat and he stood. She took his place on the round of wood and pulled the book toward her. "You're talking Christian rites like exorcism. Christianity is a new religion. All their rituals were stolen and rewritten from old religions."

"Wow, that would offend a lot of people." Michael shook his head but inched closer.

So did Ramon. "We had a friend," he said. "A scientist. Curtis said kind of the same thing. He thought mythical creatures went underground, like the first people of Ireland, when people stopped believing in them. He thought the quake just opened up faults that released them."

Gloria tilted her head to one side. "He makes sense, actually."

"He was a good man."

Gloria didn't respond, just turned a few more pages. "Christianity had the right idea, even if they stole them. There were always rituals, things you did, to protect yourself or your home."

Tommy suddenly stood and went to the older woman. With one hand he grasped his shirt front as usual, but with the other hand he tentatively reached toward the book. Gloria pushed it toward him.

Payton lifted her head. "We still do. Locking doors. Closing curtains. Zipping a tent...like that will stop anyone or anything that wants in."

There was a long moment of silence and Ramon couldn't help but look at her fading bruises and healing cuts. She met his eyes briefly and lowered her head again. Michael took a step in her direction but faltered to a stop. Ramon nodded in encouragement and he drew a deep breath, went forward, and lowered himself tentatively to the ground next to her.

Gloria broke the silence. "Exactly. Rituals."

Ramon frowned, biting back impatience. "We don't need some kind of ritual. A map would be more useful."

Gloria actually laughed. "Oh, definitely. I'm not saying any of this will work. I'm just saying that if the old ways have returned, maybe we have to go back to those old ways to survive. I mean, it must have worked back then, right?"

"No," Ramon said. "Sorry, but no. Those things worked back then only because some survived and there was nothing else to take the credit. Those people didn't know anything else. They thought sprinkling salt along your window kept evil out only because salt got the credit when something went right for a change."

"Like us thinking locked doors keep burglars out," Michael said. "Because our house doesn't get robbed and the neighbor's does."

"Maybe," Gloria said. "Except, really, how do you know? Maybe a burglar tried your house first and found the door locked."

Michael opened his mouth to speak but then fell silent, looking to Ramon as if Ramon could refute the woman's logic.

Ramon shrugged. "Okay, I see your point. But there's no way to prove it either way."

"So what's the harm in trying?" Gloria asked.

"Dying," Ramon said abruptly. "Some old ritual doesn't work and you find out it doesn't work too late when you get sucked up by soul-eating fog."

Marie had somehow acquired a buff-colored cat that was curled up in her lap while she stroked its matted fur. "We're going around then?"

"Of course we are," Ramon said. "You guys stay here, if it's okay with Gloria, and take a break. I think I remember which way Ben went. I'll see if I can find it and we'll go when I get back."

Gloria simply nodded. As Ramon left them, Michael and Marie were leaning toward Payton, talking quietly to her. Tommy stood at the table's edge, reading mildewed pages. He didn't even look up as Ramon left.

And when Ramon came back, the skinny little boy was gone.

Chapter 36

A T THE HOLE, CASEY held back, listening, scanning her surroundings, watching for shadows that shouldn't be there, or darkness that moved. The black dog, next to what had been the door to the Hole, also held still as if evaluating.

Before the quake, the scientist Curtis had worked here, in this tunnel bored into the granite of the mountain. After the quake, Sharon had gone into the dark, taking the Shadow People with her. She'd been dying of cancer and she'd never come out of the Hole. The quake had dropped boulders and trees down the high rock wall to pile before the Hole and close it off. But Casey knew that there were spaces someone could get inside.

Though no one wanted to.

Still, the place had become a shrine to Curtis, who'd died to save Ethan. She'd liked Curtis in the short time she'd known him. Why would the giant dog bring her back here? Carefully, she moved closer until she was next to the animal.

The dog shifted, dirt and small rocks sliding away under its paws as it jumped up onto the largest boulder and stood, a dark shadow against a damaged forest.

"What the hell are we doing?" Casey asked the dog in sudden irritation. "You're wasting my time."

She shifted to turn and go and, unbelievably, heard Anya's voice.

"Is someone out there?"

Casey froze for a second, and then scrambled upward. "Anya?"

"Casey! Oh, thank god! I can't get out."

"Are you injured?"

"Yes," Anya said. "And trapped. But-"

Maybe an aftershock had dropped rocks on Anya, but what the hell was she doing there in the first place? "Okay. Hold on. I'm coming in."

"No! Stay out!"

Casey ignored her, studying the rockfall until she saw a clear way in. The opening was larger than she'd expected and she was able to slip through what had been the round door of the Hole.

"Casey, no, don't come in. Go get help. Get Ethan."

"Too late." Casey crouched inside the Hole, pulled out her headlamp, and panned the area, keeping her rifle up. She saw no Shadow People, no mist or tendrils of fog snaking toward her. She saw nothing moving. She could hear water running somewhere and remembered Curtis saying his work station had straddled a small stream. Probably why the place was so cold and damp. "Where are you?"

"Here," Anya said, sounding resigned. "I can see your light ahead of me and to my left."

Max's heart was pounding.

"It's okay," she told him.

That's your heart, love.

"It's not okay," Anya said, her voice catching as if she was trying not to cry. "You shouldn't have come inside. But I'm glad you're here."

You never did listen too good.

Casey snorted. "I listen just fine. I just make my own decisions."

The headlamp beam caught Anya, who held up a hand to shield her eyes. "Well, this is one decision you might regret."

It took Casey a second to realize Anya was responding to her, that her friend didn't realize she was talking to Max. She drew closer and dropped down on one knee, letting the beam of light wash over Anya.

She had a bloody tee shirt knotted around her right forearm and a fleece sweater, half on, half off. She sat there in old black sweats and, incongruously, ugly orange crocs. She looked pale and shaky. But she wasn't injured otherwise, that Casey could see, and she wasn't stuck or restrained.

"Can you tell me what's happening here?" Casey asked, her voice slipping into the old deputy cadence of cool and calm. Routine that always shielded whatever she'd been feeling at the time. Like now, the deep frustration that this was a distraction pulling her and Max from their hunt.

She slipped her pack off her shoulders and opened a pocket one-handed. Rooting around in it, she pulled out the slim package of a space blanket and tossed it to Anya, then followed that with a protein bar and a bottle of water.

Anya tore open the packaging and unfolded the space blanket, wrapping it around herself with trembling hands. "No idea. I got up early. Went to the outhouse. The raven, you know the one, flew right at me. And then I was here." Her teeth chattered and she fumbled trying to open the bottle of water.

Casey moved closer and did it for her, then pulled her pack back on and took a better grip on the rifle. She let her headlamp beam sweep the area as Anya spoke, illuminating fallen rocks and the remains of the tunnel going back deeper into the mountain. Cold air came out, like the granite was breathing, but Casey knew it was just the change in air pressure between the depths of the tunnel and the outside world.

Still creepy though.

"Keep talking," Casey said. "And let's get you out of here."

"We can try," Anya said, and actually managed a quiet laugh. "Do you think I'd be sitting in here if it was that easy?"

"Figured you just couldn't see the way out in the dark." Casey felt the cold calm dropping over her that happened on every call she went on as a deputy, when her instinct started yelling that things were about to go sideways real fast.

"Like I said, that damn raven grabbed my arm in its talons and I was gone. It happened so fast I don't think even Bird saw it. For a second, I felt like I was in the wind, and then I was here. In the Hole."

What about the Stone Woman?

"Good question," Casey said, and repeated it to Anya who met her eyes and seemed, for a brief moment, unsettled.

"Never saw her. But with the raven I'm sure she was around somewhere."

"So, back to why you haven't just walked out."

Anya opened the wrapper of the protein bar with her teeth and took a bite. "I've tried. Each time I make it to the opening, or even a few steps outside, the damn raven shows up and I end up back in here. Not sure how many more times my arm can handle being cut open by those talons."

"Okay. Well, I'm here now, so we're going together. Can you stand?"

Anya nodded but let Casey help her to her feet.

"Put your hand on my shoulder," Casey said. "Stay close to me. We're moving for the opening."

She could feel Anya's hand trembling but her grip was strong.

Using the headlamp beam, Casey moved forward slowly, making her way around the collapsed rocks. She could actually see the exit, lighter than the dense darkness of the Hole.

They made it to the entrance with no problem, and Casey stepped out into the cool, fresh air. But then there was a tremor under her feet. For the briefest second, she thought it was an aftershock, but the movement was there and gone before the thought fully formed.

And so was Anya.

What the hell?

Casey didn't bother responding to Max. She quickly retraced her steps to find Anya back in the same spot, bent over her injured arm and cradling it as fresh blood stained the tee shirt.

"See?" Anya's voice was breathless with pain. "A couple more times and my arm's going to fall off."

Get Ethan. This is more than you can handle on your own.

"You're right."

She was talking to Max, but Anya answered.

"That's hopeful. Any solution for keeping my arm?"

"Obviously don't go outside."

Anya managed a shaky laugh.

"One step at a time." Casey put her rifle on the ground long enough to open the pack and hand Anya a couple more protein bars. She started to pull out Max's warm wool shirt but paused when her hand touched it.

She needs it.

"It's yours." She closed her fingers around a handful of his shirt. The one that still smelled of him if she held it close. "I can't. It's yours."

"What?" Anya asked, the concerned look back in her eyes.

Casey faltered for a second, confused, but then shook her head and pushed Max's shirt deeper into her pack and instead pulled out one of hers. "Sorry, fatigue is catching up to me. Take this flannel shirt of mine. It's yours. Not as warm as wool but it will help. And my stocking cap. That's wool, so at least your head will be warm."

Anya took both and pulled them on, maneuvering the shirt sleeve carefully over her arm, then tugged the space blanket back up over her shoulders. "Do you think..." Her voice got quieter, almost a soft whisper of hope. "Do you think Ethan might know what to do? If you could find him?"

Casey had never lied to anyone she'd helped as a deputy. It was one of the first things she'd learned in her training. Never lie. Never give false hope. "No idea. One step at a time."

Anya leaned her head back against the cold granite. "Got a spare headlamp? Kind of don't want to wait in the dark."

Casey did. In her pack. Max's. She pulled it out, checked the battery, and then with no hesitation this time, took hers off and tossed it to Anya. She slid Max's over her short hair. "Don't know how long the battery will hold. And take my rifle. I'm more comfortable with my service weapon anyway. Plus, I have my knife."

"Thanks." Anya's voice was stronger as she took the rifle and checked for bullets. "Get going then, and thank you. Watch out for the raven."

Casey didn't respond to Anya's assumption that she was going for Ethan. She shouldered her pack and made her way back outside. There, she stood for a moment as the woods lightened to clear spring morning around her. She didn't want to look for Ethan. She wanted to hunt. Deep inside her fury waited, coiled, for the moment she could release it.

She could find her way to their cabin, where Ethan probably was. It would take her a couple days though. She hesitated and looked where the Black Dog waited. It stood when she met its eyes and moved away a few steps, then looked back at her, clearly waiting for her to follow.

No raven circled overhead. No wind full of wolves raced through the trees. No pregnant woman with long claws followed. But the Black Dog wanted her to follow it and that must mean it knew where the woman was. Could she leave Anya? Just go back into the deep woods and keep hunting? Take down the woman who took Max?

Yes, she could. Anya now had supplies. She'd be okay until someone else found her.

No, love. Bring Ethan here. Then hunt.

"Nope." The ice-cold fingers of rage unfurled.

Stop. The Casey I love wouldn't abandon her friends.

Casey swallowed the bitterness of guilt and breathed in deeply, regaining her focus. "I'm not abandoning her. I'll get help as soon as I can. I just need to finish this Max. And I need you to understand."

Max didn't reply.

Casey headed toward the dog. It was shifting its weight, starting away from her, then stopping as if impatient. The same sense of time shortening clutched at her. The longer she waited, the more she let distractions in, the further away the pregnant woman could get. Someone else could take care of Anya. Someone with more time. Who didn't have something to kill.

Pulling that cold, clear vision around her, pushing away Max's disappointment, she left the Hole.

Left her friend.

Chapter 37

"He was right here!" Michael said, face flushed. "We didn't see him leave!"

"Well he's not right here now!" Ramon pushed back against Michael's shoulder. "What were you doing? Just-" Ramon bit back the words that wanted to fly out.

Michael's eyes glistened like he was about to cry and his face was flushed but he didn't look away from Ramon. "Go ahead! Say it. 'Just sitting on my fat ass' right? Right? Isn't that what you were going to say? That I'm stupid and useless?"

Michael grabbed up his backpack and shoved past Ramon.

"Michael, wait," Ramon said, shame eroding his fury.

Michael didn't turn back or even look back. One hand came up, middle finger saying more than words could have.

Ramon gestured to Payton. "Bring him back."

She nodded, ran after Michael who had only gone a few yards, and pulled him to a stop.

Ramon pointed at Marie. "Don't go anywhere, you hear me?"

Without waiting for a reply, he headed for the railroad berm and scrambled to the top. Fear was a sick, heavy weight in his stomach. He stood slowly and carefully, needing to be high enough to look for a scrawny kid, but terrified he'd attract the Shadow People.

He saw Tommy immediately, maybe fifty yards away, standing still on the railroad berm. With the fog flowing toward him, reaching and stretching, almost eagerly surrounding him.

"No! Get back here!"

Tommy turned in his direction, eyes wide and terrified. He ran toward the boy, with no idea what he thought he could do against the Shadows. Tommy abruptly held his hand up to Ramon in a clear signal.

Heart pounding, Ramon stumbled to a stop. "No," he whispered, starting forward again. "No, little man."

Tommy kept his hand up to Ramon, as if that alone would hold Ramon back. With his other hand he reached inside his grimy shirt and pulled out the cord that was always around his neck. A small brown pouch hung from it but from the distance Ramon couldn't tell what it was.

The bag moved.

Tommy lowered his head and his mouth moved as if speaking to the bag.

Something flew up and out of it. Small, brown, fluttery.

Like a butterfly.

Ramon started to run again, stumbling on the rough ground. Crazy kid, thinking a butterfly could do anything against killing mist. He clawed his way up and over bent railroad tracks, hit the ground and sprinted the remaining few yards to Tommy. The Shadow People were too close. Ramon grabbed up Tommy as a misty tendril reached for the boy and missed. It sluggishly turned and tugged at Ramon's ankle. A deep chill started up the inside of his pantleg.

Tommy wrapped his arms around Ramon's neck, hanging on tight, his whole body shaking. He buried his face against Ramon's chest as Ramon turned back.

The chill creeping up his leg was almost to his knee. Fog roiled, taking on humanoid shapes that gathered and came toward them. Ramon's leg was going numb. He couldn't feel the ground, couldn't pull his leg free. Frantically, he pulled on Tommy's arms.

"Run."

Tommy gripped him tighter.

"Run, Tommy! Get out of here!" He yanked Tommy's hands away and dropped him to the ground, pushing him forward.

Tommy wrapped his arms around Ramon's leg. Between the kid's sudden grab and not being able to feel the other leg, Ramon went down, hitting the ground hard. This was it, he thought. On the ground there'd be no chance. He sat up, wrenched the boy free and tossed him away.

"Go, go, go!"

Tommy bent, arms coming up over his head as he curled into a ball.

Something tickled Ramon's cheek, darted past his face, darted back. The useless, useless butterfly.

His leg was so cold it burned. He wrapped his hands around his knee even though he knew it wouldn't stop fog.

"Tommy, come on kid. Get up. You have to run."

Tommy didn't move.

The butterfly darted in close to Ramon's leg. It zipped into the fog and a tiny clear spot appeared. The little thing flew so fast it couldn't be tracked. But tiny, tiny clear spots opened and spread. The tendril writhed and pulled back.

The sudden pain was excruciating, like Ramon's skin was being peeled. He fell sideways and screamed in agony.

More holes appeared in the tendril as it stretched, coming out of his pant leg. The pain eased and Ramon sat up, gasping for air, his leg on fire. The fog thinned, looking like a sieve, like something was taking bites out of it.

He groaned, holding his leg.

Pieces of fog sifted across the ground until there was nothing left but small, wispy trails disintegrating as he watched.

All around him the Shadows were pulling back.

Ramon got to his knee, and managed to stand. His leg burned and he couldn't put much weight on it, but he stumbled forward to grab a handful of Tommy's shirt and pull him up. He didn't have the breath to speak through the pain, but he didn't let go, pulling Tommy back the way they'd come.

He couldn't walk across the bent rails with the numb leg so he sent Tommy ahead and then clumsily crawled across. On the other side, back at the top of the berm, he collapsed and rolled onto his back, struggling to catch his breath and slow his heart. Tommy came to him and curled up against his side. The boy was shaking and Ramon could feel the warm dampness of tears against his shirt.

He'd seen those holes before.

Back when all their gear had been stolen. When he'd been knocked unconscious. The body of the man that had attacked them looked the same. Hundreds of small bites all over his body.

Something flickered against his cheek again and he instinctively started to raise his hand and swipe it away, but stopped when Tommy sat up. With tears wet on the boy's cheeks, and hands that still shook, he took the cord around his neck and pulled open the little pouch. The butterfly whizzed down into the bag and Ramon had a quick glimpse of arms and legs, maybe a head, brown and spindly like a root. Tommy wrapped his shaking hands around the bag then dropped it back under his shirt and once again his hand came up to grip the material.

"It's okay." Ramon managed to sit up. "Really, it's okay kid. You're not in trouble. That's a hell of a butterfly though. Is that, whatever it is, where stuff has been coming from?"

Tommy nodded carefully and covered the pouch with both hands.

"It's okay. Whatever it is can stay right there. Seriously." Ramon shifted and groaned. "Let's see if we can get back to Gloria's camp."

Chapter 38

THE SUN ROSE SLOWLY into early afternoon. Between the restless night and the fight with the pregnant creature, Ethan ached with weariness. He stumbled on the rough forest floor and only managed to not fall because he grabbed Bird's thick ruff for balance.

They'd been moving at a steady pace since the fight, hiking back toward Index. There was no trail to follow and no easy way to traverse the torn-up landscape. He'd been hit by tree branches, struggled through thick underbrush, and once walked right into an erratic, the glacial boulder as big as a truck. Big enough he should have seen it. Big enough Bird should have seen it.

As he told the dog while fluently swearing.

He ached. He was dirty, bruised, scratched up, and sluggish. But if he sat down, he'd fall asleep and waste time he couldn't afford. He could feel a deep, shifting sense of fear and urgency rolling around inside him under the even stronger dread for Anya.

He clung to the thought that she was alive. That he would know if she wasn't. He would know.

Bird jumped a downed tree and then simply stopped, sinking down to lie, panting, in front of him. Ethan could have walked around the dog but instead he also stopped, struggling to remember if he was going in the right direction.

Exhaustion was causing him to make mistakes. He lowered down to sit with his back against the tree trunk. He'd rest for just a minute, like Bird was doing, and then keep going. Maybe Alegria and Joseph would come back.

The ground was damp and the air chilly. He crossed his arms, tucking his hands into his armpits, and lowered his chin to his chest.

Bird surged upright, stiff, alert, and snarling.

Ethan clumsily got up on one knee, raising his rifle and searching with gritty eyes for the threat.

Above him, in what was left of the forest canopy, something big perched on a fir tree that still stood in spite of a large split in its trunk.

The thing was like a roughly-shaped human torso, but with wings and trailing what looked like intestines. Ethan raised the rifle, drew in a steadying breath, and aimed. Was it a threat?

It lifted off the tree and was so big that the air pressure from the downdraft of its spread wings made Ethan's ears pop. He watched as it circled, rising, and then paused, drawing in its wings. When it dropped into a dive toward him, he fired but the thing didn't slow and he couldn't tell if he'd hit it.

Another loud gunshot echoed his from somewhere south of him and the thing veered away. He fired again and his shot was echoed by another. He pushed up to his feet, keeping Bird close. The thing above him flapped its wings. The sound was an odd clacking like small stones being moved by a river. It arced away, came back, and then rose, leaving.

Heading west.

Everything was headed west. Just like him, desperate to get to Index, to get help searching for Anya.

Ethan lowered his rifle slightly. Sudden hope that it was Anya, and the sudden airless fear that it wouldn't be, made him almost shaky. He staggered toward where the sound of the other gun had come from. Bird didn't follow him though, standing quiet, ears up.

Casey pushed through underbrush and came into full view. The brief flare of warm hope that he'd found Anya died.

She stopped, lowered her handgun, and shook her head. "Okay, okay," she said in disgust. "I get it. Happy now?"

A huge and scruffy black dog came up behind her and though she was clearly talking to it, she didn't even glance back at it. Bird, oddly, didn't react to the dog.

He just went to Casey and pushed his nose under her hand, sniffing at her skin intently. He looked back to Ethan and unbelievably, wagged his tail.

"Casey," Ethan said, hope blooming again like a lump in his throat. "You've seen Anya, haven't you?"

Chapter 39

MICHAEL WOULDN'T LOOK AT Ramon. He swiped at his eyes with the back of his hand. "Leave me alone. I'm going back to Monroe. I don't need any of you. I can take care of myself."

Ramon sat on a round of firewood at Gloria's camp, his numb leg stretched out. Michael stood at the edge of the camp with Payton next to him, hanging on to his arm as if she thought she could hold him in place. Marie and Tommy were at Gloria's makeshift table and Tommy seemed oblivious to them all, once again paging through Gloria's mildewy book.

Ramon had no idea where Gloria and her dogs were.

"Michael, stop," Ramon said.

"You thought I'd just been sitting on my fat ass!" Michael swiped at his eyes again. "I know what everyone thinks when they look at me. I know I can be an asshole. I know I'm fat. But I'm not stupid. And I *was* watching out for the others."

"Okay. I hear you." Ramon rubbed his leg and felt only tingling. What he did feel strongly though, was shame. "I'm sorry."

"You should be, man."

They managed to tentatively nod to each other but Ramon felt it was half-hearted.

"I mean it though," he said seriously. "I was out of line. I'm sorry. And I need you to stay with us. I can't do this on my own, trying to get us all back home safe plus trying to avoid helicopters and soldiers."

"Shit," Michael said. "They don't have to hunt us. They can just go to Index and wait for us to show up."

They fell quiet, staring at each other, the words hanging there between them. Ramon didn't want to admit that Michael was right. It was a reality his subconscious recognized but a reality he wished he could deny.

"No." Ramon hoped he sounded confident. "They won't waste resources having a helicopter and crew just sitting around waiting for us to show up."

"But if they are there, what will they do to our friends?" Marie asked softly from behind Ramon.

Obviously, he hadn't sounded as confident as he thought. The sick pit in his stomach came back with a heavy thud. Everything in him wanted to just quit. Maybe it was stupid to try and get home. Maybe they should just give themselves up. After all, if Marie couldn't fully sense monsters anymore maybe the crew would realize it and leave her alone. Then they could go back to...what? Monroe with its smokestack spewing the ash of all those who had died? Monroe with everyone out for themselves and no place safe?

"It doesn't matter," he said, gesturing for Marie to come closer. "Monroe isn't safe. Sultan isn't safe. Nothing is anymore. So we go where we have family and friends, where we can hide in the mountains if need be. Where we have a grizzly and a wolf. Plus, can you imagine Max or Casey if those Cascadia Protection assholes did show up? Give it a few days and Max will probably come looking for us in their helicopter."

No one laughed but Payton tugged on Michael's arm and he stepped closer to her.

"Besides," Ramon said wearily. "We have a freakin' butterfly."

"A what?" Michael asked.

Ramon told them what he'd seen, why he called it a butterfly, and how he thought it was the cause of things showing up when they needed them.

"But...that's great!" Michael said. "I could use a steak. Rare." He stared at Tommy's shirt, then up at the sky, and then turned in a circle.

"Don't think it works that way," Ramon said. "But it was worth a try."

"Can it get us out of here?" Marie asked.

"Doubt it. But hey," Ramon said. "You never sensed it? Not once? Even being this close to Tommy?"

Marie shook her head. "No. I told you. There's something drowning everything out. Sometimes it's even hard to hear what you're saying."

Tommy stood and pushed the book toward Marie. She glanced down at it, then pulled it closer.

"A Brownie? That's what your...friend is?"

Tommy shrugged.

"What's the book, like, say?" Payton asked.

"A house gnome," Marie answered. "Something that lives in old houses and, at least this one in the book, comes out at night to do housework people forgot. Legends say people would give it offerings of milk or cream. But Tommy's thing doesn't look like a little gnome."

"Might not be exactly what he has, just the closest he could find." Ramon reached for the book and looked at the water-stained pages. "But it kind of makes sense – something that's normally attached to a home and now there aren't any houses. Tommy's its home, I guess."

"Except it's not doing a very good job if it's supposed to keep its house clean," Michael said. "I mean, no offense, but Tommy needs a bath. We all do."

"Go for a swim," Ramon said, waving a hand in the vague direction of floodwaters.

"Yeah, no, I'll pass."

"Could it get us through, like, Sultan?" Payton asked suddenly.

"If we take back roads, even if it takes longer, we can go around and live." Michael reached for the book, sniffed, scrunched up his face, and pushed it back. "We take a chance on a...butterfly...and we're wrong, that's it, man."

"We take a chance here with a butterfly or we take a chance out there in the woods for days with other monsters." Marie crossed her arms. "We need the quicker route."

Ramon rubbed his leg, which was beginning to burn with returning sensation. "Tommy, you think we can make it, don't you? That's what you were doing, seeing if your friend could do anything about the Shadows. Right?"

Tommy nodded.

"And now, seeing how close they came to getting us, do you think we can get through?"

Tommy nodded again, emphatically.

Ramon stood and tentatively put weight on his leg, which made pins and needles shoot up to his hip. "We're just going on blind trust here. That you might be right. It's a big risk. Too big."

"Not if we went one at a time." Marie said suddenly. "Tommy, would the butterfly leave you long enough to get one of us across?"

Tommy hesitated, then nodded.

Ramon stared at his niece. "Are you insane?"

She looked at him steadily. "We need to get back to Index. As soon as we can. All this time, you keep telling me to let you know what I'm sensing. That's what I'm sensing. If the Cascade Protection crew believed me enough to take me, then it's time you did, too."

"Ouch," Michael said. "Right between the eyes."

Ramon fell silent, staring at his niece. It was like looking at two different girls, superimposed on each other. The fragile girl he pulled out of their destroyed home and held in his arms while she bled, and now metamorphosized into this young woman. Did he believe in her, in what she had become, or not? The logical part of him didn't. But it wasn't a logical world anymore.

"Okay Marie. I hear you. But I'll go first."

"No way, man," Michael said, his voice shaking. "We need you to get us back. They can make it without me. Not without you."

"None of us are expendable." Ramon felt suddenly like control had just slipped out of his fingers.

Michael started toward the railroad berm, his whole body trembling. "Let's do this before I shit myself."

They followed Michael to the top of the berm and stood there in a tight group, staring at the swirling fog moving over the water. Human form took shape, became low-lying mist, then reformed, as if stirred by the chill breeze that lifted from the dark water.

"This sucks," Michael said. "Wish Jennifer was here."

Payton laughed, quick like a gasp, then put a hand over her mouth.

"I mean, if we're talking expendable."

Ramon grabbed Michael's arm. "We can take back roads. We can go fast if need be. Listen to me. I'm telling you this is too risky."

Michael pulled away.

Frustration, anger, fear, shame at not being the first to take the risk, emotions he couldn't even name churned through Ramon like a tornado, destroying his belief that these were his kids and he was in charge. How could he forcibly keep Michael from doing something he was set on? Tie him up and drag him to Index? Who was he, if he failed at his duty to protect them?

"See you on the other side."

"Wait," Ramon said quickly. "No, seriously, if I can't stop you then at least listen. Go slow. Let the butterfly do its thing. If you fall into the water or slip and get stuck, we can't help you. Don't panic."

"Not helping." Michael drew in a deep breath. "I better get some sort of reward for being the hero finally."

Payton touched his arm briefly then stepped back. "Heroes always get the girl at the end."

Shock wiped out the fear in his eyes. Ramon saw the change, watched his shoulders draw back, his chin lift.

"Yeah. That's me. The hero with the girl." He took a few steps away from them and hesitated. "Even if I piss myself? Cause I'm scared shitless."

"Even," Payton said.

Tommy pulled the cord around his neck, lifted the small bag out, and opened it. Something small whizzed out and up, sunlight catching on a tiny gnarled brown form that sped to Michael and buzzed around his head.

Michael clenched his hands into fists and walked away from them, breathing heavily. But he moved carefully, although awkwardly, watching the ground at his feet, not once looking up.

Ramon, with a nauseating mix of anger and fear and helplessness watched as gentle river mist rolled and congealed and took form. He'd just sent Michael out there to die. "No. This was a mistake."

He started forward but both Payton and Marie caught his arms. He pulled against them, taking all three of them down to the ground, but they refused to let go. He tried to get up, dragging them, then froze.

The Shadows had reached Michael. The elongated humanoid things reached out for him as he carefully climbed over a twisted pile of railroad ties. He cupped his hands at the sides of his eyes and hunched forward, as if not being able to see them meant they weren't there.

A Shadow touched his hip and he went down on his knees and elbows. "Die you motherfuckers!" he screamed. "Just die!"

A small hole appeared in a tendril. A single, tiny window through the fog.

"Yes," breathed Ramon, gripping the girls. Tommy knelt next to them, staring intently at Michael.

Another tiny, tiny piece opened. Michael shoved back up to his feet and took a stumbling step forward.

And then it was like someone throwing handfuls of tiny pebbles at fragile tissue. Hole after hole appeared. Just like before, the Shadows closest to Michael writhed and pulled away, tried again, surged back, and then simply disintegrated. Others came toward him, swelling.

Michael, ignoring, or forgetting Ramon's words, moved at a stumbling run, falling, getting up, falling again. Holes formed in more Shadows.

Michael had reached the half-way point where the small bridge over the little Wallace River had collapsed. He didn't even pause, simply climbed along the steel ribs to the other side.

It took him about ten minutes to get to the far edge of the floodwaters. They could see him move to slightly higher ground, could see the fog sliding back like a shallow tide going out. Michael went down on his hands and knees and stayed there and even from where they were they could see his whole body shaking.

Payton, without a word, let go of Ramon and sprinted for the berm. He tried to grab her but she was already out of reach. And then the butterfly was there, rocketing around her head.

"Look," Marie said breathlessly.

The Shadows moved fast toward her but then washed back, recoiling into amorphous shapes.

"They know." Ramon shot to his feet, grabbed up Tommy, and jerked Marie up. "Come on. Now. Payton! Wait for us."

She hesitated, looked back, then paused long enough for them to catch up.

"Go, go, go," Ramon said, hand to her back. "Careful but fast."

They moved in a fog-free zone of clear air, like a small bubble around them. The butterfly moved constantly, tracing lines around them, darting out into fog for a bite, coming back to circle again.

Then they were across and climbing upwards to the small rise where Michael was still on his hands and knees, gasping for breath.

Ramon dropped, rolling onto his back and panting. He managed to reach out and pat Michael's shoulder.

"You did it, hero."

"Yeah. Well, let's not do that again, okay?" Michael said, and threw up.

Chapter 40

C ASEY HAD GIVEN IN to exhaustion and taken a quick nap curled in a hollow space of a root ball from a downed fir tree. When she'd woke, the Black Dog stood a few feet away, watching her with its red eyes. She got to her feet stiffly, swallowed against sudden queasiness, and pulled her pack out.

"What do you want now?" she asked the dog as she unzipped a pocket and got a small chocolate bar with almonds.

You're shaky.

"You would be, too, if you hadn't had a real meal in weeks, didn't get breakfast at all, and woke up to that thing."

The dog watched her without moving or reacting to her voice.

Last time it wanted you to follow it.

"Yeah, well, not this time. Unless it's going to take me to the wolf woman."

You won't know until you follow it.

Casey grimaced, wadded up the candy wrapper, and pushed it into a side pocket of her pack. The queasiness and shakiness dissipated as she shouldered the pack and checked her gun.

The dog looked back as the sound of a rifle shot cracked through the forest. She jumped, heart ratcheting up to race with her breath. There was an odd sound like rattling stones. For the briefest second, she thought she'd found them, the wind wolves, and exaltation flooded her like fire.

But then she saw movement in the treetops. Something huge and batlike, trailing what looked like guts rather than feet or claws. Its wings folded back as if it was going to dive toward whoever had just shot at it. The Black Dog snarled, moved forward, and then looked back at Casey as if urging her forward.

Shoot it. Now.

When Max told her to do something, she did it. She raised the gun and fired, calmly and in control, training taking over.

The thing arced away from her. She went in the same direction, gun raised in both hands, finger near the trigger. She scanned the sky and saw the dark thing, wings flapping, flying west away from her.

The Black Dog growled low and when Casey looked down, she saw movement in the trees. A man. Ethan.

And here's why the dog wanted you to follow it. Not to find monsters. To help your friends. You see?

Casey stopped, lowered her gun, and shook her head. "Okay, okay," she said in disgust. "I get it. Happy now?"

"Casey?"

Ethan looked exhausted. She could see the ragged collar of a tee-shirt under a grimy pullover, under a canvas jacket. His jeans were stained, his boots caked in mud. Bird was with him, the dog almost as scruffy as the Black Dog.

You're almost twins.

Casey shook her head.

"Have you seen her?" Ethan stepped closer.

"What?"

"Anya. Have you seen her?"

Casey took a moment to focus. She'd left the Hole. She'd left Anya.

Tell him. Take him to her. Come on, love.

"You probably can't help anyway. I couldn't."

"What?" Ethan flushed as if with rising anger.

Casey held up a hand to stop his words, to stop his interference, and tilted her head, listening.

Every time you leave to hunt, something happens to pull you back to our friends. Think about it. You're a cop. You feel it just like I do. Something's wrong.

"No. I have to go. I have to hunt. You know that." Casey held her hands to her ears for a moment, then shook her head.

"What the hell is going on, Casey?" Ethan's voice rose.

She took two quick steps toward him, fast, angry, bringing up her gun.

Casey. Stop. Now.

She froze, horrified, and lowered the gun. Sudden queasiness rolled through her and she bent, retching. When she straightened, Ethan had taken a step back and his eyes were cold with anger.

"Hunting," she said, and wiped her mouth. "I'm hunting the pregnant woman. I'm going to kill her. But you won't leave me alone. You, and this cursed dog, and even Anya!"

Ethan gripped his rifle so tightly she could see his knuckles whiten to bone. He gestured to Bird to follow him and said nothing as he walked past her.

Don't do this.

The huge mythical dog, the guardian of crossroads and ancient pathways, stared at her, red eyes intent. Its head was up, body tense. It came forward and stopped in front of her, its eyes burning like the fire in her.

Get help for those you care about. Or follow revenge. This is your crossroads.

"No." She grimaced. "Max. I need to kill that bitch. I need to!"

The heat of fury burned inside her. The weight of Max's heart in her hand, cooling. The wild rage that pushed her to killing that thing that had taken everything from her. The overwhelming *need* to pull out that woman's heart, to watch her die.

Casey, I understand. But help our friends first. Just this one more thing.

She'd never been able to tell Max no. But she'd never needed something so much before either.

"No." She raised her voice to a shout. "Ethan!"

He didn't look back.

"She's stuck in the Hole! I tried to help but couldn't. Maybe you can."

Ethan still didn't look back, but a hand came up in acknowledgement.

"Take me to the pregnant bitch," she said to the dog. "I've chosen the path."

Max was silent. So very silent.

A broken, choked sob forced its way up and the rawness of the sound was like desperation or heartbreak. Casey pressed a hand against her mouth so hard she felt her teeth split her lip.

No weakness. No grief. Max would have to understand. All that was left was the wild, enraged woman his death had created.

Chapter 41

E THAN JOGGED AT A steady pace toward the Hole, with Bird keeping up beside him. Somewhere behind him, he thought Casey followed. He didn't know what was going on with her. For a minute back there, after the winged creature left, it had been like she was listening to someone else, like maybe some sort of message had passed between her and that dog. For now, none of that mattered.

The only thing he focused on was that Anya was at the Hole. That Casey had talked to her. That she was stuck inside somehow. That was all he needed.

He left the shattered woods for the torn up back road that led to the Hole. More boulders and debris had come down from the Wall since he'd been here and it made the going rough but not enough to slow him down.

The ground under his boots still trembled, the mildly disquieting shiver that had started with the last aftershock. Movement where there should be stability made him slightly queasy, like a mild case of vertigo. Strange and unsettling, but again, not enough to slow him down.

He clambered up the boulder field that had crashed down during the initial quake and finally stopped at the round door of the Hole, barely visible behind rocks. He glanced back the way he had come but there was still no sign of Casey. Bird whined and dug at the opening.

That was all he needed, to know Anya was truly here. The round door wasn't fully blocked and he could see a way to get through, although the constant low-level hum of quivering earth was bringing down gravel and dirt to fall like rain.

"Anya?" He paused but when he heard no reply, pushed his way through the rocks.

Inside, all light was gone. It was cold and he could hear water running back in the depths. Bird whimpered as Ethan ripped open his pack and pulled out a headlamp. The light was a narrow beam showing collapsed timbers and rockfall, and at the farthest reach of his light, the edge of Curtis's broken work station.

"Casey?"

It was her voice, faint and shaky but strong. A light came on somewhere back in the tunnel, shining back to him from the depths, like a silver trail to her. He released the dog and ran.

She was on the ground, sitting up against the rock wall. He couldn't see anything else, blinded by her headlamp shining right in his eyes. He held up a hand to block it and then he was pulling her upright, one hand to the back of her head, one arm around her shoulders, holding her as she broke into sobs against him.

He couldn't seem to hold her tight enough. Bird howled and jumped, making both of them stagger. She choked out a laugh and reached one hand for her dog but didn't leave Ethan's arms.

She stood tight against him shaking more than the earth.

"Casey found you. I knew she would."

Ethan, his cheek against her hair, gripping her close, barely heard her.

"Do you know how to get me out of here?"

When her question sank in, Ethan lifted his head. "What?"

"I can't get out." Her teeth chattered.

In the beam of his headlamp, Ethan could see a space blanket where she'd been sitting and he let go with one hand to reach for it and wrap it tight around her shoulders. In doing so, he saw the blood-caked bandaging around her arm.

"You're hurt."

Anya sniffled. "Every time I try to leave."

"Who?"

"I need to sit," she said. "Not who. What. The damn raven. Every time I try to leave, it brings me back."

Ethan sat, pulled her down onto his lap, and only then realized he'd dropped his pack and rifle. He reached to draw both close and opened the pack as Bird pushed his way on top of Anya, madly licking her face. She wrapped her arms around the big dog.

Ethan pulled out a first aid kit and his backup heavy fleece pullover. "First things first. Let me see that arm. Then you can give me more details. Come on Bird, help me out here you stupid dog."

Bird rolled onto his back half on and half off her lap. With her good hand, she reached out, sinking her fingers into his thick fur.

"You and your tummy rubs." She broke into sobs again, which made Bird jump up again and start licking her again. The headlamp beams shot all over the rock walls.

"Okay! Okay!" Ethan said, trying to hold them both plus not spill the kit. "Settle down."

Bird subsided, slumping against Ethan's leg, with his head on Anya's lap.

Ethan shown his light on her arm and carefully cut away the bloody tee shirt, trying not to pull fresh scabs free. Her arm had been deeply punctured in several places, some scabbed over and some raw and new and still seeping.

"The raven did this?" He had to bite down the rising anger.

"Yes." Anya leaned her head on his shoulder as he swabbed the wounds. "I went to use the outhouse and it was there, on the deck. It was so eerie in the dark to see it just, waiting, I guess. It latched on to my arm."

Her voice grew shaky and Ethan didn't know if it was from tears or cold or relief or all three.

"It grabbed me, and then I was here. Every time I try to leave, I get outside and it's there, and then I'm back here with my arm more torn up."

Ethan listened as he worked quickly, cleaning, spreading ointment, rebandaging with clean pads and horse tape, and then working his fleece down over her head. After zipping it up, he took the space blanket and put it over her, then leaned back, holding her against his chest and under the blanket. He could feel her shivering easing as she warmed.

"Casey didn't tell you any of this?"

Ethan shook his head, sending the headlamp light back and forth. He reached up and shut it off. "No, but we didn't talk much."

"What's going on?" Anya asked. "What's happening? The raven keeping me here and now this weird aftershock."

"No idea." Ethan leaned his head back, reaction from crushing relief hitting him. He was suddenly and overwhelmingly exhausted. "Right now, I'm going to take a nap."

"What?"

"I haven't slept in...days I think," he mumbled. "But now it's okay. You're here."

He could feel himself drifting away and Anya lowering her head to his shoulder.

"Seriously? You're going to sleep?" Her voice was incredulous and there might have been a hint of tear-filled laughter.

His grip around her tightened. "You can't get out. I'm never leaving you alone again. Might...as well."

Chapter 42

T HE RIVER FLOWED AS if the world had never changed. Casey, walking its edge, imagined that, for the river, nothing *had* changed. Life and death on its banks were nothing. Fish spawned and grew and left and returned. Ice formed and thawed. And through it all, the river, unaware, carried away anything caught in its rush forward.

Their small fishing hole, where snow-melt water eddied calmly in a pool created by rocks and roots, looked exactly the same as she neared. She could even see her section of broken fishing pole still there, caught on something and bobbing gently against small wavelets at the rocky shore. The sound of the rushing water drowned out all else.

The wind gusted and the earth shivered under her boots. It was like standing on a bridge during high traffic, where the passing of cars vibrated the surface. She put a hand on a tree trunk, but more for the feeling of something solid than because she needed it. The trembling wasn't that strong.

The Black Dog was behind her and when she glanced back at it, a growing breeze brushed her face.

The broken, splintered trees bent toward her, pushed by wind that strengthened as it came down the granite Wall.

It was time.

Casey dropped her pack and slipped off her cumbersome jacket, then carefully unwrapped the bandage around the puncture wounds in her hand. The wraps would make shooting awkward. She spread her feet for balance, checked that her knife was in its sheath and her gun was loaded, then gripped her service weapon with both hands.

Rage rose cold as ice and she welcomed it with something almost like rapture.

The growing wind darkened and formed until she could see the wolf-storm coming for her. With a sudden clench of fear, she realized they could rip her to shreds before the woman even reached her. Like Max.

She heard wild laughter in the wind around her as the wolves became more solid, became a circling storm with her the center. She turned in a fast arc as they darted in, eyes solid black like the woman's, fangs long and flashing in the unnatural dark. Sharp pain flared through her left thigh and blood bloomed through puncture wounds, running freely down her leg. She stumbled and the black wind darted in again, with another bite appearing in pain and blood on her hip.

Casey fired her gun but there was nothing of substance to hit.

Something flashed red off to her right and she spun, stumbling again on the shivering earth as her wounded leg gave out beneath her. The wind roared, pummeled her, and she was thrown back, hitting the ground hard, pain shooting up her spine.

On the ground, she was defenseless against the creatures and she fought to stand but was only knocked down again. Jaws clamped on her forearm and then were gone, leaving a long bleeding tear.

A wind wolf grabbed her leg, shook her, dragged her along the forest floor. Her shirt rucked up and rocks and dirt abraded her skin, burning. She scrabbled through grit, tearing fingernails and losing her gun as she tried to hang on. She was shaken again, the pain deep and blinding. She kicked out with her free boot but hit nothing.

There was another flash of red, closer, and then the Black Dog was there watching her, still and solid as if there was no wind.

"Help me!"

She sobbed as she begged but the Black Dog didn't move.

The guardian of crossroads.

There was no help coming, from myth or friends. She could die on her back, torn apart by the wind-wolves, or she could die fighting them. She scrabbled in the dirt, searching for her gun.

You don't need it.

No. She just needed her rage. And Max. She kicked out again, and though she felt no contact, her leg was suddenly free. She rolled, made it up on her knee, then braced one hand against rough earth.

You don't need me, either, love.

Fighting the wind, she groaned with effort and stood, staggering. More wind-wolves closed in, circling.

You just need my heart.

She took a step toward the Black Dog, molten pain and rage like an inferno strengthening her.

Behind the Black Dog she saw something pale in the trees. The woman. Close. Within her reach.

"Kill them!" she screamed to the ancient guardian. "Get them the hell out of my way!"

The Black Dog roared forward as if her command released it. She heard its deep howl and felt it inside, a sound of primeval fury that she recognized. That she exalted in. Strength flowed hot like her blood. Pain faded as she raced forward, barely aware of the battle around her, the howling, the disintegrating blackness.

All she could see was the space opening before her, like a path straight to the woman.

Casey ran.

The woman brought up her hands, folding them protectively over her pregnancy. It was such a timeless thing, the mother protecting the unborn. And it was calculated. Casey didn't flinch, didn't hesitate.

The woman hissed and took a step forward, her long white dress floating around her. "You took the heart that was mine."

Heat flooded Casey's belly. She welcomed the firestorm, stepped into the rage.

The woman cocked her head to one side. "But you brought it back to me."

Max's heart in her hand, cooling as life ended. His blood soaking into the earth, into her skin. His soul, his wonderful, beautiful soul, taken.

Wrath, stoked by grief, engulfed her.

Could she kill this pregnant woman?

Of course she could.

Casey leaped forward screaming in pain and rage and the need to feel the thing's death in her hands. She grabbed the woman's throat, jamming thumbs into the soft spots under the jaw, forcing her head back. Those spots caused excruciating pain and Casey shoved in with all her strength.

The woman writhed and shrieked. Her hands came up, long nails raking Casey's face. She broke Casey's hold and shoved her back.

Focus. Steady.

Casey listened, like she always had. She braced herself against the trembling earth. The woman laughed and spread her arms wide.

"Concede. Give me that man's heart."

The fire in her burned into ash and rose cold as ice that steadied her hands, slowed her breath. One more time. That's all she needed. She charged forward, body-slammed into the woman, and punched, a perfect undercut to the jaw that snapped the creature's head back. But she grabbed Casey's neck with one hand, claws digging into skin.

"Men's hearts are mine. Always and always, from the beginning of time."

Casey couldn't breathe. She scrabbled at the woman's fingers with one hand but her vision narrowed and darkened. The woman laughed and lifted her off her feet.

Casey wrapped her left arm around the back of the woman's neck and pulled her as close as she could.

"Not this one."

Her words were nothing but a hoarse whisper. She reached for her knife in its belt sheath. Flipped it once to a reverse grip.

And took the woman's heart.

There was no blood. Just a black hole that gaped when Casey jerked the knife out.

She plunged the knife in again, twisted, jerked it out. The hole grew, the blackness spread. The creature screamed until the sound became the roar of the wind. Until she became the black wind roaring through the trees. Until the wind died to a circling draft. Until the air became still.

Casey dropped to her hands and knees and rolled to her side, gasping as pain came back with force. The gouges on her face burned, the bites throbbed deeply, and she couldn't swallow against the bruised swelling in her throat. She sensed something coming close but had no strength to move, no fight left.

A rough tongue rasped against the cuts on her face. The Black Dog stood over her, licking her wounds and she retched at the smell of its hot breath. But after a moment she pushed herself up to sit, shivering, head hanging. Her blood dripped into the earth and she wondered, in a half-dazed way, if the blood would mingle there with Max's.

The woods were quiet, the trees still, the river muted. Everything seemed to slow and all she could do was breathe deep, as if she hadn't breathed since Max's death.

The Black dog stopped licking her and backed up to stand beside her forgotten backpack. Carefully, she crawled over to it and pulled zippers open, spreading contents haphazardly around her. She found the first aid kit under Max's heavy wool shirt. The one she hadn't been able to give to Anya.

Her fingers were cold and shaky and she fumbled her blood-soaked shirt off and clumsily bandaged the wounds to her arms. Everything burned in pain as she got Max's shirt on and then turned to the still-bleeding punctures in her leg.

"Could you bring me my knife?" Her voice was hoarse and the words like grit in her throat.

The Black Dog just stared at her.

"Get my knife now!"

The Black Dog just stared at her.

Disgusted, she managed to tear wider openings in the rips in her jeans until she was able to bind the wounds. Blood soaked the bandaging, but slowed. With that done, strength left her and she eased back to lie on the cold and damp and trembling earth.

Above her, a gentle breeze whispered through tree branches and she watched the movement as her breathing slowed and her heartrate slowed and something fluttered light as a bird in her stomach.

Of course, she was hungry. And probably going into shock. She couldn't remember the last time she'd eaten. Or had any interest in food. But, oh, a cup of June's hot chocolate would be so perfect.

Does that mean we can help friends now?

Max was still there.

Still with her.

Casey rolled onto her side and sobbed, each gasp a tortured sound of anguish, hot tears the flood of pain finally, finally let go.

Chapter 43

RAMON WAS BONE-DEEP EXHAUSTED. He'd slept only fitfully the night before, even though they'd shared watches. It wasn't that he didn't trust the others to know if something happened. It was just...his responsibility. Keeping this little family of his safe was his job so even when it was his turn to sleep, he just dozed and tossed and turned.

Added to that, the day before they'd been constantly moving, pushing, with the goal of getting as far away from Sultan as they could.

Added to *that*, there was the constant low-level fear under his skin. Was something following them? Was that the sound of a helicopter? Were they running out of food? Was Payton limping again?

And finally, if all that wasn't enough, the night before Marie had nightmares. He'd heard her crying in her sleep or making small, whimpering animal sounds of fear that broke his heart. Sometimes he could soothe her back into a deeper sleep by simply touching her. Sometimes he had to quietly wake her. She'd come back to awareness only enough to turn and curl up, to sigh, and to sink back into quieter sleep. Only to dream again and start it all over.

In the morning she told him she couldn't remember her dreams and got agitated if he pressed. He quit asking even though he didn't believe her. There were shadows under her eyes and she was too pale.

Of course, none of them looked that great. He wasn't the only one exhausted. Working their way along the torn-up highway, always wondering when monsters were going to show up took its toll.

Now, in the late afternoon, they were coming into the city of Gold Bar. Before the quake there had been two thousand people living here. The two-lane highway passed between the city and the railroad tracks, similar to Sultan, but here there was no dam to flood the place. Instead, like everywhere, the damage was from the quake itself. Wrecked cars, burned out gas stations, destroyed homes.

"What's it mean when you see death and destruction and are, kind of, bored?" Michael trudged next to Ramon, carrying Tommy on his back. The day was sunny and bright and spring-cool but Michael was sweating.

"You're not bored," Payton said quietly. She and Marie were behind them, each with a pack. "You're just shut down."

Ramon looked over his shoulder at the girl and saw his exhaustion reflected in her eyes, her slumped shoulders, her lagging pace.

"As much as I want to push on to Index, get home safe, we need to find a place to rest up," he said. "Someplace secure enough we can actually sleep."

"Hell yeah," Michael said. "But, hey man, have you looked around? Not much in the way of hotels with free rooms."

Ramon snorted, slipping off his pack. "Smart ass. Give me that kid. It's my turn."

Michael didn't argue. Tommy, of all of them, was actually getting stronger. Maybe because he'd already been so malnourished that even their protein bars were an improvement. He'd been walking earlier and never admitted to being tired but when the butterfly appeared and started dive bombing them, it was time to pick the kid up. Now that they knew the thing existed, it seemed to feel safe enough to boss them around.

Just like in Monroe, there were camps here. Rough shelters made from tarps or broken timbers. Old tents. Cobbled together lean-tos scattered along the edges of the broken road. A rare house with enough structure remaining to be called a home. Ramon saw a few people working on their spaces, reclaiming what they could, creating something safe. There were a few kids, staying close to adults. People would pause to watch Ramon and his group pass and a few would nod in acknowledgement or lift a hand briefly. But no one came close or called out a greeting. It was a new world of caution and fear, of no trust, not able to risk any overture of friendship. At least there was no obvious hostility. Ramon was glad of that. His ribs still ached.

"That used to be city hall," Payton said suddenly. "My mom, like, knew that lady over there. She ran the place."

Ramon saw what had been a large two-story building with cedar siding. One half of the place still stood, listing, but the rest of the building was badly damaged. A woman stood on a broken chunk of concrete that might have once been a step. She had long hair and wore jeans with holes in them, a sweat shirt, and an old Ford baseball hat. A few people had gathered in front of her and Ramon edged closer with the others following.

"We've got one standpipe going and the water's potable," she said. "Pass the word around. And water means the old Red Hat ladies are mixing pancake batter. They don't have much to put on the pancakes but they're going to be handing them out at the fire over at Gateway Park. Pitch in if you have anything you can spare."

"What do you think took the Martini family from their tent last night?" someone asked.

The woman jumped down from her makeshift podium. "Well, hell, I don't know. Maybe a monster?" Her voice was thick with sarcasm and anger.

"What if it comes back?"

She rolled her eyes. "Kill it or be killed by it. What do you want me to say?"

Michael tugged on Ramon's sleeve. "Pancakes, man," he breathed wistfully.

Clearly, he had other things on his mind than monsters. Ramon hesitated, then nodded. "Okay. Go ahead. Take these three with you and line up. I'll meet you there."

"But...where's the park?" Michael asked.

"At a guess," Ramon said, "Where everyone else is headed."

"Oh. Yeah. Right." Michael straightened. "Okay ladies and kidlet. And butterfly. With me. We're on a pancake quest."

Ramon watched them walk away with a few others from the small crowd. He could see more people headed in the same direction and hoped briefly that there would be enough to go around. He went to the woman, now sitting on her concrete.

"I know that girl from somewhere," she pointed after his kids.

"Payton Lang. She said her mom knew the woman who ran this place."

"That would be me. She's had a hard time, hasn't she?" the woman asked quietly.

"Yes." There was no need to say more. No one came out of the quake whole. No one came out of the aftereffects undamaged. "Is it okay to fill water bottles if we're not from here?"

She took her baseball cap off, ran a hand through her hair, and put the cap back on. "Sure. Water's one thing we have plenty of now."

"Is there-"

"No," she said abruptly. "No, there's no help coming. No, I don't know when emergency management will come back with gas for our generator. No, I don't have hidden supplies of food in the city hall. No-"

"Wait." Ramon held a hand up, interrupting her as she had him. "I was just going to ask if there was some place we could crash for the night. Maybe a place we can actually get some sleep. We're just passing through and the kids are exhausted."

"Oh. Sorry."

"No, it's okay," he said. "You don't have to apologize."

She rolled her eyes again. "Yeah, I do. I'll squeeze you guys in the city hall. For Payton's mom. We've been rotating people through, everyone taking shifts at sleeping some place secure."

A man came around the corner of the building and she turned to him. "Did you find those old cots?"

"No, I looked-"

"Forget it." She cut him off with a sharp wave of her hand. "I'll do it myself."

Ramon watched her leave without another word. One overwhelmed woman trying to hold everyone together. He hoped she'd succeed.

The guy who hadn't been able to find cots looked hopefully at Ramon. "I heard there's pancakes?"

Ramon gestured in the direction his family had gone and the guy trotted off. Ramon followed more slowly. It was good, for the moment, to pretend everything was okay, that the world was like it used to be, that he was headed to a community breakfast where his family waited.

Well, they were kind of waiting. They sat on the damp grass in a rough circle around a paper plate with some small pancakes. There were people nearby, some also sitting on the ground, some standing, some still in line by a small fire with a grill over the low flames. Ramon paused, watching his kids. They hadn't seen him yet.

Michael had a plastic knife. He carefully cut a pancake into fifths, and equally carefully, handed each of them a piece. The fifth piece he set aside, obviously for Ramon. He raised his piece in his hand and said something that made the others rock with laughter. They raised their pieces of pancakes in the air as well, and then saw Ramon.

He watched their faces light up and the sudden warmth inside, the sudden sense of belonging, made him catch his breath.

He sat down in their small circle and Marie handed him a piece of pancake. He saw there were three more on the plate that hadn't been cut yet. There was no butter. No syrup. No jam. But the piece was warm and soft in his hand and smelled like rich Sunday breakfasts. He took a bite, and after weeks of protein bars and rehydrated meals the sweetness was almost too much.

Michael's eyes were closed. Payton nibbled at hers, obviously making it last as long as possible. Tommy's piece was already gone but Ramon saw a tiny bit go down the boy's shirt. Marie ate hers in two bites.

Michael heaved a long sigh, opened his eyes, carefully cut the next pancake into five pieces, and handed them around.

"We're sleeping in the city hall tonight," Ramon said. "We have one night where we can all sleep without having to take a watch. We can even sleep in some.

And then tomorrow we hit the road again. We should be home in a few days if everything goes okay and we can get across the river."

"We haven't had any problems so far," Payton said. "I mean, other than Sultan."

"Yeah," Michael said. "Does anyone find that weird or is it just me? I mean, things suck, right? Walking all day, no sleep, shitty food. But no monster attacks."

"Those people were talking about one." Ramon gestured back to the city hall. "But you're right. Nothing since the Shadows."

"Maybe," Payton said in her whispery, hesitant voice, "Marie can't sense them because they're gone."

"No." Marie rolled the edge of her shirt between her thumb and forefinger.

They fell quiet, watching her.

"There's something. Mostly at night. Like, when I'm asleep I can hear better." She raised her eyes to look at Ramon. "I didn't want to tell you."

Ramon put his arm around her shoulders. "This isn't a world for secrets, baby."

She was quiet a long moment, her head down as if thinking. "The white noise. It got a little quieter last night when the ground started trembling. For a little bit I could sense things, faintly. And it's like everything is on the move...maybe...pulling away."

"But that's good, right?" Michael asked. "I mean, maybe they're all going back where they came from."

Marie now gripped the edge of her shirt, wrapping it around her hands tightly. "No. No. That's not it."

She began to rock and squeezed her eyes shut. Ramon pulled her closer. She let go of her shirt and gripped his hand instead.

"Breathe," Ramon said. "Take your time and just breathe. We're here."

Tommy scooted over and leaned against her other side. Payton moved behind her and put her hands on Marie's shoulders. Michael closed the circle by moving in front of Marie. He looked at them as if not sure what to do, hesitated, and then awkwardly patted her arm.

"We're here with you," Ramon said. He could feel her trembling, but she breathed in and raised her head.

"It's so faint I can't be sure. But it's like whatever is coming, is calling them."

"Where?" Ramon asked, an odd weight like fear, like already knowing, sinking into him.

Marie stared at him.

"Oh, hell no," Michael said.

Chapter 44

I T WAS LATE AFTERNOON and Spike was back at the river that had almost killed him. The rushing emerald green water still held a strange fascination for him. He kept remembering what it looked like from within, how deeply cold it had been, how easily it could take life. And yet it was beautiful and full of movement, foamy white where it cascaded over boulders, spiraling where it circled in deep pools and shallow eddies. He'd never paid any attention to the character of a river before and now he kept returning.

Of course, he also kept watching for the seaweed that was Rowan's long hair, for the pale flash of her skin, hoping she would surface and return to them.

He even carefully and painfully tossed a rock. But nothing at all returned.

He shifted a little where he leaned back against one of the many granite boulders that the river, over years, had shifted and shoved and left behind. He thought his ribs might be getting better but the ache was constant and brightened to sharpness if he moved too quickly.

Clouds were sinking over Mt. Index and Persis but weren't low enough to cover Philadelphia Ridge yet. He didn't think they looked like rain, but then he shook his head. What did he know?

Homesickness was a sudden and unexpected weight in him. He'd never felt that before, never missed his home, so it took him a moment to recognize the sadness. It didn't take him long, though, to realize it wasn't his old home he missed, or the people he'd thought meant family. He even held a secret shame, that the earthquake meant he never had to go home. No, this was missing life as it used to be. A bed with pillows and blankets. The security of a roof and walls and a door that locked, even if that security was an illusion. Those greasy, cheap tacos he used to buy by the dozen and eat, cold, for breakfast on his way to school. Hell, he really missed flushing toilets. Being warm and dry.

Plus, the noise. Damn, but life had been noisy and he'd never noticed. Traffic and trains, cell phone conversations in grocery stores, canned music, manmade noise. Now it was just nature. Wind and river, rain and birds. Well, and the squeak of the rope holding Rob's oar frame boat tethered to a boulder.

He sighed, then winced. Life would never be like that again. No matter how much they were able to rebuild and restore and repair, it would never go back to what it was. Carefully, he straightened, then made his way slowly up the path and back to Avenue A. He stopped to breathe and ease the pain in his chest, and heard Tessa yelling across the street.

"No! No! No!"

He recognized fear and anger in her voice but she sounded angry more than someone about to die from monsters. He tried to jog across the street but could only manage a stumbling shuffle and by the time he got there, she had run into the fort and Samuel and Connor had come out of the fire department.

"What's going on?" he asked Samuel.

Samuel lifted his shoulders, looking as confused as Spike felt.

Tessa returned, racing through the fort gate, clutching an old coffee tin.

The three of them followed her to the small garden she had been so carefully nursing in front of the town hall. She jumped over something in the garden and peeled back the lid of the can.

"Not my miner's lettuce!"

She upended the cannister and dumped the contents. Something began to smoke and the sudden stench of rotting meat rolled over them.

Tessa, clutching the empty can, staggered back, retching. Connor went after her, stared at something on the ground, and then pulled her back to Spike and Samuel.

Spike had his coat up over his mouth and nose. "What the fuck!"

Samuel bent, hands to knees, and retched, then straightened.

"It's, kind of, like, a slug, dude," Connor said, and gagged. "A really big slug. Really big."

"We need this garden!" Tessa choked and tears ran down her face. "I've worked so hard on this, on making sure we have fresh food and now it's destroyed!"

Spike, keeping his coat pulled up, stepped carefully into the garden bed, where smoke rose behind a giant bush of rosemary. He went around the bush and stared down at a gray mass slowly turning to jelly as it smoked. It kind of looked like brain matter except it was about three feet long and almost as wide. And except that it was covered in what looked like bubbling caramelized sugar.

A wide trail of slime showed where the thing had come into the garden. The plants in its path were already blackening and dying. He went back to the others, gagged, and wiped the back of his hand across his mouth.

Tears overflowed down Tessa's cheeks. "I'm so sick of monsters. Every day. Everywhere we go. Being afraid all the time. Trying to kill us."

"Except, you know, that one was probably a vegetarian." Connor patted her arm but she pulled back.

"Not helping," Samuel said.

"I mean," Connor raised his voice. "Wow! Fast thinking! You saved the garden!"

June came out of the fort with a mug in her hand. "Tessa, dear, did you take the sugar?"

Tessa burst into noisy sobs, threw the empty cannister in the direction of the smoking slug thing, and ran toward the little trail to the river.

They stood there silently, looking at each other, and Spike wondered what the hell he was supposed to do now.

"I thought you used salt on slugs." Connor picked up the empty can and looked inside. Then he put it back on the ground and started to follow Tessa.

"I'll take care of this," June said, stopping him. "It's a job for a grannie. You boys clean up whatever that is over there. See if you can fix her garden. This life of ours, well, it's just impossible some days."

Spike looked at Samuel and Connor as June made her slow way across the street. "No shit," he said. "It's getting to all of us. Always waiting for the next bad thing to happen."

Connor pushed at the blackened plants. "She's been transplanting the stuff we forage. So we don't have to go out into the woods. Trying to make it safer for us. And she's scared about winter coming and all of us starving because a helicopter can't make it, or because she didn't gather enough food, or someone steals it all, or because she doesn't know how to preserve it."

"It's not all on her shoulders," Samuel said.

"Mayhap she needs to hear that," Ben said walking up behind them. "How about we gather around a fire this evening?"

"Yeah." Connor wiped the palms of his hands across his eyes. "Yeah. That would be good."

Chapter 45

"INDEX." MICHAEL PACED, PANCAKES forgotten, face pale and almost frantic. "We can get there. We can go fast. Well, kind of. But, I mean, we can get there. We can help."

Ramon stood, took Marie's hand, pulled her to her feet, and then Payton and Tommy. His stomach was twisted in knots and his mind raced in circles. "My first priority is keeping my family, you guys, safe. We're not going to Index. We can't."

"What are you talking about?" Michael asked. "Back in Sultan I pretended to be the hero. To, you know, get the girl. But I'm not. I'm the coward that runs. You're the hero that helps me do the right thing."

Ramon took a deep breath. "Not this time. People in Index are our friends. We've survived with them. We've grieved with them. But I need to think of you guys, here."

"But they got a shit-ton of monsters headed their way!" Michael's voice rose to a shout. "They're going to need help, man!"

Ramon struggled to keep his own voice calm, to pull up the ruthlessness he needed. "My priority is keeping Marie, and the three of you, safe. And that doesn't mean taking you where monsters are gathering."

"But...Alegria!" Marie grabbed his arm and tugged like she was trying to drag him east.

"I know!" Ramon pulled away and stepped back. Helplessness and fear rolled into anger. "You say something massive is coming. You say monsters are headed to Index. What the hell am I supposed to do? If I take you into that you're in danger. If we go back to Monroe, we face a threat we know, but then I won't be any use to Alegria. Every single choice is sacrifice!"

"Hey, man-" Michael reached for him.

Ramon shoved his hand away and wheeled around to stumble a few steps back.

Alegria was in Index. Or at least in the area. She had a wolf and a boy with a grizzly. She was half myth, beyond his help. But abandoning her to what was coming cut deep into his soul.

Friends were in Index. Old Ben and June who had saved him and his nieces. Ethan and Anya. Max and Casey. Those four would fight. But for how long? Would it make a difference if he was there? Maybe not in the actual fight, but he'd be there with his friends to at least help.

He dug his hands into his hair and gripped, as if he could pull his heartbreak out. Or pull out some decision. He had Marie, at risk from Cascadia guys who might be in Index waiting. He had Payton, still frail. He had Tommy, a little kid even frailer. Then there was Michael, trying, but not much help.

He turned back to the others. "All options are bad. But there's absolutely no way I'm taking you into a storm of monsters. Even if that means leaving friends on their own." He pulled in a shaky breath. "Leaving family on their own."

The kids stood in a tight circle hanging on to each other, watching him with pale faces and wide eyes.

"We stay here tonight." His voice steadied. "We get some rest. Tomorrow, we leave early. We'll go back to Monroe and set up a more permanent shelter. Make our home base there until things improve."

"No," Payton said in a whisper.

"Yes." Ramon's words were tight and controlled. "I'm not taking any of you where monsters are. This isn't up for discussion. You're my responsibility and my family and I'm keeping you safe."

"No." Michael's face drained of color and he trembled but he clenched his fists. "Sorry, but *fuck* no. *You've* made us your family, but I'm *not* your kid."

"Michael, listen to me."

"No! I know you need to take care of us. And I don't know how to fight. I'm scared shitless all the time. But June gave me hot chocolate!" Tears ran down

Michael's face. "I'm not going to Monroe. I won't be much use in Index but at least I'll be with them."

Payton took Michael's hand. "I'm going with you."

"And me." Marie lifted her hands to Ramon as if begging him to understand. "I need to be there."

"Marie, please." Ramon's voice was thick with pain. "Please listen. We've lost your parents. Then Alegria. I can't lose you, too. You can't go."

Michael held up a hand as if to stop Ramon's words. "It's not your decision, man."

Ramon felt queasy, as if everything was slipping away. "Look, I've kept you safe this long. You guys are my priority. But I hear what you're saying. Let's go back to Monroe. We can go to the National Guard, tell them what we know, get them to help."

"Who are you kidding, man?" Michael asked. "You do that, they take Marie. We just escaped all that shit."

"I just..." Ramon trailed off as he realized suddenly that the queasiness was fear.

All along, it had been fear. Fear of loss. Fear of not being strong enough, of not knowing what to do. And fear of more loss that would be his fault.

Payton dropped Michael's hand and stepped forward to reach out almost tentatively and put her hand on Ramon's arm. She touched, light as a bird, and quickly pulled back.

Her voice was a low whisper, for him only and he bent to hear her better. "What happened to me wasn't my fault. What happened to us wasn't your fault."

Ramon's throat felt clogged and it was hard to speak past the pain. He swallowed hard and the pain sank into his heart. He put a fist to his chest and bent his head.

"But we need to help our friends," Payton continued. "We're not the only ones in this family of yours."

Ramon drew in a breath and straightened. "I know. But it's too dangerous."

"That's it?" Michael asked.

"That's it."

Chapter 46

A NINE-HOUR EMERGENCY CANDLE in a small metal lantern sat on top of a box of FEMA supplies and sent out a tiny circle of wavering light. Clouds had come in early in the evening and now Spike could hear the soft patter of misty rain on the partial roof of the fire department. That, and the candlelight, gave a warm, cozy, safe feeling to the place.

Which was defeated by people and conversation.

He sat on a folding cot, slightly hunched to ease the pain in his ribs. Nathaniel was next to him, and in a rough circle with them sat Albert, Samuel, Connor, and Tessa. Three folding camp chairs made seats for Ben, June, and old Henry.

Spike wasn't sure what Henry was doing there, but the smelly old hermit had followed Ben and June in, toting a camp chair and battered notepad.

"Can someone open the door a little?" Tessa asked, carefully scooting a little to one side, adding space between her and Henry.

Spike grinned.

Connor wedged open the piece of plywood that doubled as a door, letting in a welcome cool, damp breeze.

June patted Tessa on the shoulder. "Well, I'm going to start this by saying we need to talk about Tessa."

"Oh, no, it's not important," Tessa said quickly. "Not compared to everything else going on. I'm better now. Really."

"Yeah, no," Spike said. "You're taking on too much. You can't be expected to feed all of us plus stock up for winter. Maybe we can make a list for the next supply chopper that comes."

"And we'll help more," Nathaniel said. "I didn't realize you were thinking about winter already. I mean, it's just spring."

Tessa interlocked her fingers, gripping her hands together. "I spent time with Anya. Talking about what she does to survive winter. The things we need like firewood and non-perishable food. I have a few seed packets I planted. We've all been foraging. There's a few survivors who know how to hunt. We could smoke meat. June knows how to can stuff."

"Okay," Albert said. "We've been caught up in day to day and not thinking long term. Good thing you have. We'll spread out tasks, like assigning a team to firewood."

"And ask for help," Samuel said. "It's the only way we're going to make it."

Henry shifted around on his chair, opening his notepad to show a dogeared page full of cramped writing. "This gathering was a good idea, as is planning ahead. But there is something more important to talk about that none of you are aware of."

Spike sighed heavily and Nathaniel poked him.

"And what would that be?" Albert asked politely. "We're all overwhelmed and trying to figure out plans to survive. What's more important?"

"Obviously, monsters." Henry shook his head. "Specifically, Betty and monsters. Would you care to hear what I have to say?"

Spike remembered how Curtis would get so frustrated when he came out of the Hole after working all day but then had to talk to Henry. And yet, Curtis always made an effort to listen. Maybe there was a reason. "Okay, old man, you got our attention."

"We have a trifecta before us that needs careful handling."

"A what?" Connor asked.

"Three issues. A trifecta." Henry folded his hands over his papers. "Monsters. Betty's death. And the decrease in domesticated animals."

Ben straightened. "Ah. Mayhap not my imagination."

"Most assuredly not. Chickens, cats, dogs. Several perished in the earthquake. We would expect to see a decrease afterwards from natural attrition. Predators, the need for food, simply wandering back into the wild. The numbers decrease."

"Well, sure," Connor looked confused. "Like you said. It's expected."

Henry shook his head. "Normally. But consider the way we live now. We are careful with our resources. Tessa in particular does a commendable job locking chickens up each night. Additionally, she has reinforced the coop. And yet she still loses chickens."

"Yes." Tessa sighed heavily. She looked pale and the shadows under her eyes showed her exhaustion and earlier tears. "I'm sure they're getting out somehow. But I can't find where and everyone's so busy and stressed, I haven't wanted to bother anyone."

"How many and how often?" Albert asked, his voice sharp.

"I don't really know. I'm sorry. I'm just so…"

Connor draped his arm around her shoulders. "Hey. No one's blaming you."

"You are losing approximately one chicken a week." Henry frowned at her. "And you would have noted how unusual such regularity was if you actually paid attention. Chickens are a valuable commodity for our town now."

Tessa flushed.

"Hey, come on, dude." Connor took her hand. "We're doing the best we can."

"And if you don't like it, pitch in and fucking help," Spike added.

Henry shook his head. "I am helping. As I am about to point out if you will all be quiet."

Spike suddenly realized he would never be as good a person as Curtis had been. "If you have something to say, do it. If you're just going to piss all over us, then get the hell out."

Henry's eyebrows shot up like startled bushy caterpillars. "Yes, thank you for the reminder. I…do not like people. I…forget occasionally, how to interact."

"No shit."

"I apologize. However, returning to my point. Albert wisely began an inventory of our dead immediately following the quake, and has kept the death roster updated. It occurred to me a roster of our living population and resources would be equally important. With little else to occupy my time, I began a ledger." He patted the notepad on his lap.

"I didn't know you were doing that," Tessa said. "I could have helped."

"No one did, which means I was unobtrusive, which was not my intent but had beneficial consequences."

Spike sighed heavily again and Henry seemed to get the point as he nodded quickly.

"One chicken a week goes missing at night. Regularly. Not during the day when they are allowed to roam freely. Our cat and dog population is quite small, commiserate with our small human population. Again, the cat population is decreasing regularly. As well as dogs. Although only small dogs."

"At night, from inside the fort?" Albert's eyebrows went up in shock. "I heard things were missing from the barter shed, but the fort? With all of us right there?"

"At night, from inside the fort." Henry closed his notepad. "Now you understand. This is a much bigger problem than a few cans from the barter shed."

"Well actually," June said, "It's been more than just cans. It's soap and-"

Henry waved a hand in the air as if brushing her off. "Still not as important as our fresh egg source and what the cause might be."

"After all we've been through, I can't believe someone would steal from us." Tessa wiped at her eyes.

"Yet it is happening." Henry shrugged. "I have not yet fully formulated a working hypothesis."

Spike's heart raced with sudden anger. "Well, here's an idea. Maybe someone feeding fucking monsters."

Ben leaned back in his chair. "And mayhap escalating to something bigger than a chicken. Like an elderly person on their own."

The soft rain had stopped outside and a light wind rattled the plywood. Spike looked around at the others but no one seemed to want to speak the name in all their minds.

Old Henry stood suddenly and gripped his notepad over his chest like a shield. "I have passed on the information I wished to give you. I am not needed for anything further. Additionally, it should be noted that while I am elderly and alone, I am not defenseless."

Connor shifted to give the old man room to leave then pulled the plywood closed. There was silence for a moment after he left.

"Now what?" Tessa asked.

"Fuck it." Spike sighed heavily. "I'll say it if no one else has the balls. Jennifer. It's obvious. All the times we've seen her going out with her foraging basket. But does she ever bring anything back?"

"Innocent until proven guilty," Nathaniel said quietly. "She made a horrible choice once because of her terror when we were at Anya's."

"Terrified, yeah. Like all of us. But we didn't sacrifice anyone." Spike shifted uncomfortably and rubbed his side. "What do we do about it?"

Connor scowled. "I'm going to start guarding Tessa's chicken coop at night, that's what."

"We could warn people," Tessa said. "Like, maybe, those who still have pets."

"Fuck that." Spike shivered and reached for his old coat, struggling to pull it on.

"No, she's right," Nathaniel said, pulling the coat up and patting Spike's shoulder. "We could warn people quietly. Without directly accusing someone who might be innocent."

"Not happening," Spike said. "I'm talking to her tomorrow."

"What?" Tessa asked, fear making her voice suddenly shaky. "She could be dangerous."

"No shit. Which is why I'm going to tell her we know what she's doing and it's going to stop." Spike lifted his hands in question. "I mean, why the hell not? What's the worst that can happen? She denies it, but then she'll know we're watching. So it stops."

"Mayhap that's not a good idea," Ben rubbed his knee as if it ached. "Might be better to catch her in the act."

"And risk another Betty?" Spike asked. "We catch her in the act, but we're too late? I'm talkin' to her tomorrow."

Chapter 47

RAMON SLEPT, BUT UNEASILY, slipping from lying awake to falling into nightmares. Around him, the Gold Bar City Hall was full of people. He could hear faint snoring, the rustle of sleeping bags and old blankets, the sound of a baby whimpering. He kept listening for signs his family was sneaking out in the middle of the night but they slept, heads on packs, military surplus wool blankets covering them.

He thought of Monroe, the long line of heart-sick people searching the lists of names while the ashes of the dead settled on their shoulders. He'd thought getting his family out of there, getting them to the mountains, was the right decision.

He was wrong. They had to go back. The kids wouldn't like it, didn't like it, but he just couldn't take them forward to face whatever was coming.

He finally gave up on sleep and quietly made his way outside. The sun was coming up behind the mountains, not visible yet but turning the undersides of scattered clouds pink. The air was cool and smelled of the lilac bush next to the city hall. Part of it had been broken away but the bit that remained was blooming.

The woman from the day before was sitting on her chunk of concrete with a blanket around her shoulders, a large handgun in a holster on her hip, and still wearing the old ratty baseball hat. She looked up as Ramon joined her and wiped her eyes with the palms of her hands. He pretended not to notice as he sat.

"What's your name?" he asked.

"Jean."

"Ramon."

She just nodded, watching the coming day.

"Did you live here, before?"

She nodded again. "Me, husband, daughter. We survived. But I have another daughter and a granddaughter I haven't had any news about. My husband wants to go to Monroe. Heard there was a way to add names to a search list."

"Monroe is nothing but death," he said. "But I'm going back. I'll take the information with me and post it for you."

Her shoulders sagged. "Thanks. I didn't want him to go, you know? Not that I don't want to find my granddaughter. God, my husband used to drive me nuts. Seems like I hated everything about him."

"But disaster puts things in perspective."

She snorted. "Oh, he still drives me nuts. But yeah."

They sat shoulder to shoulder, the new world slowly turning around them, shadows and fear and hopelessness.

Ramon shivered in the cool morning air, just beginning to warm with the rising sun. "What do you think is going to happen?" he asked, not sure what he was really asking.

"I think we're going to rise from these fucking ashes and burn monsters." She coughed out a laugh. "That's what my daughter says. Me? I think...I hope, we just manage to live."

"Me, too."

Ramon went back inside and worked his way through the semi-darkness to their sleeping area. His bag and pack were as he'd left them, but the allotted space around them was empty, except for one grimy little boy, clutching his shirt in one hand, sitting wide-eyed on a sleeping bag. They hadn't sneaked out in the middle of the night. They'd waited for daylight. They'd waited until he let his guard down and looked away.

Anger flushed heat through him. He'd explained it to them. He'd made it clear. And they'd gone off into danger anyway. He sank down to sit cross-legged on his sleeping bag, fists clenched as he thought through options.

"Those stupid, stupid kids." He wanted to shout but managed to hold his voice tight and low for those still sleeping. "I have to go after them. Bring them back.

But I can at least make sure you're safe in the meantime. I'm going to talk to that woman out there. See if she'll watch out for you."

Tommy vigorously shook his head, sending his hair flapping into his eyes, and pointed at Ramon, at himself, and out the door.

Ramon blew out a heavy breath and sat for a moment, chin to chest. Then he looked up at the little kid who had stuck with him.

"Yeah. I know. If I try to leave you here, you'll just follow." He got onto his knees and started rolling up his sleeping bag. "Think the butterfly can find them? Maybe keep an eye on them until we can catch up?"

Tommy shrugged, but then pointed outside.

"Pack up then." Ramon stood, thinking about what lay ahead. "They can't be that far ahead of us. I wasn't gone very long. Damn kids."

Outside the city hall, Jean stood in a small circle of men and women, holding a clipboard and pen. A pair of reading glasses had replaced the ball cap on her head. She glanced over her shoulder as they came out the door, Ramon shouldering his heavy pack, Tommy already wearing his bright pink plastic one.

"Thanks for letting us sleep here. I'm sorry, but we're not going to Monroe after all. Don't let your husband go, though. Wait for FEMA or someone else to take a message. You don't want him out there."

She rolled her eyes. "No shit." She turned back to the group and spoke to them, as if Ramon and Tommy were already gone. "People can smell gas at the station. One of the underground tanks cracked, maybe. Someone figure out a way to siphon up that gas."

Ramon wished her luck but she didn't turn. He took Tommy's cold little hand in his and gave it a gentle squeeze. "Last chance, kid. You could stay here where it's safe. I bet she'd take care of you."

Tommy gripped Ramon's hand tighter and scowled.

"Yeah, I figured you'd say that." Ramon, with a heavy weight of dread in him, worked his way past quake mayhem and out to what had been the highway. "East it is. Again."

Chapter 48

T HE MORNING WAS CHILLY with scattered clouds that didn't seem able to commit to clearing up or gathering. Spike shivered as he stood by the general store, watching Jennifer come out of the fort with a basket over her arm. He thought about the conversation the night before, about Betty's death. There was no way he was letting that happen to anyone else.

"Hey, Jennifer!"

She turned quickly, as if startled, and Spike went to her.

"Come on, I'm going to the river."

"Why?" She frowned.

"So we can talk with no one interrupting."

"Sorry, I've got things to do that are more important than visiting."

Jennifer started away from him but he caught her arm. "You can come talk to me where we can have some privacy or I can yell for some people to come see what you have in that fucking backet."

She jerked free of his hand and paused, clearly thinking, and then smiled. "There's nothing in it. But how about this? I'll go with you, give you five minutes. But then you have to go with me to forage. You don't trust me? Then fine. Go with me and see for yourself I'm not doing anything wrong."

"Deal."

If she wanted to believe he was that stupid, he'd let her. He started for the trail to the beach, not sure she'd actually follow, but she did. When he reached the small beach and sat down on his customary boulder, she came slowly to stand beside him.

He picked up a small rock and tossed it from hand to hand.

"What did you want to talk about? I have chores to do." She put the empty basket at her feet.

Spike stood and threw the rock. The movement hurt, but he got the rock further out into the current than he had before.

Within seconds it came flying back and he caught it.

"What is that?" Jennifer's voice was high and startled, but somehow forced.

"Nothing to worry about." Spike threw the rock again. "Just Rowan. But I think you already knew that."

"What?"

"Rowan. You know. When I almost drowned trying to save her? She and her friend like playin' catch."

Jennifer stared at the water.

"If you look close, you'll see them. Bright blue, and if direct sun hits them they disintegrate into something like an oil rainbow on water. Kind of pretty, if you like that shit. Of course, if they hit air, they turn skeletal. Kind of creepy, if you like that shit."

He watched her for some sort of reaction, but Jennifer just looked at the rushing emerald water and shrugged.

"She made a choice. She's happy."

"Sure. You can look at it that way."

Jennifer turned to Spike. "Talk. You're wasting my time."

"I know you fed Betty to a monster. Plus, I know you've been stealing chickens and pets."

He saw her hands shaking and she quickly crossed her arms over her chest. "Prove it."

He shrugged and tossed another rock. "I don't have to. Everyone knows it's you. I mean, fuck, it's what you do, right? Kill friends to keep yourself safe?"

"No! Everything I do is to keep all of you safe."

Spike slid off the boulder and caught the rock that came flying back, droplets of water scattering. "You keep telling yourself that. But what I wanted to tell you here, alone, is that everyone knows. And you're going to stop that shit because after Betty, no one wants you around."

Jennifer took a quick step backward and her chin trembled. "But, I do it *for* them! You have no idea what's out there in the woods. What will come here if I don't feed it."

"I was out there in those fucking woods with you right after the quake." He took a fast step forward, so close she had to tilt her head up to see him. "We went through a lot of shit together. That's why we're talking. Last chance. Stop, now. No one else dies."

"Max is dead. Casey is gone." Jennifer raised her hand and pushed him back. "There's no law anymore, nothing anyone can do about it. Besides, when people see what killed Max, what it feeds on, they'll *thank* me for keeping it out of town."

"Like I said, last warning."

Spike started up the trail but a sharp cry of pain made him turn back.

Jennifer was holding a dripping rock in one hand and rubbing her shoulder with the other.

"Threw a rock at you, did they? Toss it back. They just want to play. She was a friend of yours, once."

He went up the trail and stopped at the top. He understood, now. The way tragedy could change you. The things you'd do to keep those you loved safe.

Or the things you'd walk away from and let happen.

Jennifer stepped to the river's edge, hesitated, and then threw her rock.

Chapter 49

Before the quake, Zeke's had been a popular spot. The parking lot was always packed with people lining up for fat burgers and wandering around the drive-in's signature red caboose. Ramon, carefully climbing over the collapsed railroad overpass with Tommy, was sure he could still smell the faint whiff of grease in the air.

The building itself had been lucky and fared better than most. There was damage to the roof from a huge fir tree and the quake had thrown the caboose on its side. As he neared, he could see that the place, like everywhere, had been scavenged for anything useful. There would be no burgers today.

His stomach rumbled and he absently rubbed it as he reached the tipped over caboose. Tommy, next to him, imitated the movement.

"I know. Time for a break and-" He froze.

Michael stood at one corner of the building, his face white with fear, his eyes wide. Payton knelt on one knee next to Marie, one hand on the chest of his niece.

Adrenaline slammed Ramon's body and he sprinted forward. "What happened?" he shouted.

"Don't know, man," Michael said as Ramon dropped down next to Payton. "We were waiting. She said you'd follow us. Then she just kind of, like, sighed and fainted."

"How long?" Ramon's voice was in more control than his racing heart. "Get me some water."

"Just a minute or two," Payton said.

Tommy reached them, breathing hard. He pulled a zipper on his plastic pack and handed Ramon a half-full bottle of water.

Ramon opened it, poured a little on the edge of his shirt and wiped Marie's face. She was flushed and her skin hot. She was breathing, but shallow and rapid, and her eyes moved quickly under closed lids.

"Marie," he said gently. "Hey, baby. Come back now."

Nothing.

"In my pack," he said. "First aid kit from McCausland. See what's in it."

Michael grabbed the pack, tugging it off Ramon's shoulders and ripping open a zipper. He tossed things out until he came up with a small red bag. He sat back and opened it.

"Bandages. Neosporin. Tylenol."

"Not helping." Ramon lifted Marie so her head rested on his legs. He brushed her wild, sweaty curls away from her face.

"I don't know," Michael said, frantically digging through the bag. "She's not bleeding, she's not poisoned, she's not – wait. Here."

He tossed a small Chapstick-size tube to Ramon who caught it one-handed and then twisted off the cap. Carefully, he held it under Marie's nose.

"What is that?" Payton asked, her voice high and shaky.

"Smelling salts," he said quickly. Marie moved her head slightly but didn't come around. "Come on, you can do it."

"No." Payton stood. "That noise."

Ramon heard the faint thumping rhythm of a helicopter and glanced up.

"Oh shit, oh shit," Michael turned in place.

Ramon stood and lifted Marie. "Michael. Grab our packs. Payton, can you carry Tommy?"

She nodded, lifting Tommy onto one hip.

"Run. Hide." Ramon watched the sky, clutching Marie to his chest so tight he could feel his pounding heart against her.

Payton, with no hesitation, ran the few yards to the red caboose on its side with Michael following. She put Tommy on the ground and tugged on the bent and twisted small door at the back. Ramon scanned the sky as he carried Marie to them. No helicopter yet but he could clearly hear it, the sound almost subliminal under his fear.

"Michael," Payton said breathlessly.

He dropped Ramon's pack and helped, wrenching back the door. Payton pushed Tommy inside, tossed in Ramon's pack, and then climbed through. Michael went next as the noise of the helicopter grew louder. Ramon bent and handed him Marie, then crouched down and followed.

"Get against the back wall."

The windows on both sides were now the floor and skylights. But if they were in the shadows, in the corners, maybe they wouldn't be seen from the sky, from a fast-moving chopper.

Broken glass crunched under Ramon's boots as he squatted down next to Michael and took Marie back into his arms. She moaned and twisted but then stilled.

The sounds of the chopper grew loud, faded slightly, grew loud again. And then grew even louder. A strong downdraft came through the broken windows above them, scattering grit.

"They're landing!" Michael said. "What do we do?"

"Quiet!" Ramon said as the sound of rotors slowed. "Might have nothing to do with us. There aren't many places to land choppers."

But then he heard the sound of boots on gravel and dirt and McCausland's familiar voice.

"Heat signatures. Might as well come out."

Payton curled into a tight ball, shaking so hard it was like a seizure. Michael started to move but Ramon pointed at him.

"No," he whispered. "Take Marie. Stay here. None of you come out unless it's me telling you to."

He made his way back to the small door, suddenly oddly calm. The worst had happened. They'd found Marie.

Outside, the helicopter sat in what had been the parking lot, the rotors slowly turning. Next to it stood a woman in the dark uniform of the Cascadia Protection

Force. Near the end of the helicopter a man stood with a big military style rifle in his arms. And near the caboose was McCausland, in his National Guard uniform with his arm in a sling and the shirt stained with old blood.

"They want your niece and they're tired of looking."

"Not going to happen."

"Of course it is," McCausland said.

"She's no use to them now." Ramon blocked the little door, arms folded across his chest. "She can't track monsters anymore and she's unconscious."

The woman came closer and took a hand gun out of a shoulder holster. "You're lying. We're done messing with you."

"I mean it," Ramon said, resisting the urge to pull his own gun out. That would be a fast way to die. "Listen to me. She can't sense them anymore."

The other man came closer. "She *was* having trouble the last few times we went out."

"She was faking." The woman's dark eyes were cold.

"She wasn't." Ramon drew in a deep breath struggling to sound calm and in control. "Look, in the days you've been flying around, have you seen any monsters? I'm guessing you haven't. Before Marie collapsed, she said something big was pulling monsters to Index."

"Oh, come on." The woman looked to her companion. "Now there's some kind of monster magnet. One more lie."

There was the sound of movement in the caboose and a hand pushed against the back of Ramon's leg, almost making his knee buckle. As he moved to catch his balance, Marie crawled out and stood. She looked dazed and flushed, and sweat glistened at her temples. Her breathing was shallow and too fast. She looked around at all of them but said nothing, simply starting to walk away. Headed east.

"Stop right there!"

The woman gestured to McCausland but Ramon reached his niece before the other man could move. Marie struggled briefly against him but couldn't get free and after a moment she sagged against him.

"You want me to find monsters for you to kill." Her voice was almost too low to hear and they all drew nearer. "The one who's coming waits in Index."

Michael and Tommy came out of the caboose and stood tentatively behind Ramon.

"Take us there." Marie's voice strengthened. "And then I'll help you find it."

"I knew you were lying," the woman said. "We'll go to Index and kill this thing. And then you're ours to hunt again."

"You aren't going without all of us," Ramon said quickly. He glanced over at Michael and met his eyes, nodding slightly. A quick way to get to Index, and once there they would have Max and Casey, Ethan and Anya to help.

"And just how do you see that happening?" the woman laughed and waved her gun. "You walk."

Something fluttered past Ramon's cheek.

Michael grinned. "Not happening, man. We got us a butterfly and you're about to be Swiss cheese."

Ramon saw confusion in the faces of the helicopter crew. The pilot raised her hand and swatted the air as if brushing away an insect. A second later she flinched and ducked, and he saw blood dripping from her earlobe and down her neck.

"What the hell?" She flinched away again and blood appeared on her cheekbone.

"What is this?" the man shouted. He moved toward the pilot, raising his rifle and aiming it at Marie. "Whatever you're doing, stop. Now."

The pilot cried out and dropped her pistol as blood appeared on her hand. Ramon could actually see the small holes appear, the bits of skin and meat being pulled and dropped. One hole on her wrist began to bleed heavily.

McCausland ran to the pilot and squeezed his hand over the wound on her wrist. "Ramon, call it off!"

A larger chunk flew from the pilot's neck and blood ran freely down and across her chest.

McCausland flinched back and his temple began to bleed. The other man was on his knees, his face pockmarked with holes.

Ramon stepped in front of Marie and fumbled in his pocket for the handgun McCausland had given him. But Tommy, the skinny, half-starved little kid, gripped Ramon's hand before he could get the gun out. There was blank coldness in Tommy's eyes as if the child was gone.

"Ramon!" McCausland shouted. "You kill her, you have no pilot!"

The woman had collapsed, curled up with her bleeding hands over her head. Her clothes were shredded on her back, holes in her skin raw and bleeding through the material.

"Enough." He squeezed Tommy's hand tightly. "Enough!"

Tommy pulled against Ramon's hand but then hesitated. He looked up and Ramon saw the moment when the child came back, when his eyes widened with shock.

"Come on, kid," Ramon said, taking his shoulder. "Call your pet home. Now."

Tommy straightened and lifted the pouch around his neck. Ramon had a brief glimpse of the humanoid stick whiz back toward the boy. The pouch bulged then went still. Tommy cupped his hands around it and lowered his head, almost as if warming the creature, then carefully dropped the bag back under his shirt. He looked up at Ramon, tremors moving through his small frame.

Ramon scooped him up and Tommy's little arms went around his neck, squeezing tightly.

"That's some butterfly," Michael said with awe, or maybe horror, in his shaky voice.

McCausland and the man pulled the pilot to her feet. She bent, grabbed her gun with a blood-slicked hand, and screamed as she surged forward toward them.

"I'll kill that kid!"

Ramon turned his shoulder to her, as if he could shield Tommy from a bullet.

McCausland grabbed her, dragging her to a stop only a few feet from Ramon. She held the gun up and even though it shook in her hand, it was pointed right at his head.

In that frozen moment Payton spoke in her soft voice. "Oh, god, something's there."

A man came from behind the ruin of the drive-in, moving slowly, with no head. For the briefest crazy second, Ramon wanted to rush forward to help him, as if he was injured.

"What the hell!" Michael's voice was high with fear and it jolted Ramon back to the moment.

It wasn't a man with no head. The creature had eyes but they rested on its shoulders. Something that looked like a pulsing brain bulged grossly in his groin area.

Ramon shifted Tommy to one hip and grabbed Marie's arm. He raced for the chopper and hoisted both of them up inside it. Guns fired behind him but he ignored the sound, going back for Michael and Payton, both frozen in shock. He grabbed Michael's arm and shook him, hard.

"Move your ass!"

He scooped up Payton who was bone-white and shaking and ran, not waiting to see if Michael followed.

He lifted her inside, then turned to face the thing, pulling his handgun out but not firing yet. His mind worked coldly and calmly while his heart raced. He had a limited number of bullets. He'd only use them if the thing got past the other three and made it to the helicopter.

The pilot and McCausland stood a few feet apart, firing methodically. Even with one arm in a sling, McCausland's bullets were hitting the thing right in the brain matter. The pilot, with the gun slipping in her blood-soaked hand every time it kicked back, was having a hard time hitting it. But one shot hit an eye and the thing twisted away.

The third soldier raised the rifle. "Down!" he yelled.

McCausland and the pilot both immediately dropped to one knee, still firing. The man opened up with the rifle, shooting over them at the thing. It flailed silently but didn't fall.

Of course the thing was silent; it had no mouth. Even as that thought raced through Ramon's brain, a hole opened in its chest and it roared.

Fetid air washed over them, smelling of decomposing flesh. The soldier kept firing, moving forward now, as the thing hit the ground, writhing. And then was still.

Michael, beside Ramon, retched.

The soldier walked over to the creature and stood, pointing the rifle at it and breathing hard. McCausland and the pilot stood and he helped her stumble back to the helicopter. When they reached it, Ramon could see fury in the woman's eyes. She leaned into the opening.

"You could have helped, you little bastard." She jabbed her gun toward Tommy who was squeezed tight against Payton. "You could have released that thing of yours."

Ramon pulled the woman from the chopper opening and pushed her against the side of it. He twisted the gun out of her hand and raised it.

The pilot surged forward, using her weight to take them both to the ground. Her fist slammed into his still-healing ribs and the pain was blinding. She was breathing heavily and bleeding even more heavily. Ramon rolled, got his knee in her chest, and tried to grab her arms but her fist caught him under the jaw and he was knocked sideways off her. The pain was bright and sharp and he tasted blood.

"Stop!" Michael yelled, pulling Ramon back. "It's not dead!"

Ramon shoved himself up, grunting with pain.

"Get us out of here!" McCausland shouted at the pilot.

She awkwardly pulled herself up and into the pilot's seat. With one hand held to her neck wound, she started doing something with instruments and the rotors slowly began to move. Not once did she look back at what was happening.

Ramon brought his gun up. The thing had caught the soldier in a tight hug. Even as Ramon fired, the soldier deflated, as if collapsing inward.

It happened so fast that by the time McCausland was also shooting, the soldier's torso was gone. His arms, legs, and head fell to the ground, scattered. When the thing turned toward them, McCausland and Ramon ran below the turning rotors and climbed into the helicopter.

Michael's mouth hung open, his eyes dilated with fear. He had one arm across Payton and Tommy as if holding them back, or in place. Payton's head was down and Tommy's face was buried against her shirt.

Marie was unconscious, limp, and slumped to one side.

McCausland scrambled into the seat next to the pilot. "Move it, Chen."

He pulled out a first aid kit and jerked the zipper open as the rotors picked up speed, throwing debris toward the thing coming for them.

Ramon grabbed restraints and tightened them around Marie, then Payton. Michael fumbled with his but managed to lengthen it enough to get around him and buckled. Ramon buckled in next to her, and then pulled her toward him and braced his arm around her.

The chopper lifted, wobbled, lifted a bit more, and tilted.

McCausland slapped a thick gauze pad on the pilot's neck wound and wrapped bandaging around her neck.

"You're leaving the other guy?" Michael asked, horror in his voice. "I thought soldiers never left anyone behind!"

"There's nothing left, kid," McCausland said loudly over the rising sound of rotors. His voice was flat and controlled, but Ramon saw the heat of anger in his eyes. "There's nothing left."

The pilot looked over her shoulder at Ramon as the helicopter lifted higher and banked to the east. She was bone-white and shaky but her eyes were cold and he saw their unfinished battle there. She pointed her forefinger at him and mimed shooting a gun, then turned back to her controls.

Ramon didn't respond. He was shaking with cold and pain, and nauseated from adrenaline, shock, and fear. Her posturing meant nothing to him.

All that mattered now was that they were headed east. Into the mountains.

Home.

Chapter 50

SPIKE WAS AT THE barter shed with Nathaniel. His goal was to secure the building but he had to have Nathaniel screw in the heavier bolt because it still hurt too much to even use a screw driver. Pissed him off.

"Did you talk to Jennifer?" Nathaniel asked.

Spike handed the new padlock to Nathaniel and didn't meet his eyes. "Yeah. Told her we knew what she was doing and she'd better stop." He hesitated. "She wasn't too happy. Headed down to the river."

Nathaniel started to speak but Spike held his hand up as he heard a faint, familiar sound from down valley, almost a low throbbing. "Chopper."

"Finally," Nathaniel said. "Hope they brought us some more soap. Supplies are low."

Except this helicopter was all black and didn't have the FEMA logo on the side. Spike's stomach clenched in dread and he wished suddenly he had his rifle. But it had been painful to carry the weight so he'd left it in the tent, trusting that those around him would be armed. Most people were these days.

The few locals were leaving tasks and standing on the street, watching as the helicopter grew closer, blew up debris, then landed.

Samuel walked up to Spike. "That chopper look familiar to you?"

"You're right," Nathaniel said. "Like the one that took Ramon and Marie. Maybe it's bringing them back."

Relief washed through Spike's whole body so suddenly he felt weightless. "Those asshole military wannabes. They've brought Ramon back. About fucking time."

As the rotors slowed, they headed to the park with the others.

One man, with his arm in a sling, jumped out of the helicopter as it shut down and the rotors slowed. "Medic! Medic!"

The weight plummeted back, the heaviness of knowing it was all going to shit again. The man in the sling pulled a woman out of the pilot's seat. She was covered in blood, with a soaked bandage around her neck. Samuel raced past them and reached for her, but she shoved him back and turned on the man with the sling.

"Your gun! Now!"

The pilot staggered but struggled to get to the guy's handgun. He held her back one-handed and gestured to Samuel. Spike started toward them even as he knew he wouldn't be any help. But then Nathaniel caught his arm, pointing.

"Look! It's Ramon."

Spike stared. "And that idiot Michael."

"Is that..." Nathaniel's eyebrows shot up. "It's Payton. My god, what's happened to her?"

"Can't be." Spike barely glanced at the beat up homeless-looking girl. He watched Ramon lean into the helicopter opening and lift out Marie, who draped in his arms. "Shit. Marie. What did they do to her?"

"I need help here!" Ramon yelled.

The pilot was now on the ground with Samuel working frantically on her, hands deep in her blood. Spike started for Ramon but he couldn't move fast and Nathaniel reached them first.

"She's unconscious. I can't rouse her." Ramon's voice was controlled but Spike saw the fear in his eyes.

Samuel barely glanced their way. "Take her to the fire department."

Ramon stood there as if he couldn't process the words and Spike nudged Nathaniel. "Help him. He's in shock."

"Come on, Ramon. This way." Nathaniel cupped Ramon's elbow.

The woman looked like she was full of holes but there was nothing Spike could do that wasn't already being done by Samuel and the man in the sling. He cussed under his breath and carefully made his way to the fire department, one hand pressed against his side. By the time he got inside the rough makeshift first aid space, Marie was on a cot and Ramon was spreading a wool blanket over her. She was still unconscious but her eyes moved fast under her lids like she dreamed.

"What happened?" Spike asked.

Ramon looked up at Spike. His face was haggard. He'd lost weight since Spike had last seen him, but then they all had. Even Michael, who sat awkwardly on an old ratty couch. Payton and a skinny, terrified looking kid came through the doorway and hesitated. When Spike nodded to them, they went quickly to Michael and joined him.

"They kept Marie." Ramon pulled a folding chair next to the cot and sank down, gripping Marie's hand. "I got her back with McCausland's help. The guy in the sling. Then they found us." Ramon looked around as if just realizing where he was. "We need Max and Casey. That woman, the pilot, she's going to take Marie."

June came quickly through the door, breathing heavily and followed by Ben.

"Good to see you, son," Ben said, squeezing Ramon's shoulder briefly. "Move aside now and let Mother have a look here."

"Ramon wants Max and Casey," Spike said slowly, wondering who was going to break the bad news. "Says that pilot's after Marie."

"Not anymore," Ben said, his voice heavy. "She's dead. Come outside now, all of you. Let Mother take care of Marie. We need to share some news."

"Even us?" Michael asked hesitatingly. "I mean, you want us, too?"

"All of you," Ben repeated.

Spike and the others followed Ben outside. Samuel was there, rinsing blood-soaked, shaking hands in a bucket of rain water. He stood and viciously kicked the bucket, spilling red water and sending it in the air with a loud crack.

"I'm so sick of this shit! I can't save anyone! I'm just a fucking EMT! People die and it's my fault!"

Spike didn't know what to say. Every little injury or illness, every impact, from monsters to someone constipated from eating nothing but protein bars fell on Samuel's shoulders.

"It's not your fault," Nathaniel said.

Samuel raised a hand in the air as if pushing Nathaniel's words away.

The man with the sling crossed Avenue A and came toward them, wiping his hands on a blood-stained cloth. He nodded to Samuel. "There wasn't anything you could do with that arterial wound, but I appreciate you trying. Is there...is there some place I can put her body?"

"Back in the chopper?" Spike said in sudden helpless anger. "So you can go back where you fucking came from?"

"Can't do that," the man said. "She was the pilot. And I'm not the threat here. Lose the attitude because I sure as shit don't need it right now."

Samuel gripped Spike's arm, then released it. "It's okay." He motioned to the man with a shaking hand. "Give me a minute. Just...give me a minute."

"I'll go find Albert." Nathaniel took a deep breath. "We'll take care of it."

Samuel pushed at the air again with his hand and walked away.

Spike watched him, useless to know what to do.

Ben rubbed a hand over the gray stubble on his chin and then pressed his palms briefly to his eyes as if exhausted.

"Maybe we could get him more help from the Red Cross. Someone that could stay here." Nathaniel shrugged.

Michael shook his head and sat on an old bench. "There's no help coming, man. There's nothing coming but monsters. Ask Ramon."

"First," Ben said, putting a hand on Ramon's shoulder. "We need to give you some bad news, son. Casey's missing. And...and Max was killed."

Chapter 51

MAX WAS DEAD. RAMON stared at Ben, the old man's words not making sense. A deep hole of grief for his friend opened inside him. Max, who always knew what to do, who was always the calm eye of the storm, couldn't be just gone.

Payton, still holding Tommy, gasped out something like a soft cry, sank to the bench beside Michael.

"No way." Michael's eyes were wide and dilated with shock. "No way, man. Not Max. He's tough. He's a cop. Nothing could get him. You're wrong!"

Michael's voice rose with his words. Ramon went to them and stood behind the bench, a shaky hand on each of their shoulders. Tommy slipped off Payton's lap and came around to press himself against Ramon's leg. He could feel the boy shaking. Tommy hadn't known Max, but it was clear he knew something new and awful had happened. Ramon squeezed Michael's shoulder, put his hand briefly, gently, on Payton's head, then picked Tommy up. He struggled to draw in a deep enough breath to form words, to fill the void, to hide his own grief and sudden helplessness. For his kids, he needed to find a way to hide his own hopelessness.

"Tell us."

"You don't need all details right now, son," Ben said. "Just that Casey is gone and we don't know where. Max died fast. Probably didn't even know what happened but-"

Michael interrupted, face pale, eyes wide with fear. "Tell them, man. Tell them. With no Max, we're screwed."

"Tell us what, shithead?" Spike asked.

Michael stood so abruptly he lost his balance and had to catch Payton's shoulder to keep from stumbling. "Quit it. Just quit it. We've been through..."

His voice trailed off as if there were no words strong enough. He wiped tears from his eyes and turned away as Payton stood and caught his arm.

Spike's eyebrows went up as if in surprise and he looked from Michael to Ramon, and then back.

"It's bad." Ramon struggled to find words but Michael's voice, getting louder, cut through the wall of grief.

"Max was nice to me. When none of you were! Even when I was being an asshole. He'd call me on it and give me another chance. He was supposed to fix all this and now he's gone and everything's wrong and...and...and you don't get to talk to me like that anymore!"

Spike's eyebrows climbed even higher. Nathaniel poked him.

"Uh, look shithead," Spike said. Another poke. "I mean, Michael. It's nothin' personal, you stupid shit. It's worse since you left, our friends are dying, and you're not the only ones that have been through hell."

"Enough," Ben said. "What's going on, son?"

Ramon sank onto the bench, heart aching with loss and suddenly defeated. "The monsters are headed here. All of them. There's something big trying to come through every time there's aftershocks. Marie's overwhelmed with the white noise, as she calls it, drowning her ability out. And now she's unconscious."

Spike felt gut-punched and saw the same shock in the others around him.

"And we need a plan, man," Michael said, drawing in a deep breath and wiping his eyes again before straightening his shoulders. "We need to figure out how to fight these things with no Max here to show us."

"You sure?" Nathaniel asked. "Index is some, like, monster magnet?"

Ramon nodded. "I'm sure."

"Then we need to get out of here," Spike said. "There's probably a radio on that helicopter. We call for evacuation, right? That guy with the sling will know how. Take us all to Monroe or something."

The earth shivered and Ramon grabbed Tommy, bracing them for the aftershock. But instead of throwing them around, the low-grade trembling just continued. "What the hell?"

"It's been doing that more and more," Nathaniel said. "It's even lasted a couple days."

"Doesn't matter," Spike said, spreading his feet to maintain balance. "Get that guy and get on the radio and get us out of here."

"It's too late." Payton's voice was quiet but they still heard her. She pointed to the berm that had once been a railroad crossing but was now just a rough path that led down Index Avenue and into the destroyed forest. A large raven circled down to land on the twisted railroad tracks and fold in its wide wings. It waited, perched there, watching them.

There was movement behind it, something heavy and dark like a solid shadow that came up and over the berm and took on the shape of a giant dog. Its black fur was matted and wild, its eyes red-tinged and wilder. It stopped next to the raven. Waiting. Watching.

And behind it, came Casey.

Chapter 52

C ASEY DIDN'T COME ANY closer. She stood next the giant dog looking slightly confused and just watching them.

"What the hell?" Spike asked.

"The raven." Nathaniel took a hesitating step forward. "We need to get her away from it."

Ramon glanced at the others, but when no one moved, he walked across the rough pavement to her. The fine trembling of the earth under his boots made him slightly off balance. He stopped a couple feet away, not wanting to get too close to the massive, wild-looking dog.

The slanted late morning sunlight shown starkly on her. There was dried blood on her ripped clothes revealing what looked like bites or puncture wounds, raw and still oozing. Deep red marks circled her neck, she had three or four long gashes down one cheek, and dirty and scabbed wounds on her hand. Her pack hung off one shoulder, dirty and ripped. Her gun was covered in dirt and her knife was black with dried blood.

She looked beaten. She should have looked defeated.

But she didn't. Her eyes were direct, looking straight at him. She shifted from foot to foot as if barely able to restrain herself from moving.

"Ramon. You're back." Her voice was hoarse. She coughed, then looked past him. "Is Marie with you?"

Ramon stepped closer. "Yes, but not well. Casey, I just heard about Max. How can I help you? What do you need?"

Casey tilted her head and looked briefly distracted, her eyes not focused, but then she seemed to refocus. "I'm okay. We're okay."

He tried not to look at the raven and the dog. "Can we go the fire department? Some place a little...safer, to talk? Samuel should take a look at you."

The raven flapped its wings and she tilted her head again, almost as if she was listening.

"He keeps nagging me," Casey said. "Max is...Max would be glad you're here. He trusts...he trusted you."

Ramon, at a loss, glanced at the raven again. She clearly wasn't fully functioning, but then who would be after losing someone they loved? He hesitated, wanting to do something, to find the right words that would show her she wasn't alone in her loss. It felt like his grief was hers, like he could spread it over her and draw her in and find some way to heal them both.

Casey gestured to the raven, which rose with a loud call and lifted up, headed downriver, then stepped around Ramon. "Marie."

He turned to see Samuel, arm around Marie's waist in support, behind him. She looked pale, fragile, vulnerable.

"Samuel? What the hell?"

The young man shrugged. "You try keeping her down. I sure can't."

Marie pulled away from Samuel, walked past Ramon, touching his arm lightly, and went straight to Casey. "Alegria is coming. With Anya's son. We need to go."

The huge black dog backed away from them, went a few feet down Index Avenue, then stopped and looked back. Waiting.

Marie's voice was calm, stronger than it had been. Controlled. In contrast, Ramon could see the fine shivering throughout her body, as if she matched the trembling of the earth under their feet. She took Casey's hand, tugging her after the dog.

Ramon started forward to catch her but Marie stopped suddenly and stared at Casey, her eyebrows up in alert surprise. He saw Casey tug as if to free her hand, but Marie didn't let go.

"Such a strong, strong heartbeat."

"Max." A smile illuminated Casey's face, almost as if the old Casey resurfaced. "He never left me."

Shocked, Ramon saw an equally beautiful smile light up Marie's face. Happiness that he hadn't seen in too long.

"Yes, he's with you, of course," Marie said. "But the little heartbeat is just as strong."

Casey went white and staggered. Ramon jumped forward and caught her before she could fall. He could feel her rapid gasping for air.

"I thought...I thought she meant Max's heart."

Ramon heard the rough whisper. He didn't know what she meant, but he knew grief and he knew tears and he knew loss. He tightened his arms around her and her head came down briefly on his shoulder.

"Take your time," he said.

Casey stiffened and pulled away. "No. No time."

Ramon pulled her to her feet and he saw something like fire come into her eyes.

"Ethan and Anya are at the Hole," she said. "They need help."

Marie moved to Casey. "Yes. I need to be there."

"Hang on," Ramon said sharply. "Just wait a minute. If they need help, we'll go. But I need you to be safe. You stay."

She held her hand up, palm out, stopping him. "Don't do this again. I'm going. Quit wasting time and trust me."

Taken aback, he stared at her. "Right. Okay. You say want me to trust you and I do. Honest. But convince me why you're the one that needs to be at the Hole."

"I can't because I don't know. But just like the monsters being pulled there, so am I. I'm shaking. My heart is racing." Marie put her hand to her chest. "It's like a massive panic attack. I *need* to go. Whether you're convinced or not."

Ramon met her eyes and slumped. He knew with sick certainty that if he fought her on this she'd somehow slip away, just like she'd done in Gold Bar. So, did he go with her this time, or did he follow her again?

"Okay. Okay. I give in. But we need to think this through, especially if we're about to be overrun." He gestured to McCausland, standing back with the others. "You got more weapons on the chopper?"

McCausland came forward. "A few."

Ramon pointed to Spike. "We divide up then. You get everyone here organized. Use McCausland. He's got training. Tell Michael and Payton to keep Tommy safe. Listen to Ben. I'll get Casey and Marie to the Hole.

Spike paled.

"Just do the best you can. I trust you. Once we get Ethan and Anya out of the Hole, we'll get back here to help. Keep everyone safe until then.

"We're so fucked."

Chapter 53

Ramon helped Marie over the torn-up pavement on Avenue A, watching Casey stride ahead of them as if impatient with their pace. But Marie could only move so fast and she moved awkwardly, as if not fully with him. She was distracted now, occasionally looking around as if clueless where she was.

The late morning light strengthened as the sun lifted away from the mountains and maybe, somewhere else, it was a peaceful spring day. But not here.

There was a familiar, yet strange rumble behind them and when Ramon looked back, he recognized the big, old, battered pickup coming toward them. It had been so long since he had seen a vehicle actually moving, heard an engine actually running, that it was disconcerting.

The truck stopped, idling roughly, the door squeaked open, and Ben got out.

"Someone's been stealing gas from the barter shed so there's only the little left in the tank," Ben said. "But mayhap enough to get you to the Hole. Just like old times."

Ramon grinned. "Just like old times."

The beater truck had brought them to Index on old logging back roads. With its winch attached to a massive slab of hardwood that made the front bumper, the truck would get them over the remains of the road a lot faster than walking. Especially if he had to carry Marie.

"Casey!" Ramon yelled, then gestured to the truck. He shook Ben's hand as she came back toward them. "We can use the winch depending on how trapped Anya is."

"That's what I was thinking, son."

Casey pulled open the passenger door and climbed in. Ramon boosted Marie up from the driver's side and she carefully slid across to the middle of the bench seat. He climbed in and lifted a hand to Ben then pointed at Casey and Marie.

"Seatbelts."

Both stared at him.

"One messed up niece. One pregnant friend. One quake-destroyed road. One old truck. Seatbelts. Now."

Marie reached for the lap belt and stared at it as if it was something foreign. And in a way it was. Their life no longer revolved around cars, highways, traffic.

Casey grabbed Marie's belt, latched it, and jerked her shoulder belt down. "Move it, Ramon."

"Moving it."

The truck lurched and tilted up and over a small splintered tree. Ramon didn't let up on the gas and the solid bumper slowly and inexorably cleared their way down what had once been a nicely paved two-lane scenic road through the woods. The Black Dog loped ahead and was lost to sight in the ruined woods. The raven simply flew off. Ramon was a little envious.

"Tell me what happened to you," Ramon said, jerking the steering wheel back as they hit something. The old truck creaked and groaned and kept going.

Casey jumped as if his words startled her, broke into her thoughts. She hesitated and then nodded to herself. "Okay, okay. I hear you."

Marie leaned against Casey's shoulder and took her hand. Casey stared at their hands and Ramon saw her stiffen as if to pull away.

"Three auras," Marie said, so quietly Ramon almost missed it over the noise of the truck. "Three, but one. I see, and you hear."

Casey used her free hand to wipe her cheeks. "Okay. There was a woman. A pregnant woman. I killed her."

Ramon looked at her in horror, the truck veered to the right, and he jerked the wheel back, then stopped. "A baby? My *god* Casey!"

"No," she said wearily. "It wasn't like that. Keep going and I'll tell you from the beginning. From Max."

Ramon stared at her a moment longer, gripping the steering wheel. A pregnant woman. A baby, when this world had already seen too much death.

"Trust her." Marie straightened and gripped his arm. "And drive. Now."

With no other choice, Ramon took his boot off the brake, glancing over his niece's head at Casey. "Better explain things."

Casey rubbed her eyes. "Max and me...Max and me went fishing."

As Casey talked, Ramon worked the truck down the ruined road. He listened, hearing a story worse than his time in Monroe. He wondered briefly how any of them would ever come back from this, come back to a life without black memories and nightmares and deep scars.

The earth still trembled but it didn't impact the big truck too badly. He had to focus on steering as it felt like driving with four flat tires. Casey paused in talking only when he had to get out of the truck and use the winch to get a downed tree out of their path, or she had to take the wheel while he guided her in pushing a boulder out of their way. They were almost to the Hole when she finished her story and held out her arm, staring at the gashes and puncture wounds.

He ached for the loss of Max, what that loss had done to Casey, for her anguish, and for the grief they all carried now. Wounds that might heal and scar, but would never, ever fade. He started to reach across for her but hesitated and the moment was lost.

"So," she said, dropping her hand back into her lap. "How was Monroe?"

Chapter 54

S PIKE STOOD AT THE railroad berm as the ground shivered under his feet and watched Ben coming back down the street. He wondered if the hollowed out feeling inside him was abandonment or fear.

"They'll get to the Hole faster with the old truck," Ben said. "Now then, son, what's the plan?"

He looked at the old man, wondering why Ben thought he had a clue what to do. He had no idea. He wasn't a leader. He wasn't Max. He was a fucked-up kid from a fucked-up home. All he was good at was being mad and cussing.

Ben put a hand on his shoulder and the smile on the old man's whiskered face was gentle. "We mayhap got fights coming on two fronts. We only need to focus on one. Mother and me are going to move supplies from the barter shed to the fort. We could probably use some help."

Spike's whirling, overwhelmed, scared thoughts slowed as he looked at the old man in his bib overalls and black glasses and grandpa haircut. The fort. Barricades. Supplies. He could do that. He caught sight of Tessa in the street and yelled for her.

"Ben needs to get stuff from the barter shed to the fort. Priorities on weapons and food. Can you help?"

Tessa didn't waste time replying. She simply nodded, went to the old mayor, Albert, and tugged him along behind her.

Spike searched the small crowd until he spotted Connor and Nathaniel. "Need you two to help Tessa get stuff moved to the fort. Then get people inside. See if there's something else we can do to fortify the gate. Make sure no one's left outside."

"How about the backhoe?" Connor asked. "For moving stuff?"

Spike waved his hand as if shooing Connor off. "Go for it. You don't need me to tell you what to do."

"I'm going for that guy. From the chopper. Tell him to get on their radio for help." Nathaniel didn't wait for any response but as he moved away, Spike grabbed his arm.

"Make sure he's in the fort. With anything he's got that we can use."

Spike heard his name called and turned as Michael ran up to him and bent, struggling to catch his breath.

"Tessa said you need help. What's next, man?"

"We need weapons." Spike gestured to the others at the barter shed. "See what you can find."

"Tommy, the little kid, has a butterfly. Only listens to him but the thing's wicked. He's with Payton."

"Okay. Sure. A butterfly. Whatever works." Spike struggled to sound supportive when he wanted to shake reality into Michael. A butterfly for fuck's sake. "You take care of that end, okay?"

"I can do that, man. I'll get Payton to help."

Spike flashed on how dramatically she'd changed since before the quake. "What happened to her?"

"Didn't ask. Not going to." Michael grabbed Spike's arm. "Don't you ask, neither."

"Didn't plan on it." Spike tugged his arm free. "Just make sure she's safe. Have her help get shit into the fort or something, so she's inside. Ring the old schoolhouse bell in case any morons don't know what's happening yet. And hey, remember the old guy, Henry? Check the school. He's usually hanging out there. Might not hear the bell. I got something to do."

He crossed Avenue A, then jogged as fast as he could down the rough short trail to the river, where he stood at its edge, staring into the rushing water. Was Jennifer out there now with Rowan? He hadn't seen her since he'd left her here. No one had even asked about her. Someday he'd have to deal with what he'd done. Or not done. But not today.

"Hey! Rowan!" He waited briefly but nothing happened. "Bunch of fucking monsters coming. Watch yourself in there."

He turned back for the trail, feeling kind of stupid talking to the river, but she'd been a classmate once. She'd become a friend. She deserved a warning.

Coming fast down the trail was Rob, the only kayaker left in town. Before the quake he'd been known as a world-class extreme kayaker for running some of the most dangerous rivers in the world. After the quake, he kept running the Skykomish but in his oar frame raft, ferrying supplies across the river to a few families.

"I'm going to get as many people over here as I can," Rob said as he neared Spike. "They got no way to shelter from what's coming."

"What do you need?" Spike asked.

"Probably help getting them out of the raft and to the fort. We're going to need to move them fast."

Rob continued down to the river where his raft was tied up and Spike went up the trail as quickly as his bruised ribs would let him.

The tiny community was in chaos, but it looked like controlled chaos. Samuel came out of the fire department bay with his arms full of supplies and went in the direction of the fort. Connor and Ben, with a local mom and her three teens, stacked cartons and canned food from the barter shed onto two garden wagons.

He jogged painfully over to the park where the helicopter was. The guy, McCausland, was getting out of the cockpit and Michael stood by the opening.

"I got through to the National Guard," McCausland said. "My battalion. Told them we needed help. Not sure they believed me about a mass monster attack though."

"National Guard?" Spike gestured at the helicopter. "Thought you were with these fuckers."

"Not willingly. Helping your friend Ramon didn't do me any favors. What's next?"

"Rob is ferrying people across the river. Don't know how many are coming, but we need to get them to the fort."

"Me, too?" Michael's eyes were wide but Spike couldn't tell if it was fear or hope.

"I got bruised ribs. He's got a broken arm. Shit, yeah, we need help, asshole."

Michael's face lit up. "You got it, man. I'm your man. Whatever you need. I can do it. I can-"

"Let's move." McCausland cut off Michael's words.

Spike turned back toward the river, one arm tight against his chest. The pain was sharp, making his breath come fast and shallow, but he was still faster than Michael, who lagged behind, still talking.

At the rocky little beach, he tried to catch his breath while Rob, already across the river, was eddying his oar frame out of the current. Spike could see him yelling at some people, gesturing back toward their side of the river, then rotating his hand in the age-old 'hurry up' motion.

Michael came up behind Spike, panting heavily. "What's taking so long?"

Spike turned his head and stared. "What took *you* so long?"

"Focus." McCausland's voice was calm as he gestured across the river with a nod. He pulled the slide back on his handgun and checked for a shell.

Spike saw men and women coming out of the trees. One guy carried a small child on his hip.

They were scrambling. Faltering. Sliding down steep rocky bank in their haste to get to the water. Looking back over their shoulders. Except for the dad. He went fast, straight for the raft. A woman screamed, fell hard, and struggled to get up.

A large goat came out of the trees. Michael grabbed Spike's arm and Spike wanted to shake him off, to say there was nothing scary about a goat. But then it jumped almost gracefully onto the boulders and shimmered like light reflected on water.

"Come on, come on," Michael whispered.

"Run you fuckers!" Spike yelled, and then gasped in pain.

McCausland didn't say anything. He just raised his gun and fired. But the thing was too far away.

The goat elongated, stood, took on a humanoid shape, solidifying. In seconds the thing grabbed the fallen woman, pulled her head back, and bit into her throat. Dropping the body, it lunged down the rocks toward the river.

Rob had the oar frame untied. The dad tossed his kid into the boat, then grabbed the rope, steadying the raft. People screamed, panicked, stumbling on rocks and falling. They scrambled into the raft, rocking it dangerously. Six or seven were now in it and three more were pulling their way up and over the side.

The dad shoved the boat out into the current. Rob pulled against the flow with his oars, steadying the raft until the dad waded out and clambered in.

There were still four or five people on shore. Spike's heart pounded and he clenched his fists as the goat thing caught another, bit into another throat, dumped another body. Rob didn't wait any longer. He didn't even look back. Spike could see the grim determination on his face as he dug in with the oars, fighting rapids and the overloaded oar frame.

Two women jumped into the water, threw themselves forward, grabbed D-rings, and clung to the side of the oar frame. A man followed but the current swept him downriver. Rob grabbed a small bag with a loop on one end and tossed it to the dad, yelling something. The dad held the looped end and threw the bag. Rope uncoiled and the bag hit the swimming man on his shoulder as he was going under. He grabbed it, surfaced, and hung on, dragged with them and against the current by Rob's muscle at the oars.

"He's overloaded," McCausland said.

"It's Rob." Spike had faith.

The oar frame, riding lower in the water than it should, was mid-current and barely moving. There seemed to be a tie between Rob's strength and skill and the power of mountain white water.

"Oh shit," Michael said.

The thing had shifted back into something half goat, half human and was swimming out into the river. And more were coming out of the trees.

"Oh, fuck me." A huge mass of fear solidified in Spike's stomach.

McCausland started forward shooting as he went but stopped with his boots in the water when his gun was empty.

Spike knew the force of that river. He knew how fast it could take a person, knew that freezing cold intimately. There was no way they could help Rob. Or the people clinging to the sides of the raft.

The oar frame lurched forward so suddenly that Rob momentarily lost his grip on an oar. The raft rocked again, throwing people around. Rob leaned far to one side and looked into the whitewater. He straightened, shouted something, and bent to dig in against the current. Slowly, he began to win against the strength of the river.

The boat lurched again.

"Oh shit." Michael backed up a step. "Those things are in the water. They got the boat. What do we do?"

"No." Spike grinned so broadly it hurt. "Look."

One creature was jerked down into the river. The water around it frothed and turned black before the goat thing floated up and was washed away.

"Yes!" Spike pumped a fist in the air, barely noticing the sharp burn of rib pain.

"What the hell?" McCausland stared as another goat was pulled under.

"It's Rowan." Spike said. "And her fucking friend."

Rob dug and pulled with oars again and again until the overloaded raft beached so hard it came up a few feet onto the rocks, tossing people off. Spike, Michael, and McCausland wasted no time, grabbing them, pulling them up, yelling at them to go, shoving them toward the path.

Rob got out, face pale with exhaustion. "Got as many as I could."

Spike punched his shoulder. "Fucking hero, Rob."

"Listen. Three things out there," Rob said, breathing heavy. "Looked like blue people. Maybe two females and a male?"

"*Two* girls?" Spike stared at the river. "You sure?"

"No, I'm not sure. Between white water and killer goats, I'm not sure of anything. Nothing makes sense anymore." Rob went up the path after the others, rubbing a shoulder.

Spike hesitated a second, watching him, then went back to the river's edge.

There was no one left alive on the far side. Just a few limp, bloodied bodies. A goat creature's body floated, caught in an eddy between two boulders. As Spike watched, it was jerked underwater and disappeared.

He bent carefully and picked up a piece of jasper. He rubbed a finger over the rock's smoothness, and then tossed it into the water. It was a lame attempt that made his ribs burn. He wasn't sure if he should thank Rowan or apologize to Jennifer.

The clanging of the old school bell made him realize he needed to be at the fort, but as he turned for the path, the picture rock came up out of the river and hit him in the back.

He painfully bent and picked it up. Rowan and Jennifer both had just fought for them. He didn't know if he felt grief or shame or pride.

Maybe there was room for all three.

Chapter 55

Spike stood inside the fort with his back to the closed gate, scanning the area. High log walls. A few ramshackle shelters made from scavenged wood and leaning like Max had built them. Boxes and bags and piles of supplies stacked wherever there was room, with people trying to organize them. FEMA military-green tents and tarps that flapped in the rising wind. All the locals who had survived the quake and stayed, survived injuries and elements and monsters. Maybe thirty total, all crammed in the little fort.

Old grandma June sat on a sagging, folding camp chair with the kid from the raft on her lap. Ramon's kid, Tommy, stood next to her, holding her hand. Spike watched the dad from the raft cross to them, bringing Samuel who knelt to talk to them.

The heavy gate behind him vibrated and he heard a low bass rumbling almost too deep for hearing. He didn't know what it was and didn't want to look. The sound moved, following the wall of the fort.

The rising wind shifted and an odd, sweet smell came to him. It reminded him of the one Christmas he'd spent with a friend's family, and all the baking. It smelled of home and homesickness, an almost overwhelming desire to go, to be there where family waited. He longed to follow it and even took a step forward before realizing the smell was a trap, a lure, sure death. He'd never once been homesick for his family. He'd never once longed to go home.

There was a cry, drawn-out and harsh that came from the river, and then from the granite Wall, and then from somewhere upriver. Something airborne.

Airborne.

Spike breathed in, sudden, sharp, hopeless.

His knees gave out and he sank to a squat, head hanging, elbows on knees, fingers digging into his scalp, pulling his hair. He shook with the weightlessness of adrenaline, the helplessness of fear. They'd screwed up. No, he'd screwed up.

They had all gone to the fort for protection because he'd told them to.

Max would have known better.

Ethan would have known better.

Instead, they'd left a fuck-up behind and he'd fucked up again. Just like always. Letting people down, making stupid, stupid decisions. No good, like his parents told him. No future like his teachers told him.

For a brief time, he'd fooled himself into thinking he'd beat them all, become a better person, deserved someone like Nathaniel. He'd believed he belonged. That he'd found family, that he was as good as they were. That he could be valuable in this new post-quake life.

He rocked back and forth, then stood and slammed his fist into the logs of the gate, over and over. His ribs screamed, bones in his fingers broke, skin split and bled and still he hit the wood.

"Spike!" Nathaniel was there, grabbing his arm but not able to stop him.

He hit the gate one more time then stood, head hanging, blood-soaked hand hanging, pain sharp and bright and burning. And still unable to drown out the awareness of what he'd done.

Nathaniel took the edge of his shirt and gently pressed it against the split and bleeding knuckles. "What's going on?"

"We're going to die."

"Well, yeah, but why did you just do this?"

Spike pulled free and stepped back, waving his good hand in the air. "Look at this shit."

Nathaniel's eyebrows went up in confusion as he glanced around the fort. "We're getting stuff organized. We're getting people ready."

"No. No, we're not. All we've fucking done is corral everyone up. We should have gone to the fire department. Even with one collapsed wall, and not enough room, it had a roof."

Nathaniel still looked confused. "The fort is sturdy. This is what we built it for."

"There's no fucking roof!" Spike gestured at June and the little kids. "I've just killed them. Telling everyone to get in here. All these fucking monsters. They can climb. They can fly. Hell, they can probably dig under the walls."

Nathaniel paled. "We'll figure it out. This isn't on you. You've seen the danger when we didn't. Now we can prepare. Right? I mean, sure, maybe the fire department would have been better, even partially collapsed. But we're here and you've seen the weak points and we'll make a plan and we'll-"

Spike shook his head, once, and Nathaniel faltered to a stop. "No. Max or Ethan, or hell, even Ramon would have seen this sooner. This is on me and I should never have been trusted. See if you can find Albert. Tell him what's going on."

Nathaniel hesitated.

"Go." Spike's voice was harsh. "Get out of here. Get Albert, Connor, Tessa, the smart ones. Maybe they can figure something out."

"Spike..." Nathaniel hesitated, reached out tentatively, then dropped his hand and turned, jogging toward Samuel, June, and the little kids.

Little kids. Trapped now in a stupid piece of shit fort.

Spike closed his blood-slick hand, deserving the deep, grinding pain of broken fingers. He watched Nathaniel talking, gesturing, not looking back.

He pushed up the bar on the gate, pulled it open, and left.

The tiny town was broken, destroyed by the quake, hunkered down at the base of the Wall, hemmed by forest and granite and river. And now empty. Everyone was in the fort behind Spike. The collapsed buildings and cleared paths and debris of living among destruction looked like an apocalyptic ghost town.

Except there was movement all around him.

Shadows that shifted and solidified among the buildings. Shapes of things unimaginable sliding down trees. Coming up through still-trembling ground.

Surrounded.

There was nothing he could do. He'd failed everyone. This was their end. He was terrified and hopeless and accountable.

The gate creaked behind him.

"What's the plan, man?" Michael came out and stood next to Spike, back against the fort wall. He was shaking with fear, his eyes darting around wildly.

Spike stared at him.

Nathaniel slipped out behind Michael and stood on the other side of Spike. "Plan?"

Michael gestured with a trembling hand. "Them. What's first?"

"There is no fucking plan." Spike took hold of Nathaniel's arm and tried to push him back inside. Nathaniel grabbed onto the gate.

"Yeah, right." Michael caught Nathaniel's other arm and pulled him loose from Spike. "This is where the plucky red shirts become the heroes. You know, we rush forward all together and fight valiantly until we win. We could use some swords though. Or at least a battle cry."

Spike stared at him. "You're insane."

"Well, yeah man, but so are you."

Nathaniel gestured to Spike. "He's given up. Wants to be the first to die. Thinks he deserves it."

The low, deep rumbling came again from the far edge of the little fort. There was a sudden downward pressure of wind and a shadow passed over them. Spike looked up to see a huge winged creature circling, trailing what looked like intestines.

Michael blew out a breath. "So. No plan. Okay. Just out here risking ourselves for the scenery." He wrapped his arms around Spike's torso and heaved him up.

Spike groaned with pain but couldn't get loose.

Nathaniel tugged the gate further open.

Michael staggered but managed a step forward. "This isn't all on you, man."

Spike twisted again but the pain in his ribs from Michael's grip cut his breath off.

Michael managed a few steps inside the gate then let go of Spike and put his fist to his chest, gasping.

Nathaniel quickly shoved the gate closed and dropped the bar down, then stalked to Spike and shook him hard.

Spike sucked in a pained gasp.

"Stop it," Nathaniel said in a quick, fierce voice.

"This is my fault," Spike managed to say.

"You're not that important," Michael said. "Yeah, we screwed up. We're still acting like we're in a world where walls mean safety. Even Max and Ethan. That's why they wanted the fort."

"I don't care whose fault this is." Nathaniel slapped Spike's arm. "You're smarter than me so do something."

Spike flushed in anger. "Like what? Exactly what am I supposed to do? I can't fix this!"

"Dude!" Connor yelled, running up to them. "Come on, we've got napalm!"

He turned and raced toward the backhoe sitting against the southern side of the fort.

They stared at each other.

"Ummm...okay." Michael started forward. "Napalm. Didn't see that coming."

Chapter 56

T HE TRUCK DOOR SQUEALED as Ramon shut it and the sound was loud in the quiet of the broken landscape around the Hole. He shouldered on his pack, checked for his gun still in his jacket pocket, and stood with his hand on the warm hood listening to the tick of the engine. He saw no monsters. Trees shivered in response to the trembling earth. Rocks occasionally fell from the Wall and dirt and debris filtered down through cracks in the granite.

Casey got out of the passenger side and helped Marie out. They came around the front of the truck to stand next to him. "Anya's inside." She tilted her head, then nodded to herself. "Yeah. Right. Ethan should be, too."

Marie started carefully making her way up the boulder field in front of the Hole door.

"Hey!" Ramon went after her. "Watch our backs, Casey."

"Got it." She pulled her gun out and followed them.

At the narrow opening, Marie started to slip inside but Ramon caught her arm and tugged her back. "Nope. Not happening. You stay here with Casey until I see what's going on."

"You'll need a light." Casey had taken position with her back against a boulder and was turned away from them, watching the woods.

Ramon unzipped his pack, put on his headlamp, and gave Marie a quick hug. "Listen to Casey. I won't be long."

He worked his way around rocks and debris until he was inside, standing on the threshold between light from outside and dark from inside. He flicked on the headlamp and the beam was the warm amber of dying batteries.

"Anya! Ethan!" His voice echoed around the quiet sound of trickling water.

"Ramon?" Ethan's voice sounded oddly hollow, showing how far back under the granite he was. "Hang on, we'll come to you."

Ramon waited, confused.

Twin headlamp beams bounced around as they came out. Ramon caught glimpses of Ethan and Anya in the moving light, flashes off a rifle, a backpack, Bird between them with his tail up and wagging.

"Man, it's good to hear your voice." Ethan grabbed Ramon and hugged him tight, thumping his back.

"Marie? Is Marie with you?" Anya asked, catching his hand. It looked like blood had seeped through her fleece.

"What the hell's going on?" Ramon asked. "Why are you in here?"

"*Is Marie with you*?" Anya said again, her voice intense, her hand tightening its grip.

"Outside, with Casey." He tugged his hand free. "Don't think I want her coming in here until I know what's going on."

"Anya hasn't been able to get out." Ethan spoke fast, explaining about the raven. "But with Marie here, she thinks she may have a chance."

The tremors beneath their feet paused and all three looked down in surprise. Before they fully registered the stillness though, there was a loud crack like a gunshot back in the Hole, followed by the thunder of a boulder hitting the ground.

"All this shaking." Ethan said. "Bound to break more rocks free. Let's go."

"Sure." Ramon moved to the opening, shutting off his headlamp. None of them wanted to give words to the sudden worry that something other than falling rocks might be back there.

The light of early afternoon was bright enough to make Ramon's eyes water. He blinked and stepped out of the way for Anya and Ethan to follow.

They all heard the downdraft of wings. They all saw the black sheen of the raven, coming down fast.

"Marie!" Anya's eyes were wild, focused on the raven. "Help me!"

Ethan pushed Anya toward Marie and lifted his rifle.

"Casey!" Ramon yelled as he raised his own gun. He saw her step in front of Anya and Marie.

The raven swooped low, wings beating wind into their faces. There was a sudden drop in pressure and Ramon's ears popped painfully.

"No!" Anya screamed.

Ethan was gone.

Chapter 57

S PIKE CAREFULLY FLEXED HIS broken hand. It hurt, but Samuel had just bound it up so the pain wasn't as bad. He stood inside the fort as Albert maneuvered the backhoe, lowering the bucket to the ground. Connor was nearby with two pint-sized mason jars filled with something thick and white.

June shepherded children toward a rough A-frame type shelter near the tents. Ramon's little kid was there and as Spike watched, something small darted out of the boy's shirt and circled the children's shelter. He remembered Michael's words about a butterfly. Fat lot of good that was going to do.

Ben had an open tote at his feet and handed out bullets. Tessa stood next to the backhoe with her foraging basket over one arm.

Spike moved closer to her and saw several more jars in her basket. "What is that shit?"

"Old Henry made us napalm and FEMA gave him the ingredients," she said, and laughed.

Albert raised the bucket with Connor balanced precariously inside it, legs spread for balance and hanging on to the bucket with one hand.

Tessa tugged Spike back a few feet. "He's been working on it for a while in the school. Remember the soap missing from the barter shed? And the gas Ben saved? Napalm."

"Henry was the one stealing from the barter shed?" Nathaniel asked.

"Napalm. Focus." Tessa pointed upwards.

The bucket stopped even with the top of the fort wall. Connor leaned out to look over the logs and then ducked down.

"What do you see?" Tessa called.

Connor stared down at them, eyes wide. Spike could see the fear turning to terror, and recognized the same hopelessness that filled him. Oddly, Connor's fear settled his. It didn't go away but it was like the tremor of the earth under his feet, terror under his skin, there but not drowning everything else. He drew in a deep breath and winced.

"Hey!" he shouted. "Suck it up! What do you see?"

Nathaniel stared at him. "Suck it up?"

Spike shrugged.

Connor straightened and looked over the edge, then ducked back down. "Okay."

"Louder," Spike said.

"Okay." Connor's voice was shaky but loud enough to hear. "Couple things underground, almost to the walls. Like *Tremors*, dude."

Ben came up and handed a rifle to Spike. "It's loaded, son."

Spike took it and nodded, still watching Connor.

"We got some of Tessa's slugs out there," Connor continued.

"They'll hang in the garden." Tessa waved her hand dismissively.

"No, sorry, they're on the fort wall, down by the corner kind of, like, eating the wood. Better get someone down there."

Albert shouted to Rob who was helping June. Rob waved a hand in acknowledgement, picked up a big gun and headed for the corner, gesturing for a few people to follow him.

"Sugar!" Tessa yelled after him, and he raised a hand again, not slowing down.

"We got some weird goat things coming up from the river," Connor said. "And...holy shit...we got a fish thing. Three of them."

"Details, son," Ben said.

"Like a stingray on ground. Or flying carpet. Weird eyeballs all around the edges. They're coming kind of fast. And oh, fuck, here comes a flying thing with its guts out."

A huge shadow passed over them, turned, circled back.

"What do I do?" Connor sank down in the bucket again. "Spike?"

"You got fucking napalm! Why are you asking me? Throw that shit!"

Visibly shaking, Connor pulled himself up with one hand. As the intestinal thing flew overhead, he pulled a lighter out of a pocket, lit the white goop in the jar, and threw it so hard he almost toppled out of the bucket. And missed. They all heard the shatter of broken glass and all saw the small plume of smoke come up over the wall.

"It didn't work," Nathaniel said, his voice rising. "What now?"

"Henry says it doesn't explode," Tessa said. "It just kind of clings and burns forever."

Connor leaned over the edge of the bucket. "Hey! It landed on one of the stingrays!"

A gunshot cracked loudly and Michael, next to Spike, flinched and ducked. Another shot came, and then a barrage.

Connor lit and threw his last jar and it hit the flying thing in its underbelly. The scream from the creature was piercing as it wheeled away in flames.

"Lower me down!" Connor yelled. "I need more jars!"

Ben came up behind Spike and grabbed his arm. "I need you boys."

He headed for the piles of supplies. Spike didn't hesitate and Michael and Nathaniel came with him. The tremor of the earth beneath Spike's boots suddenly grew stronger and he stumbled, caught his balance, and kept going.

Ben stopped by a stack of crates with disaster supplies from FEMA. He tipped two of them, dumping their contents on the dirt, and pulled out a Coleman propane cylinder and a pack of flares.

"We go outside the fort," Ben said. "Put these cylinders around the perimeter. Light these here flares. Put them on the ground next to the cylinder."

Michael started to speak but Ben cut him off.

"Listen, son. Don't talk. Samuel's pulling out a couple ladders. Those go up against the walls. We get guns up them ladders. When something gets close, we shoot the cylinder. Flare makes the ignition. Whole thing explodes."

Spike picked up a cylinder and turned it in his hand. "Then let's go blow shit up."

Chapter 58

"**R**AMON!"

He whipped around to Casey where she stood with the Black Dog next to her. She gestured toward the woods.

"We need to get the hell out of here."

The Black Dog backed up against Casey and stood, head lowered, lips curled back on fangs, eyes like flames. The sound coming from its throat wasn't a snarl. It was the deep rumble of the earth itself, a primeval guardian called up from myth.

Marie went to the animal and stood with her shoulder against Casey's.

Anya, holding a fistful of Bird's ruff, came up next to Ramon. "What do we do?"

The Black Dog never took its attention off the trees, at movement in the damaged forest, at movement all around them. In the treetops, in the ground, in the air, shifting shapes from an ancient world.

Terror was just as ancient, something deep and now resurrected. Death was in front of Ramon and he was frozen in its face. His mind shut down even as Anya and Marie fell to their knees. He was only barely able to comprehend that Casey still stood or that Bird had gone to the Black Dog.

The Black Dog looked straight at him. He saw the deepness in its eyes as if something moved in the blood-light there. Something he felt he should recognize, or maybe remember from a time beyond remembering. The guardian was with them. His pounding heart slowed.

He caught Anya and Marie and hauled them to their feet with shaking hands. "Get in the Hole. We can't make it back to Index."

"We'll be trapped," Casey said.

"Trapped but with an entrance we can guard," he replied. "Or out here overwhelmed and nothing to get our backs against. Anya goes with Marie to keep her safe. You and me cover the entrance."

"I can't go in there." Anya pulled free of his grip. "I won't get back out."

"Fine." Ramon was jittery with the need to move. "Casey, get Marie inside and keep her safe. Anya and I will guard the entrance."

Marie went without hesitation into the darkness. Casey did hesitate, then met Ramon's eyes and nodded once before following his niece. The Black Dog didn't even look at him. It simply followed Casey into the darkness.

"Could have used the dog."

"We've got Bird." Anya touched the top of her dog's head.

Ramon gestured her to follow him and they backed up between boulders and debris until they were just outside the narrow entrance. He brought up his gun and looked out at the destroyed world, the trees shivering with the unquiet land, the movement all around them as things closed in. The shifting movement under Ramon's boots strengthened and somewhere back in the dark he heard the crash of rocks falling. He had a brief moment of fear for Marie and Casey but before it could fully form, Anya spoke, her voice shaky.

"Here they come."

Chapter 59

MICHAEL JOGGED UP WITH packs and Spike opened one. He stuffed propane cylinders inside one-handed. Michael dropped to one knee with a grunt and grabbed flares for another backpack. Behind the tents someone screamed. Guns fired and smoke billowed up and something crashed to the ground. Connor, up on the backhoe, still had a few jars of napalm at his feet but he'd quit throwing them whole. Spike saw him dig out some with a stick, light it, throw the stick, and grab another.

Spike stood and slipped an arm through one strap of the heavy backpack.

"Over here!" June yelled. "We need help!"

The ground near the tent with the children heaved upward and something like a giant lizard broke through. Children inside the tent screamed but before anyone could reach them, Tommy ran out of the tent and caught June's hand. He pointed up and Spike saw the kid's pet butterfly plummeting down. The lizard spurted dark blood from a sudden small hole. Another darting dive, another spurt of blood.

"Spike!" Ben said sharply.

Spike jumped, startled, and turned away from the lizard thing starting to look like a colander. Michael heaved himself to his feet and picked up the pack he'd filled. His face was white, his hands were shaking, and his teeth chattered with fear.

Ben reached to take the pack from him.

"No way, man," Michael said, a tremor in his voice. "You and Spike shoot better than me. I'll place the bombs, you guys blow 'em up. And don't let any monsters eat me, okay? Please?"

Ben simply nodded and squeezed Michael's shoulder briefly.

Spike didn't know how to give someone courage, not even himself. He wasn't Max. So he simply started for the gate without waiting for the others. Outside, he went right, following the fort wall. After a few feet he dropped the pack and pulled out a cylinder one-handed. Michael, right behind him, took a flare from his pack, removed the cap and struck the flare against the strike patch. The flare did what it was supposed to and Michael put it down next to the cylinder. The flame sputtered and smoked but burned, ready for the cylinder to be hit, to release gas, and ignite.

Beside them, Ben stood, rifle up. He fired at something in the direction of the ruined school, but Spike didn't waste time looking. He caught the pack strap, stood, and jogged away. His broken fingers throbbed with the pulse of his racing heart. A few feet further on, he stopped again. Michael made it to him, breathing hard.

"Not too close to the walls," Ben said, his voice still calm. "And speed it up."

Three more cylinders and burning flares took them to the south corner where Tessa's slug creatures were chomping on the wood. As they neared, there was a loud boom and one exploded into gobs.

"Hold fire!" Ben shouted.

Rob poked his head out of the hole his big gun had made as Spike dropped a cylinder. "Bombs. Cool."

"Last resort, son," Ben said with his back to the wall and rifle up. "When your gun won't be enough."

Rob saluted and pulled back inside the fort. As they moved around the corner there was another loud boom and more globs fell around them.

They were halfway down the last wall and almost out of bombs when Ben grabbed Spike's arm in a tight grip.

"Drop your packs and run."

"Oh shit. Oh shit. Oh shit." Michael dropped his pack but didn't run.

Spike hadn't paid attention to their surroundings, trusting Ben to have their backs. Now he looked where Ben had his rifle trained and saw movement beside the standing wall of the fire department.

The creature was massive, moving on four legs, its body covered in bristles. Claws like a bear churned up the ground.

"Seen this before," Ben said.

"Shoot it." Spike grabbed the lit flare from Michael's shaking hand and dropped it next to his last cylinder.

"Tried that. Ran over it with the Crusher. Smashed it between the truck and Connor's jeep."

"But you killed it. Right? You killed it?" Michael edged behind Ben.

"No. The grizzly killed it. The one with the boy. You two go on now." Ben stepped away from the wall, raised his rifle, and aimed at the cylinder. "Mayhap I can slow it down some."

"No way." Spike pulled his rifle around and brought it up, but with his bandaged hand, he couldn't fire. "Michael. Take this."

The thing reached the corner of the fort and didn't even slow down. Its massive claws ripped into the logs. Spike heard screaming and, horrified, saw a second one coming around the ruined fire department wall.

The top of a ladder clanged against logs and Nathaniel's head popped up over the wall. He brought up his rifle and fired. Dirt kicked up next to the closest creature. It bit into the wall, ripping out logs like they were twigs. The ladder slipped and disappeared.

Spike threw his empty pack on the ground and grabbed Michael's shirt, shaking him hard. "Shoot it!" he yelled.

Michael fumbled the rifle up.

"Shoot it, shoot it, shoot it!"

Michael's first shot went wild. His second shot went wilder, hitting something long and snakelike that blew into pieces.

"Fuck!" Spike grabbed the rifle from Michael and raised it, right hand useless, left hand awkward on the trigger.

Ben was there, beside him. "Slow and steady, son. Fire together."

Spike caught movement and looked to the side in time to see Michael jog past. Sweat, or maybe tears, ran down his face and his stomach heaved up and down with each step.

He held a sputtering flare in one hand and the last cylinder in the other.

Chapter 60

E THAN LAY ON HIS back, hips twisted as if he'd been thrown. Or dropped. The ground was hard and cold and rocks bit into his shoulder. His headlamp was still on and the beam of light canted up to show rock above him, glinting with dampness. His arm was oddly warm and he realized it was blood.

The ground under him still trembled like a mild aftershock and he could hear falling rocks back in the darkness. He was in the Hole. He'd been outside with Anya, and then the beating downdraft of wind, the sharp, deep pain in his arm, a brief sensation of falling.

That damn raven.

Carefully, Ethan rolled to his side and pushed up with his good arm. Nothing seemed broken. Nothing hurt beyond bruises and the punctures. He couldn't argue with the raven's trade. He'd gladly have stayed voluntarily if it meant keeping Anya out of here.

But damn, why hadn't he grabbed his pack?

He checked his arm in the yellowing light of the headlamp. The bleeding was slowing and getting sticky so for a first raven-trip, not bad. He got to his feet and turned, letting the beam illuminate the Hole. He clearly wasn't in the same area where Curtis's workstation had been or where he'd been with Anya earlier. The bored walls were rougher here as if he was near where the engineers had stopped experimenting with granite.

The ground under his boots suddenly lifted and tilted violently. He stumbled, fell back, was thrown around, and then managed one final toss against the rock wall before he was able to brace himself. Crashing rocks echoed like thunder. He curled inward and wrapped his arms around his head.

The shaking ground eased but didn't stop. It also didn't go back to the gentle trembling. This movement was stronger and hard to balance against as he struggled back to his feet.

Which way was the opening? He had to move, find a way out, before the whole damn tunnel came down on him. He felt the lightest touch of a cold, damp breeze against his face and turned his back on it. Caves and old mines breathed out with the change in air pressure.

He worked his way forward a few yards, expecting falling rock to brain him at any second. The darkness grew slightly lighter. He went as fast as he could over the rough and lurching ground, breathing hard in his sudden desperate need to get out. Light meant the exit, meant Anya, meant fresh air and no collapsing mountain over his head.

Except the pearlescent light wasn't coming from the opening.

She had existed before time. The Stone Woman. The Cailleach. The Hag. The original wise woman. She'd worn many, many names throughout legends and cultures and the turning of eons. She brought winter. She brought death with a tap of her staff on the earth.

And sometimes, sometimes she brought help.

Ethan felt the sudden overwhelming need to drop down and pray. Not to new religions but to the old one. Because that's what she was.

She stood there with long wild white hair, aged and craggy face, and raised a bony hand.

The earth convulsed under his boots and then stilled. In the sudden cessation of motion, he still shook, still struggled to find balance.

"Now it comes." Her voice was rough and hoarse and like the call of the raven.

Ethan stood before her with awe or holiness or complete terror leaving him cored out, breathless, boneless.

"Do you remember?" she asked.

What? What was he supposed to remember? What would she do if he told her no?

Rocks still cracked and heaved and fell somewhere in the darkness behind him.

"He claimed you." She gestured at him with her staff. "The daughter was mine, but he claimed you and the others, to keep you safe. But you, his friend, he loved."

"Curtis."

Ethan remembered suddenly, clearly, the day the Stone Woman came. Curtis had pulled old language from some book and told her that they were his. Curtis had been so terrified but with his words, she'd let them go. Except for Sharon, the daughter she claimed, the woman who had gone into the Hole and taken the Shadow People.

"I remember." Ethan caught his balance with a hand to the wall.

"Will you help him now?"

"But..."

He didn't know what he wanted to ask. Curtis was gone, burned to death holding back the Windigo from killing Ethan. He couldn't seem to catch words within his roiling thoughts. Did she mean Curtis was coming back, transformed, like Alegria, like Anya's son? His friend. His heart soared, and then plummeted into overwhelming panic.

"He didn't die alone."

The Stone Woman nodded once. "And he does not return alone."

Chapter 61

ASEY GLANCED BACK WHERE Ramon and Anya were shoulder to shoulder at the entrance. Something outside screeched, long, loud, and high pitched, starting an avalanche of deafening sound. A goat-shaped creature moved across the narrow opening and Ramon tugged Anya back into the Hole.

Casey hesitated and took a step toward them, bringing up her handgun.

Stop. Get Marie out of here, love.

Max was right. She clenched her jaw, bit down on the fear for her friends, and grabbed Marie's arm as the girl tried to move past her and to Ramon.

"No. Focus."

"But-" Marie pulled against Casey's grip.

"You said you need to be in here. So go." Helpless anger made Casey's words cold and sharp.

Marie, with tears in her eyes, looked past Casey at her uncle. She tugged against Casey's grip one more time and then her shoulders slumped.

"You can't help them." Casey gave her a shake. "Move."

The Black Dog, red eyes glowing, lowered its head and suddenly launched past them, disappearing ahead of them. Both of them jumped, startled.

Follow it.

"Follow it!" Casey pushed Marie back toward the depths of the Hole.

Marie hesitated a brief second, clearly torn, but then her fists clenched and she ran. Casey was right behind her, both of them stumbling over rockfall and rough ground in the darkness that wasn't as dark as it should have been.

"There's light ahead," Marie said breathlessly.

Casey saw it now, too, a faint pearly light, but before she could say anything, the ground lifted up, dropped, twisted, broke the world apart. The thunder of falling granite drowned out all other sound and pain drowned out all thought.

This quake was worse than the aftershocks and as it slowly ebbed, Casey struggled to throw off debris, get to her feet, find Marie. She caught the scent of wet earth and rotting vegetation on the cool exhaled breath of the cave. She scrabbled in the darkness, fingernails breaking against stones.

"Marie!"

A few feet away, Marie screamed.

The sound was wild and deep and throat-tearing. And up ahead, where the faint pearly light came from, there came an answering eerie wail.

Chapter 62

Sounds of rockfall slowed and Ethan braced himself with a hand against the bored tunnel wall. The place was no longer recognizable as a manmade tunnel. Too much granite ripped loose to crash down, too much debris. And one wide, long fracture reaching back into the depths. His headlamp flickered once and died, but he didn't need it in the pale light surrounding the Stone Woman. He reached up to pull it off, his bruised shoulder aching.

Something moved in the darkness and a huge black dog came out of the shadows. Its lips were curled back to show fangs and the pale light gave its eyes an odd red glint. Ethan instinctively reached for his rifle before realizing he had nothing. And then he remembered seeing the same dog with Casey. His heart rate kicked up.

"Casey. Is she here? Is Anya?"

The Stone Woman simply watched the darkness behind him like he was not even there.

"Is Anya back in this damn Hole?"

Anger and fear were indistinguishable. He lunged forward. Let the Stone Woman and her pet deal with whatever was happening. His overwhelming need was to get past them, get back to the opening, get to Anya.

The Stone Woman raised her hand but not her voice. "Remain."

Ethan tried to go forward again but the Black Dog blocked the way. "You're all-powerful. You don't need me."

She didn't respond, simply watching him with those ageless eyes.

He froze as something hollow, like despair, or maybe betrayal took his breath like a punch to the gut. "All powerful. That's what we believed. But then, if you truly were, all this...this death, this horror, you could have stopped. The friends who died. The terror we live in now. The myths unleashed."

The ache of hopelessness bore down on him like the weight of the mountain above him. He hadn't realized the faith they'd all had in her until it was stripped away.

"I could not have stopped this, to my sorrow," she said. "But put that aside. Show your face to what now comes. To what *does* need you."

Somewhere in the darkness the thunder of breaking earth rolled. When Ethan looked where she gestured, he saw only darkness.

"Come forth."

As if in answer to her words, a terrifying scream came from behind them, back towards the entrance. The Black Dog raised its head and howled in response, an eerie and deep and ancient keening.

Ethan whirled around, flooded with adrenaline, fueled by the need to *go*, to get to Anya. Maybe he could slip past and run...except the old woman turned eyes as gray as stone on him.

"You will remain. Come here to me now."

He hesitated, poised between overwhelming need and the realization she could so easily stop him. He clenched his fists until knuckles cracked. And took the few steps that brought him to her side to face the depths. The Black Dog stopped howling and shifted so Ethan stood between them. Something back in the ruined Hole collapsed with a crash. Cold wind came through, smelling strongly of decay and charred flesh.

Ethan saw the antlers first.

Terror seized him, sucked away all thought, sucked away breath, sucked away all sense of self. This wasn't Curtis. This was the Windigo, the predator of the forest, the thing that had cut strips of skin from his face, killed his students, fed on them.

The antlers were high and branching, touching the top of the Hole. Soil fell from them as the thing moved and took form in the small circle of light.

Humanoid. Fingers too long, nails even longer. Cadaverous, eyes black and hungry, focused intently on Ethan.

He could see nothing but death in this creature, this atrocity that had burned, that had taken those he knew, that had killed his friend.

Rage pushed back against his terror, like fire melting ice in his blood, in his pounding heart. He put his hand on the Black Dog's back, dug his fingers into rough fur and pulled.

"Kill it."

The Stone Woman angled her staff to block him. The Dog was coiled and ready beneath his hand but didn't move.

"Look closer. Look deeper."

The Windigo's hair was long and snarled with dirt. And blonde.

The face was bone-white and made of nightmares. And yet familiar.

The eyes, though, were bottomless night.

It made a deep guttural sound and stumbled toward them, those black eyes fixed on Ethan, the hands coming up, the claws curling as if in anticipation.

The Stone Woman thrust her staff forward to push against the creature's chest and hold it there, frozen.

"Speak. Call its name."

Ethan stayed silent. This was his friend made into an abomination, the final cruelty, something so vile created from the kindness and gentleness that had been Curtis.

"Speak!"

Ethan lifted his hand from the Black Dog. "Kill it."

Chapter 63

R AMON SAW SOMETHING THAT looked half-goat and half-human cross the opening of the Hole. Without thinking, he pulled Anya back from the threshold and fired. The sound of the gun echoed so loudly pain stabbed his eardrums. The goat thing spewed blackish blood from the center of its chest and collapsed.

So did Ramon, when the earth dropped away from under his boots, then rose up to slam into him as he fell. Beside him, Anya dropped and rolled into a ball, arms up over her head. Something hard hit him between his shoulder blades, knocking the breath out of him.

Marie flashed through his mind, sharp as terror, but all he could do was ride out the quake. As movement slowly subsided, Ramon called for Anya but his voice sounded muffled under the weight on top of him and the ringing in his ears. A hand came down on his shoulder, grasped a handful of shirt and tugged on him.

He pushed up through layers of dirt and rock to see Anya, bloodied but upright. There was still daylight from the Hole opening and the sight sent relief cascading through him. At least his family wasn't buried. Anya tugged on his shirt again and said something but he couldn't make the words out. He got to his hands and knees, breathing shallow through the pain of bruises, and then managed to stand and stagger sideways.

Anya let go of him and bent, hands to her knees and breathing hard. He saw raw and bloodied knuckles, the wounds on her arm freshly opened, and a shallow cut that ran along her jawline. The ringing in his ears eased and he put a hand to his aching side.

"I told you," she said breathlessly. "I couldn't come back in here. That I might get trapped again. And yet, here I am."

"Killed by a goat out there. Trapped in here. Crushed under a mountain." Ramon winced as he rubbed his shoulder. "Take your pick."

The light at the opening flickered as something moved across their way out, and a massive roar thundered outside.

"What was that?" Ramon asked in sudden hope. "Your grizzly?"

Anya straightened and suddenly stomped her boot down on something trying to crawl out from under a rock. "Oh, I hope so. We need help."

Ramon climbed carefully up over fallen rocks, then turned to give Anya a hand. They both moved slowly and painfully toward the entrance, stones shifting under their boots. The world outside was fully alive with sound and movement, some of it overflowing into the narrowed Hole opening.

Creatures beyond imagination, moving sluggishly or scuttling, crawling or floating, visible or just shimmering suggestions of movement in the wind. The noise made Ramon want to drop down and cover his ears. Sounds that were felt in the blood like drumming or throbbing. Sounds that were painfully high pitched.

It was sensory overload and it made each movement a struggle against gravity, against the eons of ancestral memory that screamed for him to run, to hide, to do *anything* but move toward the terror.

Anya slipped beside him but grabbed his arm and steadied herself. She was breathing fast and shallow, eyes wide, pupils dilated in fear. She was bone-white except where bright blood from wounds seeped. Her fingers, clenched around a fistful of his shirt, shook. And yet she pulled herself up and forward a few more feet.

Ramon didn't know why they were going forward, what they thought they could do. And yet, there was nothing else they could do. He stopped near the entrance and found a relative stable place to stand.

Something fluttered against his hand and stung deeply. He slapped at it and felt the ache of the sting go deeper under his skin, like when a needle found a vein.

He shook his hand violently and saw something dark green and insectile drop to the ground.

Anya let go of his shirt and went past him, kicking something smoking that was rolling toward her, back out the entrance. The toe of her boot smoked from contact but she didn't stop. At the edge between the dark Hole and the brightness of day, she hesitated, then stepped out.

No raven grabbed her.

Ramon, gun up, followed and took up a position to the right of the entrance with the granite wall against his back.

Anya nodded once to him and raised her gun. "Ready to die?"

Chapter 64

Somewhere behind Spike, inside the fort, he could hear screams and multiple guns firing. But all he could do was watch in horror as Michael ran toward the huge four-legged monster.

"Michael! No!"

Michael didn't even pause. He ran straight for the thing, throwing the cannister and flare underneath it and then tripped and fell, slamming into the side of the thing.

"Oh for fuck's sake!"

Michael managed to get up on one knee but seemed stuck there, gesturing wildly at the cannister and sputtering flare. Ben raised the rifle.

"No! Wait!" Spike pushed down on the rifle barrel. "He's too close!"

The creature twisted around toward Michael.

"Blown up or mauled. Die fast or die slow." Ben grimaced but raised the rifle again.

Horror twisted Spike's insides. Michael was moving, crawling on his elbows and knees, his mouth open in a scream Spike couldn't hear. Didn't want to hear. The thing caught Michael's leg, dragging him backward.

Ben's finger tightened on the trigger the same time someone fired from inside the fort.

The creature flew backward and rolled.

"Rob." Ben pointed at the kayaker, coming out of the hole in the fort with his big gun. "Come on."

The creature wasn't dead. It slowly shifted. Spike stared at Michael, moaning and bleeding on the ground, the creature slowly coming upright. His thoughts moving sluggishly as if his brain and body weren't connected. There was a roaring coming from somewhere. Gunshots still sounded in the fort. Spike couldn't seem to process any of it.

Ben shook him. "Move! Now!"

The tremors strengthened and Spike stumbled and fell to one knee. He heard the muffled crack as an abused rib finally gave way. The pain stopped his breath, narrowed his vision, and for a brief second, he passed out.

"Get up, son!" Ben jerked on him, sending sharp pain arcing through his chest.

"Wait," Spike gasped out. "My ribs."

Ben slipped an arm around Spike's back and pulled him up into a seated position, then dragged him to his feet. He broke out in a clammy sweat of shock and pain, his breath fast and shallow.

"Get in the fort." Ben raised his voice. "Rob! Need help out here!"

Spike staggered to the opening in the fort wall, arms tight across his chest, as Rob came through, a gash on his head dripping blood down over one eye.

"Michael," Spike said.

Rob swiped a forearm over his face and sprinted toward Michael. Ben was already there.

"Drag him," Ben shouted, gesturing widely.

Spike looked past Ben. There were too many. Crawling and flying and swarming, every nightmare bringing death. And the not-dead one getting to its legs. Groaning in pain, he turned from the fort and joined Ben and Rob, taking Michael's arm.

Spike forced his eyes away from what was coming for them. Forced down his terror. One-handed, gasping in pain, he pulled in tandem with Rob. Michael screamed and his eyes rolled back in his head.

Connor came over the broken timbers of the fort and took Michael's arm from Spike. "Go. I got him, dude."

Spike looked inside the fort, the collapsed and broken walls, the dead and dying and fighting. Go where, exactly?

The ground rose in a sudden, violent wave that threw people like they were weightless. The remaining walls of the fort crashed down, the small structure where June and the children were tilted. The kids were screaming and he saw June pulling children out of the opening. She grabbed a little girl and was thrown down by the heaving earth. The roar of movement was deafening, the destruction violent, the strange, high screams of creatures like the torture of the very earth.

And June collapsed suddenly, fist to her chest.

Chapter 65

The Black Dog surged out from under Ethan's hand but instead of attacking the Windigo, it circled the creature once then stopped in front of it. The Stone Woman lowered her staff and the Windigo stumbled, catching itself from falling by placing a clawed hand on the Dog.

"I see you." Marie came from behind Ethan. "I know you."

Ethan reached for her but she pushed his hand away and kept going until she stood next to the Black Dog within reach of the Windigo. "Marie, get out of there."

"She knows what she's doing." Casey stopped beside him.

The Windigo sank to squat, one hand digging into the dirt and rocks.

"Ethan." Marie's voice was soft. "Stay here. Casey, go with the Grandmother."

The Stone Woman had already turned. As she moved away, the pale light went with her, as did Casey. And the Black Dog. Ethan watched the shadows grow, the darkness return, leaving him with Marie and that thing. Anger still burned inside and he welcomed it. With the Stone Woman gone, he could kill it, take revenge, not just for Curtis but for all that had happened.

"Be still and listen." Marie sat down in front of the creature as light died. Darkness was alive only because of the sounds of their breathing.

"Marie." Ethan struggled to keep his voice calm and level. "You don't know what that thing is. You didn't see it kill. Move back here."

"The fight out there?" Marie asked. "They were pulled here, by this, to kill it."

"Then let them through. Let them have it."

Ethan heard the creature stir, the sound of old bones and rasping cloth, of falling dirt and a catch of rattling breath.

"He is lost and confused and scared," Marie said. "His heart is broken from the loss of his friend. He is angry at what happened to him. He is angry, too, at all that has broken this world."

Ethan had no idea if she was talking about him or the creature, and in the darkness, couldn't see who she faced. He felt his way forward to her voice and bent, finding her shoulder and then down to catch her elbow. But as he lifted, she grabbed his wrist and held on so strongly he couldn't pull free. Too strong for such a slight girl.

"I remember." The creature's voice was rough, the words slow as if unknown. "I remember the taste of your flesh."

"No. Remember his kindness." Marie's voice was as rough as the creature's, as if it came from it instead of from her.

"I remember the sweetness of their blood."

Ethan couldn't stand it, couldn't allow this to continue. "You see? This isn't Curtis."

"No. He is not Curtis," Marie said. "He is not the Windigo. He is the Gatekeeper."

The thing gasped out something unrecognizable and a deep chill shook Ethan.

"You are the Gatekeeper," Marie repeated. "You are dual, a two-soul being, our otherkin, and you are here to guard the fractures in us, in the earth, to control what comes through."

Ethan sensed movement but couldn't tell what the thing was doing. He could hear it though, and the quiet, softly whispered sound in the dark was like weeping.

"Marie. Please." He didn't know if he was asking her to stop, to leave with him, or to help the thing. His heart raced like it was shattering.

"He will help us now," Marie said. "And the Gatekeeper couldn't exist without the blood of a killer and the sacrifice of a friend."

"We remember your strength in our fear." The voice, still hoarse, came from the creature, and rocks shifted as it moved. "Give us your strength again, our friend, because the Otherkin who would kill me are here."

Chapter 66

T HERE WAS AN EXPLOSION near the south wall of the fort and Spike saw Nathaniel and Tessa with a bucket. McCausland, with his army-issue rifle, shot with deadly accuracy at creatures coming through the breach. Nathaniel fired his rifle with less than deadly accuracy. And Tessa threw another small white blob of burning napalm on a stick.

Rob jacked a shell in his big gun and ran toward the small structure where the children were. There, he bent to June and she moved as if to stand but Rob gently put a hand on her shoulder and shook his head. Spike saw Ben and yelled for him, gestured toward June, and then stumbled forward over the uneven ground.

"You okay, grannie?" Spike asked.

Ben dropped to his knees. "Talk to me, mother."

"No time, dear," she said breathlessly. "Help with the children."

There was a sudden drop in pressure and a shiver in the ground like the earth moaned so subliminally that it was felt rather than heard. Everything went still, paused, held its breath. No sound, no movement. And then with a gust of wind, an earth-exhale, monsters turned.

"What the hell?" Rob asked.

"Are they...are they quitting?" Spike asked, eyebrows up in disbelief.

"Don't think so," Ben said. "They're leaving. Look. All going in the same direction. Toward the Hole."

"We can't help them," Spike said in desperation, trying to convince himself. "We'd never get there in time. We can't win. There's no fucking way I can run, and the others aren't in much better shape."

"I'm not leaving her." Ben put his arm around June's shoulder and pulled her to rest against his chest.

June patted him with a shaky hand. "Regroup."

"She's right," Rob said. "Take care of the injured, gather, maybe get to the fire department. See if it's usable. For when they come back. Get ready for the next fight."

McCausland came running up, followed by Nathaniel and Tessa. "We need to regroup while we have time. Let's get out of here. Find someplace more secure."

"No shit," Spike said. "We kind of figured that out."

"Help me with mother," Ben said to Tessa. "Please. We'll need Samuel as soon as possible, but Michael needs him first. Spike? Can you take over?"

Spike saw the others look at him like he had the answers and this time, there was no fear, no doubt. "Tessa, make sure Michael is taken care of. McCausland, get people together and moving. We'll need everyone to fortify the department as much as we can. Nathaniel, you and me will head there now."

"Fast, son," Ben said. "We don't know how long we have before they come back."

"Maybe they won't," Tessa said.

No one responded to the single voice of hope. Spike figured Tessa was the only one left holding on to faith. That was okay. Someone needed to, for the rest of them.

Chapter 67

CASEY MADE IT OUT of the Hole and stood between Anya and Ramon. The outside world was a maelstrom. Everywhere she looked there were unimaginable horrors, not only ringing the Hole, but fighting among themselves, rending monster flesh. The sound of death was deafening, there was no place to go, no place that was safe. She saw the raven, swooping, diving into the things with hanging intestines. Each time it sank its talons into one, the thing disappeared.

Probably piling them up in the Hole.

"Better than here," Casey said, managing a strained smile. "I don't know what to do. We can't win this."

Doesn't look good.

"There!" Anya pointed, hope bright in her voice.

Casey looked where she pointed and saw silver light, saw Alegria and her wolf struggling against something that looked like a human with long fangs and wings. Its body separated in half and attacked Alegria on two sides.

Casey put a hand to her stomach, to the precious, fragile, so-vulnerable life there. She took a step from the rock wall and raised her gun. Nothing, nothing, was going to get past her and Max, to hurt their child or the people she cared about.

She took aim and fired at the half-creature. She hit the half-head and bright red material blew out in chunks as it collapsed. She fired at the other half and missed. She fired again and hit it. Alegria whirled toward her wolf and Casey saw Bird beside it, both of them snarling and ripping into something rolling across the ground. She fired and the gun clicked on empty. Ramon moved up beside her, shooting. When his gun also fired on empty, he threw it to the ground and started toward Alegria. Casey reached into her pocket for the last of her shells.

Wait, love. The Stone Woman is here.

Casey grabbed Ramon's arm. "Wait."

She looked behind her, back into the Hole, and as she did the Stone Woman came out, the Black Dog at her side. The raven lifted from its prey and rose with strong wings, flying toward her. Alegria, her wolf, and Bird left their fight and moved toward the Hole. Back in the woods, Casey heard the roar of the grizzly and then saw it, with the boy, coming out of the trees. Creatures all around them paused as the air grew chill.

The Stone Woman, the ancient bringer of winter, slammed down her staff and brought death.

Chapter 68

C ASEY SAT IN SNOW that was already melting as the air warmed. Icicles dripped from tree branches, and she knew, in a weird remote sort of way, that she was wet, cold, and covered in blood and bits of creatures she didn't want to identify.

There was movement all around her. There was death all around her. The stench was deep and heavy, blood and decay and rot. Creatures smoked and liquified and turned to husks blown by the breeze. Some were still encased in tombs of ice. Others crept close to the thawing ice pillars, waiting to end any signs of life.

Light from the afternoon sun slowly filtered down to where winter ended and something in her soul thawed just a tiny bit. She raised her face hoping for warmth and the baby stirred, a faint butterfly movement there and gone. It felt like hope and she wasn't sure what to do with that, with the absence of rage.

Ramon stood by the Hole, holding both of his nieces in a tight hug. She saw the three of them clinging together, shaking. Reaction or fear? She didn't know.

Anya was gone but Casey was sure she had gone into the Hole after Ethan.

Alegria's wolf panted, its muzzle blood-caked. Bird sat beside it, and a few yards away the grizzly stood, its massive head swinging side to side as if surveying the carnage. The boy stood with it, one hand on its shoulder.

It wasn't quiet but oddly, it felt quiet.

Casey heard movement back in the Hole. Rocks being dislodged, debris crunching under someone's boots, an odd rough breathing. Exhaustion and cold left her disinterested. There was no fear left, no energy for even a small burst of adrenaline. She simply looked over her shoulder and saw Ethan first.

He stopped in the entrance with one arm out as if holding back Anya. But then she saw the antlers. The sight of it broke through Casey's fatigue and she scrambled to her feet. Where was her knife? Where did the Stone Woman go?

"Ramon!" she shouted as she stepped back from the entrance.

Ethan raised both hands. "Easy, easy."

Ramon ran to her. "Ethan, what the hell?"

Alegria and Marie walked calmly past them and went right up to the antlered creature, each one taking hold of its long, clawed hands. The antlered head dropped toward them.

"It's not going to kill us," Ethan said.

"Gatekeeper," Alegria said, and the thing touched its forehead to hers.

Marie, still holding its hand, turned to the others. "This is what the monsters came for, what drew them. They felt his struggle to come through, they knew what it would mean if he did. They came to kill him. But there were others, like our wolf and bear, that came through to live again, not kill. They are the ones that helped us. Our ancestors. Our myths. Our otherkin."

"Gatekeeper for what? It looks like the same killer to me." Ramon took a slight step forward as if to move in front of Casey.

Ramon's a good man.

Casey snorted, moved around him, and went to the creature. "What do we need a gatekeeper for? The monsters are already here."

"No," the creature said in its raspy, earthy voice. "Each tremor, each fault, brings more. Now that they have been awakened, any quake, anywhere in the world, brings them forth."

Casey realized the thing spoke with the cadence of Curtis's voice. But this thing wasn't Curtis. It was a forgery.

"So, what then?" She made no attempt to hide the rising anger in her voice, or to wipe away the hot tears that fell. "You're going to save the whole world? We're supposed to trust you, a killer, just because you sound like our friend? You are *not* Curtis."

"Casey." Its voice was hesitant, as if testing out the word. "Yes. Casey. I am your friend. But I cannot save the world. I can only fight to keep the killers from coming through faults here, in the mountains where part of me once lived. I can help the ones who would be our friends come through and stop the ones that are not."

Ramon put a hand on her arm. "Maybe this is what we need. There was this woman we met, she said we needed to go back to old ways, old rituals, to survive. Whatever he is now, he's part of those stories."

Casey pulled away. All that had happened. Max's death. Her revenge. The quake. So much death and terror and heartbreak. And this monster said it was her friend. Said it was going to magically help them all. She didn't believe anything it said. The only thing that remained constant, the only thing she believed in, was Max and the fire inside that kept her alert, strong, and able to keep her baby safe. No more myths. No more stories.

"You're not Curtis. You're not my friend. You don't get to speak to me." She turned away. "I'm going to Index. Our *friends* need help."

Chapter 69

Spike leaned against the one solid wall of the fire department bay, scanning the woods, the path to the river, the ruined, quiet town. Late afternoon light slanted into his eyes, making him squint against it. He saw no monsters yet but it was only a matter of time.

McCausland came up to him, holding a rifle across his chest, one finger near the trigger. The sling on his other arm was ragged and blood-stained, but still in place. "Your friend is asking for you. The fat one. I'll take over watch."

"He's not fat." Spike straightened. "Just, kind of, well-insulated. And yeah, he's my friend so watch your fucking mouth."

"Sorry." McCausland lifted a hand. "Didn't mean anything by it."

"Apology accepted, old man."

"Old?"

"Sorry. Didn't mean anything by it."

Spike went inside. Or what passed as inside. At least it had a fairly stable roof, although the back part had sagged down when the wall collapsed so it looked like a lean-to with holes. Holes they could guard though. Better than the fort with no roof at all.

All the military cots were set up and full of injured people. He counted three unknown mounds with sheets over their faces. Three more people, gone forever. Samuel, Tessa, Connor, and Albert moved among the cots with blankets and first aid supplies. It was easy to find Michael, near the back with both heavily bandaged legs propped up on a couple of rolled sleeping bags. But first, Spike went to the cot Ben sat next to, holding June's hand.

He carefully lowered himself down to one knee, holding his breath briefly against the sharp pain in his ribs. "Hey grannie."

June smiled and raised a hand to his cheek. "There's my boy."

Something warm bloomed inside and felt like, if left to grow, would come out in tears that would never stop. Spike rested his forehead against her soft arm and felt her hand brush his hair.

"I'm fine, dear. Just angina. Like a baby heart attack. Samuel will get pills for me with the next supply run."

Ben rubbed the back of his hand across his eyes. "And mayhap no more fighting monsters for a while."

"No. I plan on making hot chocolate shortly though."

Spike raised his head, leaned over her, and gave her a tight hug. "We'll need it. Just not right now, okay? You got to rest."

"Yes, dear."

He could hear the fatigue in her voice and, worried, met Ben's eyes. But Ben smiled.

"She'll be fine. And son, you did real good out there. I'm proud of you."

That warmth deep inside turned into an aching lump in his throat. Spike coughed and carefully pushed up to his feet. "Yeah. Thanks. I'm going to, uh, check on Michael. Then go keep watch."

"I'll take a turn shortly," Ben said, taking June's hand and kissing the back of it.

Spike wove between cots and stood over Michael. "Hey, asshole. That was one of the most stupid fucking things I've ever seen. Running right up to that thing."

Michael shrugged. "Guess so. Sorry."

"Wish I'd thought of it. Then I'd be the hero."

Michael blushed.

"How you feeling?"

"Not losing my legs or anything. That's good. But there's a ton of stitches and it's going to be a while before I'm walking, I guess."

"Pain?" Spike raised a fist like he was going to thump a bandaged leg and Michael flinched.

"Not funny, man. Pain is bad but Samuel has pills. Payton went to get me some."

"Payton, huh?"

The blush went incandescent. "We're friends. I'm safe, you know? Fat and harmless. No threat like most guys. That's all."

Spike laughed. "You're such an idiot. I'm going back outside. Check for monsters."

"Yeah. Okay. Spike?"

"What?"

"Don't call me an asshole."

Spike thumped Michael's shoulder and headed for the bay opening just as McCausland poked his head in and gestured for him. His stomach bottomed. So soon?

"How many this time?" he asked when he reached the man.

"None so far. Our friends are here."

Spike went outside and saw Casey, Ramon, and Marie making their way across the rubble. They looked as beat up as everyone else. Torn clothes, dried blood, exhaustion. For a second, he wanted to go back inside, back to June, like a child to his mother for comfort from nightmares. For just a few more moments of ignorance. He straightened, sucked in air from the quick jab of pain, and went to meet them.

"Glad you made it." He pushed down the sudden dread, the fear of news he didn't want to hear, forced a smile, and gave Ramon a quick hug, thumping his back. Then he pulled back and hesitated, not able to ask the question.

"They're okay," Ramon said quickly. "Ethan and Anya. Beat up, but okay. They'll be here at some point."

The rush of relief left him lightheaded. "Good. And, you know...glad you guys are alive. We need the help. We did okay the first round. Fucking napalm and homemade bombs. But we're out and they'll be back any time."

"Napalm?" Ramon's eyebrows shot up.

"They won't be back. Not like the first wave anyway." Casey gestured back in the direction of the Hole. "The Stone Woman and her friends killed a lot of them. And Ethan has a gatekeeper but I don't trust it."

"Wait, back up," Ramon said. "Napalm?"

Something pushed against Spike and he moved aside as Tommy threw himself at Ramon. He bent and picked the boy up and Tommy wrapped his arms around Ramon's neck in what looked like a chokehold.

"June kept all the kids safe," Spike said. "June and that butterfly."

Ramon laughed, then coughed. "Okay, ease up some there." He shifted the boy to one hip. "Hell of a fight here. Everyone okay?"

"Michael won't be walking much. June, neither. We lost a few. A lot are beat up. You sure the fight's over? Because if they come back, we're in deep shit."

"Not all were killed," Casey said. "I'm sure some are out there in the woods still. But I think it will be skirmishes, not a battle. And skirmishes we can handle. We'll help you though. And maybe we can start recovery work."

"The fort was a huge fucking mistake," Spike said. "No roof."

Casey's eyebrows shot up and then she laughed. "What idiots we were."

"You did the best you could with what you knew at the time." Ramon shifted Tommy to his other hip and the boy rested his head on Ramon's shoulder.

Casey tilted her head to one side as if listening, then smiled sadly and shook her head.

"No, really," Ramon said. "You guys did better than most. Trust me. You didn't see some of the camps that we saw on our way here."

Casey looked around the ruined town. "We need a plan for recovery. Decide what comes first."

"That's easy," Spike said. "We throw a fucking party."

Chapter 70

E THAN SAT ON A boulder shivering slightly in the cool air from fading winter. About a hundred yards away, the Gatekeeper was ranging among the remains of battle, pausing before the living monsters that filtered out of the shadows to gather near him. He watched as the creature bent to them as if speaking, then moved to rest long claws on the bodies of those that been killed, almost as if in benediction.

Anya was several feet away, with her arms around her son. Alegria, with the wolf and bear, waited at the edge of the woods. Bird, limping, came back to him and sank with a human-sounding grunt at his feet.

He bent and ran his hands over the dog, checking wounds. "Banged up like everyone. Nothing looks deep enough for stitches. They'll need to be cleaned though. Who knows what germs monsters carry."

Bird thumped his tail briefly then closed his eyes.

Ethan knew what was coming and sure enough, Alegria came to take the boy's hand and together they left for the woods, the wolf and bear following. As they moved through the trees, amber light haloed them, marking their progress until they were out of sight. Anya stood still, watching, until they were no longer visible, then she came to sit next to Ethan and put her head on his shoulder. He turned slightly and wrapped his arms around her.

"They're going home."

"I figured." He put a hand to her hair. "What do you want to do?"

"I want to go home, too." Her voice was rough with tears and exhaustion. "More than anything."

"But?"

She sighed heavily. "We should go back to Index. See if they need help."

Ethan nodded, watching the Gatekeeper, now heading back to the Hole. "How much of Curtis is there, do you think?"

"No idea." Anya sat up, wiped her eyes, and put her hand on his thigh. "It knows you though. That's something."

"That's something."

He didn't want a long trek to Index through rough woods with everything aching followed by an even longer hike to get to the cabin. He wanted nothing more than to be in Anya's bed, warm under a thick pile of quilts, and nothing to do but sleep without being on guard, without fear and worry. She was right though.

"Give me a minute then we'll go." Ethan stood and headed to the Hole.

Inside, the dark was deep but he sensed movement back in the depths and waited as the Gatekeeper's features became visible. The tall, branching antlers. The long blonde hair, tangled with moss and dirt. The too-long arms, too-long fingers, too-long claws.

"We're leaving," he said, not exactly sure who he was talking to. Monster or friend? "What will you do now?"

"Rest. This place will be mine but I will come out when there are earthquakes and faults open."

Ethan remembered in what seemed another lifetime, when Curtis had told them what a Windigo was, the legends that it hibernated until earthquakes woke it, when it would come forth to kill.

"So, just like before then."

The Gatekeeper tilted its head. "Part of who I am now. But when I come forth now it will be to send back those that try to break through into this world."

"Curtis was a good man," Ethan said. "Gentle and kind and intelligent and scared of everything. I miss him. Knowing a little of him is still here, in you, helps, but it's not enough."

"No. But come visit. Tell me of the world even if I sleep. I missed you, Ethan."

How could emotions hurt so deeply like physical pain? Grief and loss. Endings and beginnings. Ethan couldn't breathe against the pain in his heart. He put a hand to his chest and swallowed down the ache of tears.

"Missed you, too, buddy."

He turned away and was almost to the entrance when the Gatekeeper spoke again in its raspy voice.

"Ethan, my friend. Bring coffee."

When he went out the entrance, left the darkness for the cool sunlight, went to Anya waiting for him, he was laughing.

Chapter 71

A HUGE BONFIRE BURNED in the middle of what had been the fort, keeping the darkness of early night away. Those who were able wandered from person to person, hugging, talking, sometimes just standing together, hands out to the warmth of the flames. Casey stood slightly apart, watching, holding a rifle loaded with shells she'd found in the barter shed.

It wasn't a party or even a celebration, but it was a gathering. Not quite a memorial, still almost solemn, but at the same time, there was muted laughter. Signs of hope. Spike had done a good job bringing them together, realizing they needed something to start healing. There was food, scrounged cans of beans and fruit, dehydrated meals now simmering at the edges of the bonfire, and June, wrapped in a blanket and sitting in a chair, serving her hot chocolate.

Occasionally there was the loud pop of gunfire out in the darkness where the first team had watch for the night. People would pause as if holding collective breath and wait to see if anything came out of the shadows. When nothing did, it was one more tiny, tiny step toward feeling maybe things were going to be better.

Spike and Nathaniel had taken plates and mugs inside the bay to Michael and Payton. Connor and Tessa sat together near the fire, laughing about something and Casey watched them, wondering if laughter meant all would now be okay.

Of course it didn't. But let them have their moment. In the morning the real world would be back, with foraging and subsistence living, with repairs and rebuilding, and still with monsters. Some felt, with the Gatekeeper, monsters wouldn't be so bad anymore. Casey, remembering the strength of the pregnant woman she fought, wasn't so sure. The Gatekeeper would have to prove its ability.

"What do we do now?" she asked out loud.

Who was she without wild grief and rage? Could she go back to living in this tiny town, being the one responsible for law and order? Could she leave on a helicopter and start a life somewhere else, someplace more suitable to bring up a baby?

Is there any place suitable now?

Max had a point. It sounded like Monroe was bad. Refugee camps were probably not much better. Here, at least, there were friends, even if she still felt unsettled around people. Grief was still deep and aching, rage was banked but still warm, and strangely, the solitude of the woods pulled at her. Maybe she needed to build a cabin where she could be alone.

Remember how that worked for Anya and her baby?

Okay. Maybe not for a few months yet. She put a hand to her stomach and was answered by the now familiar, and reassuring, flutter.

She watched Ramon settle Tommy on a chair near the fire next to Marie and then bring them both plates of food. A small skeletal creature darted in and out of the boy's hair. Ramon looked up, met her eyes, and came over to her.

"Everything okay?" he asked.

Casey nodded.

"Look, I've been wanting to talk to you." Ramon shoved his hands in his jean pockets. "I don't know what your plans are, but if you're thinking of staying here, you need to know I'll help you any way I can."

Casey could only nod again, not sure what to say, a little afraid of where he might be going.

"I'm not Max," he said quietly.

No one's perfect.

Casey felt a sudden desire to laugh, clearly picturing Max's face. She bit the inside of her cheek and managed to swallow down the inappropriate, and unfamiliar, emotion.

"But Max was a friend and someone I respected."

All desire to laugh disappeared.

"And I'd like to honor that friendship by being here if you need anything. Especially with the baby coming."

"I appreciate that," Casey said.

Come on, love, give him more than that.

"I can't," she said.

"Can't what?" Ramon asked.

"Can't...say for sure yet where I'm going to end up. But while I'm here...thank you for your offer. And your friendship."

Ramon nodded. "Just let me know if you need anything. We're family. Those of us still here. Nothing more important."

Nothing more important. And Casey, love? He's going to be a good father.

Acknowledgements, Music, and of course, Monsters

Many thanks to Donna and her weekly question of 'how's my book coming?'. Though it took a long time, her persistence pushed me back to the pages. It was that, or start avoiding the bank.

Susan, where would I be without you to edit and turn ramblings into stories? All these years and you stick with me. Can't believe you haven't shaken your head in exasperation, given up, and rode off on a horse, scattering rough draft pages to the wind.

The town of Index, Washington is a beautiful, unique place. Seriously. You should visit. Don't let this story keep you away, or out of the woods.

All characters here are from my imagination, with the exception of Rob, kayaker extraordinaire, who asked if he could have a big gun this time. If you see him, say hello. Oh, and the character of Jean and her eye rolls might be familiar to a few...

The Hole in the Wall is closed now, but I'd like to thank Keith Curtis again for allowing me to interview him about his work there.

After doing a beta read of the draft, the same Donna turned to a co-worker and said 'she seems like such a sweet person'. In order to convince you that I am, I want to assure you that the creatures here didn't originate in my imagination. To prove it, here they are.

House Gnomes

Typically, tiny creatures attached to a home and that help the people who live there, as long as they are treated with respect and given treats. I wondered what would happen to them if they no longer had a home, and gave the one in this story a little more...bite.

Anthropophagi

Headless cannibal. What little brain he has is reputed to be near his reproductive organs. Eyes rest on shoulders and mouth is in center of chest. Shakespeare talked of them in the *Merry Wives of Windsor* and *Othello,* but were part of folklore well before then.

Ashrays

Both male and female, they appear about twenty years old in human time although they are ancient. Whitish almost translucent bodies and are often mistaken for sea ghosts. Cannot live on land. If touched by sunlight they melt into a rainbow pool of water.

Manananggal

Able to separate its upper torso from lower parts. Fangs and huge, bat-like wings that give it a vampire-like appearance. Often seen with intestines trailing.

Pontianak

Spirit of a woman who died while pregnant. Pale, with lang dark hair and red eyes. Preys on men and appears at full moon. Feasts on bodily organs of victims.

Glaistig

Shape-shifting from woman to goat, or half and half, and cuts throats.

Manta

Huge flat extent of skin, like a flayed cow's hide, with eyes around its edge. Lures people in, enfolds them, and sucks out all vitality and goodness.

Amarok

A giant wolf in the folkore of the Inuit people. Also similar to the Black Dog or Fairy Dogs of Celtic mythology. And also similar to the wolf Fenris of Norse mythology. All are giant dog-like animals that are either the guardians of the places they haunt, killers of those they stalk, or herald the end of the world.

The Grizzly Bear

Common in legends of the Pacific Northwest, these bears renew the world. They are both ancestors and way-showers. They are teachers, guardians, and healers.

Cailleac Bhuer or Stone Woman

An old woman with a walking stick and carrion crow on her left shoulder. She can be either dangerous or, if treated with respect, a guide. In some myths she dwells in a land of winter. In some, her staff is buried under a tree and retrieved after Samhain to bring forth the spring. In Scotland she is known as the Blue Hag, who walks the highlands at night. Some see her as the crone goddess. Variations of the Stone Woman can be found in many cultures. Because she walks the Pacific Northwest in these pages, I have chosen to give her a raven.

Shadow people

More of a ghost story than a myth, these are humanoid forms made completely of featureless shadow. Some say these are other-dimensional beings with their realms occasionally intersecting with ours. Some see them as travelers, scouts, or invaders. They commonly are seen as a sign that evil comes.

Wendigo or Windigo

A creature of North America, most commonly seen as a man-like cannibal that keeps its victims alive while it slowly eats them. Sometimes described as a tall, thin, man-like shape with talons and antlers.

Wood nymphs, dryads, and naiads

Spirits that live within trees. Combined in this story with spirits of yew trees, which, in pagan beliefs symbolize psychic awareness, spirits, and the death passage. I keep hoping these will show up when I walk in the woods.

Matlose

Matlose is a famous hob-goblin of the Nootkas. He is covered with black bristles and has teeth and claws like a bear.

A wonderful resource for every mythical creature imaginable is *The Element Encyclopedia of Magical Creatures* by John and Caitlin Matthews.

Finally, if you're still with me here, while I may revise in quiet, I write to music. Here is a very tiny sampling of the songs that helped create this one.

I Am – Stan Walker

The Gaels - Artesia

You - Oryn Etheria

If You Fall I Will Carry You – Efisio Cross

The Wolf Song – Jonna Jinton

When the Spirit is Calling – Jon Henrik Fjällgren

Mountain Dance – Jon Henrik Fjällgren

With You 'til the End – Tommee Profitt

Paralyzed – NF

10,000 Miles – Mary Chapin Carpenter

The Kiss – Trevor Jones

I Will Find You – Karliene

The Expanse – Clinton Shorter

On the Nature of Daylight – Max Richter

Burial at Sea – Draugablikk

Adagio in D Minor – John Murphy

Pusel ov Akis Song – Nytt Land

Carry Me – Eurielle

Did you love Otherkin?

Check out the prequel, *This Deep Panic!*
Available in print and eBook.

Also by Lisa Stowe

The Wallace, Idaho Mystery Series

collection of four books taking place in historic Wallace, Idaho, this series follows Cody Marsh as she discovers her mysterious past and more than a few dead bodies.

About the author

 Writer, editor, and forest dweller, Lisa Stowe hides out in the Pacific Northwest with husband, son, dogs, and visiting bears. She has lived in the story world since before she could write (to the chagrin of teachers) and now enthusiastically shares those stories with anyone who will listen. Or read. She would love it if you would step into her mountain world.

Lisa was born and raised in the Pacific Northwest, her upbringing and connection to the area being unique and special. As an example, she lived off-grid for several years. She has been writing her entire life, and cherishes and embodies the landscape of the Pacific Northwest and the art of writing.

Lisa Stowe is an accomplished author with four published books in the Wallace, Idaho Mystery Series; *Ghost Roads, The Memory Keeper, Sparrow's Silence,* and *Sunshine On My Shoulders;* and with the conclusion of *Otherkin,* two books in the Index Rift Series. Additionally, Lisa provides editing services for writers.

You are invited to connect with her at thestoryriver.com.